The Art of Surprise

By Cameron G. Acosta

© 2015

"Fool me once shame on you, fool me twice shame on me."

Randall Terry

For my beautiful daughter, Alexis, the love of my life
and my toughest critic.

And for my best friend Sue
who inspired me to make lots of lemonade from one tiny lemon.

Chapter 1

I was wedged in the space between fear and exhilaration, between dread and wonder, between… well…between the big guy who smelled more like cigarettes every time he returned from the bathroom and the tiniest piece of glass you could call a window. How he'd managed to not set off the smoke alarm was beyond me. Maybe he'd dabbed eau de cigarette behind his ears on every trip.

A voice over the intercom instructed us to turn off our electronic devices and I checked my phone. My fingers tingled with anticipation as I clenched my cryptogram book. I must have deciphered a hundred puzzles in the last eight and a half hours and my eyes deserved a rest. I turned off the overhead light and focused my attention on the darkness below.

Through the tiny window Manhattan looked red-orange. From a few thousand feet up the buildings seemed to sizzle in rows like one of those car cigarette lighters my grandmother used to have that popped out with red hot ridges. I hoped that once I was away from the wall of stink sitting next to me I might stop thinking about cigarettes.

As we dragged closer to the hot ridges I lifted my feet ever so slightly to help us glide over the buildings into LaGuardia Airport. I hoped the stranger sitting next to me didn't notice, but I felt compelled to do it because if I didn't do it this time then this would be the time we wouldn't make it…you know…because I didn't do it. Lifting my feet was my way of ensuring our safety and a stranger's glare wasn't about to stop me.

From a thousand feet up I saw a fiery red hand reaching to snatch my independence. Or maybe it was already gone, abandoned back in Los Angeles. I didn't want to be here, but I was taught that family is important, a concept I'd put on hold for a few years. I was coming here to do her a favor. That's all. I thought I knew the way it would go. It would be like a dull vacation. I'd be back in L.A. in no time.

What did I know?

Chapter 2

I wheeled my suitcase through the airport and out the automatic doors to the sidewalk. The late night spring air was pleasant, not at all hot like the red glow had predicted. I entered the line with cordoned rows of people inching toward the waiting taxis. The line turned back on itself like the lines at amusement parks and banks, where, as you turn you keep passing the same people.

I enjoyed being able to look at strangers and study their faces and make up stories about them. I faced a woman, maybe in her thirties, who was talking like a schizophrenic conversing with the voices in her head. Then I realized she was having a phone conversation, her earpiece buried under her long hair. Her inattention to her surroundings allowed me to study her without notice.

She glanced my way as she spoke but her eyes were fixed on the air in front of her. I was invisible, as were the others in line. Her fingers were loosely wrapped around the handle of her rolling luggage bag, revealing her long acrylic nails pressed flat against her palm. She was wearing a business suit with a feminine touch and tall pumps.

I understand why people take business clothes with them on a business trip but I don't understand why people dress up for plane flights. Sitting in the same seat for eight hours next to who-knows-who is uncomfortable enough. So why worsen the already painful experience by wearing uncomfortable clothes?

That reminds me of the cliché about wearing clean underwear in case you get into an accident. It must be intended for little accidents like car accidents in which a paramedic might need to clip your blouse or pants to examine some wounds. I wouldn't want anyone to see my plain white bra and stretched out underpants, the ones that had been laundered so many times they were dingy gray, when I could give the young strapping EMT a glimpse of my Victoria Secret bra and a translucent thong. But who cares what you look like when you might be hurled from the sky to a fiery crash? If people don't survive jumbo jet crashes then my guess is their underwear doesn't either.

On the other hand I suppose the end could come at any time. They say most accidents happen within a few miles of home, so, statistically speaking, this trip should ensure my safety. I could possibly be locked inside a protective bubble as long as I'm in New York City. Anyway, live or die, I wanted to travel as comfortably as possible in my favorite jeans and Nikes.

The woman was still talking, to her husband I think, complaining about something that had to do with his care of their children, Rebecca and Thomas. Traditional names, Bible names. She used their whole names as many mothers do, not Becca and Tom or Becky and Tommy. She asked how Rebecca's paw was healing and said that since Thomas had chewed through his leash she'd bought him a new one when she was between business meetings. Hmm…not traditional names for dogs. She checked her watch and said she'd be home soon if the line ever got moving. I thought it was moving just fine.

I couldn't see the front of the line from where I was standing, but I was pretty sure that someone who worked for the airport or the taxi service had planned just the right amount of ropes and posts to keep things civilized. It's faith that kept me passing back and forth. I had faith that there was actually a point at the front of the line which would deliver me to the next available taxi.

Without the ropes this would have been a chaotic mass of human piranhas devouring each other to get to the front, everyone thinking that life was unfair and that they had to fight to uphold the philosophy of "first come first serve." But the inventor of the switchback waiting line proved that there are still things in life that are fair, as long as you stay in line.

I was silently practicing how I'd tell the driver my destination. I wanted to act like I knew New York City, like getting a taxi was a regular occurrence for me. I had to practice for the eight million people I was about to encounter who might take advantage of my unfamiliarity with their town.

Before leaving Los Angeles I'd googled the area map with the cross streets and the community name. A slip of paper with the name of the hotel and the street address was tucked away in my purse just in case my phone ran out of juice on the way. But as I stood there I checked my phone and it was good to go.

I tapped the screen a few times and a street map appeared with the hotel in the middle. I didn't know how much I needed to tell the driver and how much to hold back. When I got to the front of the line a man holding a clipboard asked, "Where are you going?"

I kept it simple. Shouting over the traffic noise I said, "Manhattan."

He waved the next taxi forward. As it rolled to a stop the trunk popped open. The driver jumped out, swept up my bag, tossed it in the trunk and slammed it shut with a clunk. He opened the back door and I climbed in. As he slid into the front seat he asked in some foreign accent, "Where are you going?"

I leaned forward. With my eyes focused on my phone, it all spewed out, "Manhattan, International Traveler's Inn, 155 East Fifteenth Street, west of Third." I sensed that I had just revealed that I needed a little more practice at being a New Yorker. The address or the name of the hotel probably would have been enough.

As we edged our way onto the freeway or parkway or whatever it was called in this part of the country, the driver swiveled his head, keeping his eyes on the road and asking, "Where are you from?"

I was right. He could tell I was a tourist. "Los Angeles," I said, "but I grew up in a small community in Connecticut that no one's ever heard of and I visited New York City with my family a few times when I was a kid."

"New York has great restaurants. Do you like Cuban food?" he asked.

"I don't know. I've never eaten Cuban food," I said.

"Well, if you like spicy meat you'll love Cuban. There's a great Cuban restaurant near your hotel. A friend of mine is the chef there," he said, "on Eleventh Street. Reasonable prices too."

I said, "Oh" and, "That sounds good," having no idea if I would like Cuban food.

As we emerged from a tunnel the tightly packed skyscrapers loomed over the narrow streets like jail bars promising to keep me captive. I leaned sideways to look out the window, attempting to get a glimpse of the night sky. I strained to see beyond the tops of the buildings but even as my forehead touched the glass I couldn't see more than a few stories. The building walls seemed to push down on me and enclose around me.

4

I pulled away from the window to see the smudge my forehead left on the already-smudged glass. I was not the first person to ride in that cab since the glass had been cleaned. I pulled out an antiseptic wipe from my purse and gave my forehead a swipe. As a courtesy to those who would follow me, I also swiped the glass, depositing the wipe in the ziplock bag I carried in my purse.

L.A.'s mountainous terrain with its low urban sprawl had been like New York City turned inside out. I could drive over the city on freeways that ribboned above the streets and most of the buildings. The lights in the houses dotting the rolling hills twinkled like stars in the night sky. The city's energy floated up and out into the stratosphere.

But here the energy boiled like a pressure cooker clamped shut by the urban walls. This place had never been home, it was just the place I'd visited a few times as a child, the place from which I managed to escape before college drew me into its abyss.

The city's force roared around me and rumbled inside me. The dread I had been feeling about the days to come now transformed into excited anticipation. I was so close. And somewhere nearby was my mirror, my twenty-five year old twin sister just walking down some street looking like me. She was the reminder of who I could have been, and I tried so hard not to be.

Whether or not things went well with Chloe, I was in the city that might revive my stagnant life, even if it was only for a few weeks.

Chapter 3

The taxi pulled up to the hotel. The trunk made a thudding sound as it opened and the driver met me at the back. He removed my bag from the trunk and as I paid the fare he handed me a scrap of paper with the address of the Cuban restaurant. I said, "Thank you so much. If I have time I'll try it." I meant it. I thought New Yorkers were supposed to be rude, but this man was being helpful and I felt like I would have to go to that restaurant at least once during my stay.

I looked up and counted eight stories. This building was shorter than the ones around it but still indistinguishable from its neighboring buildings. I couldn't see any stars and I felt a velvet mist on my face. As I entered the empty lobby I inhaled a musty odor that reminded me of my grandmother's house. The décor was teetering on the edge of cozy and shabby.

My friend had told me not to get a hotel below Thirtieth Street because as the numbers got lower so did the safety for a lone woman, but when I perused websites that displayed photos I noticed that as the street numbers advanced, so did the prices. So I ended up here, the most economical hotel I could find.

After scanning the lobby I decided that the hotel's marketing director must have spent the majority of the website advertising budget on an extraordinary photographer.

I wondered when technology might discover how to produce odors, like smell-a-vision or like the 4D movies at theme parks where odors and water and fake spiders shoot out of the seat in front of you. I imagined that if this hotel's website had offered a sample of its lobby's odor through an additional hole in the computer screen I might have become nostalgic for a moment, but I might not have booked a room here.

As I stepped to the small front desk, a middle-aged woman walked through a doorway from the back. She was chewing something and wiping her palms with a napkin. Her face was shiny as if she'd just applied cold cream. I told her my name and that I had a reservation. She lifted her index finger indicating that she would be with me as soon as she finished her last few chews. She plunked a couple of computer keys as she made sucking sounds with her lips and tongue, attempting to extract something from between her teeth.

A printer spit out a piece of paper which she slid on the counter in front of me. In silence she handed me a pen and pointed to the line where I was to sign my name. I signed, she handed me a key, we exchanged smiles and I walked to the elevator. As the elevator doors creaked to a close I watched her return to the backroom.

The doors opened onto a narrow hallway with threadbare carpet and drab walls. Pungent odors escaped from under a couple of the doors. My room donned the same threadbare carpet and disappointingly only one single bed.

I placed my suitcase on the luggage rack and unzipped it. I removed my make-up pouch and walked into the bathroom. I flipped on the light and a ceiling fan started with a clanking sound. As its motor settled into a whir, I glanced in the mirror to see a tired face looking back at me. A small basket with a bar of soap and miniature bottles of conditioning shampoo and lotion sat on the counter. A hair dryer was perched on a wall bracket.

I don't understand the concept of conditioning shampoo. Isn't shampoo supposed to wash everything from the hair? How can it wash and simultaneously leave conditioner in the hair? It's puzzling. Maybe, like the smart phone, it's smart shampoo. The shampoo molecules know to first wash out all traces of previous oils, shampoo and conditioner, then the conditioning molecules cling onto the hair shafts. Except whenever I use conditioning shampoo my hair feels like it hasn't been conditioned at all, like a comb would end up knotting my hair into globs. Too much to think about. I slid the basket off the counter.

Now that the tiny counter was clear there was room for my ablutions. Mom used to say the word ablutions. I thought it was old-fashioned, but I guess I'd heard it so many times it stuck.

I opened my make-up bag and removed the items one at a time. I mentally took myself through my morning ritual and arranged the items next to each other on the counter in the order of how I would use them, left to right. I gave each item a little nudge to make sure they were all parallel to each other and evenly

7

spaced.

At home everything had an assigned place, but in the hotel room I had to assign my personal items to logical usable spots. By placing them in order of use I made sure I wouldn't leave out a step in my hygienic and beautification regimen. I knew I wouldn't get any sleep unless I'd gotten things ready before I went to bed.

When I was satisfied that the items were in proper order, I removed a few pieces of clothing from my suitcase and hung them in the closet to air out the luggage wrinkles.

I took my cell phone from my purse and placed it on the bed. Then I picked up the TV remote and set it on the bed. I pulled back the bedspread and propped up two pillows against the headboard. I slid off my shoes and reclined on the pillows.

Chloe invited me to stay at her apartment but I needed one night to recover from the flight. Once I got to her place I'd be sleeping on a futon on the floor in her second bedroom, which was vacated by her roommate a month ago. After the long flight I just needed to relax and have some time to myself.

I picked up my phone and noticed that the time displayed on the screen had automatically changed to Eastern Time. I called David's number. He would probably be home from work by now. His machine picked up and I said, "Hi, it's me. Just thought I'd give you a call and see how you're doing. Three days is a long time for us not to talk. I know we said some things that were hurtful and I'm sorry. I wish I could be there with you but being here is the best thing for me right now. I miss you."

I hung up, called Chloe's number and took a breath.

I remember the day I announced to Chloe that I was going to UCLA instead of NYU. Mom would have been shocked if she had still been alive. I didn't think of moving out of state to go to college until after she died. Maybe her sudden death was what changed my thinking. She was the glue that held our tiny family together - me, Chloe, Aunt Jane, and Dad…sometimes Dad. With Mom gone I felt like something was missing, something I had to find elsewhere.

And Chloe…well…Chloe who is seldom shocked by anything, who is usually the shocker rather than the shockee, was sent into a momentary stupor because I had never made a decision that veered from the expected. Her over-inflated opinion of her own acting ability, or what I call her deceptive nature, made her

8

think she was hiding the fact that she would miss me. I suspect she knew how hard it was for me to leave and I think she also knew then that I'd be back.

I didn't think about coming back until after the mass layoff at Curran, Sanders and Fray. Being a newbie at the accounting firm just two years out of college didn't afford me much clout when it came to holding a position. I was one of the first to go.

After discovering that getting another job was almost impossible in this depressed economy even with a college degree, it took just a nudge from Chloe to get me to come back, temporarily of course. Now I was only hours away from being employed by her.

"Hello," the woman's voice said over the music in the background.

"Hi, it's me. I'm here," I said.

"Hi, Sophie," she said with her annoyingly bubbly flair. "You're at the hotel?"

"Yeah. It's been a long day. What time do you want to meet tomorrow?" I asked.

"Around ten. Do you have the address?" she asked.

"Yeah, I have it."

She giggled and said, "I can't wait to see you."

"Me too," I lied. I hung up.

I didn't want to stay at her place, but living at a hotel, even one as rundown as this, would cost more than I could afford so I appreciated her offer. She asked me here to help with Aunt Jane's business, but I was approaching her vague request with some trepidation. I needed to ease into this fast city and I was glad I had at least one night on my own.

The clock on the night stand displayed ten-thirty but my body was still on LA time. I was wide awake and I hadn't eaten since breakfast. I hadn't realized that the airline only offered nuts and overpriced dehydrated snacks on the flight, so I managed to get through on orange juice and Diet Coke. With the excitement of the trip I didn't notice until now that my stomach was growling.

I walked to the window and looked at the street below. A block east of the hotel the bright lights reflected off the cars and crowded sidewalks. I felt a twinge of excitement but was thankful that my window faced a quiet street. The room was stuffy and I would probably need to keep the one small window open all night if I was to get any sleep.

The lights were on at a small deli across the street. A young man dressed in jeans held the door for a young woman and both entered. Deli food was not my favorite but it would have to do. Until I was familiar with this part of town I wasn't venturing any further from the hotel.

I put on my sweater, the white one David gave me last year. I pulled some bills from my wallet and tucked them into my left jeans pocket. I thought it would be harder for a mugger to reach into my pocket than to grab the handles of my purse. I made sure I had my room key and I took the stairs to the lobby. I put on my "I'm totally comfortable on this New York City street at 10:30 p.m., so don't mess with me" face and crossed to the deli.

Once inside the deli I felt safe. The small room was brightly lit. Old photos of New York City donned the walls. Everything was clean and tidy. Behind the counter was a hefty woman with her back to me wearing a white apron and a pony tail. She turned around to reveal that she was a middle-aged guy who could have bench-pressed two of the deli tables, one in each hand. I felt even safer.

The deli offered all types of meats as well as chopped liver. I remember ordering a chopped liver and corned beef sandwich at Saul's Deli in LA a couple years back. I loved it so much I taught myself to make chopped liver. My roommate at the time would leave our apartment on the days I cooked it, saying the stench was overwhelming.

I had since been eating healthier food so I ordered a "California" sandwich, something with avocado, turkey and sprouts. I ate at the deli rather than take my sandwich back to the room. Even though it was more food than I usually ate in one sitting I managed to get it all down.

Back in my room I checked my phone. No messages. I leaned back on the bed and turned on the television.

I took my Sudoku magazine from my bag and flipped to the medium section. By midnight I was getting groggy even though my internal clock said nine. David wouldn't call back this late. My eyes began to close so I turned off the television and succumbed to fitful sleep.

Chapter 4

Morning sung through the open window to the tune of horns honking and trash trucks. In LA the flat urban skyline hung under the rising sun's horizontal rays that blasted into my window, but in this city the tall buildings sheltered my hotel room from direct light. The sun's rays wouldn't hit the street for hours. I had set my phone alarm, but between my internal clock and the bustling city I was awake before the alarm sounded.

This was it, the day I'd finally see Chloe. Since I left for UCLA six years earlier she and I had talked on the phone now and then but we hadn't seen each other. And our phone calls had become shorter and less frequent. I didn't know what to expect.

I showered, did my make-up and hair, packed my things and checked out. I walked, dragging my rolling bag behind me, until I came to a quaint cafe. Just inside I was surprised to see that it looked like a barn, complete with weathered wood walls and a hodge-podge of knick-knacks scattered throughout.

One wall was made of red bricks with too many paintings crammed upon it from floor to ceiling. Bushel baskets of onions, potatoes and melons adorned the floor. A scythe and a pitchfork leaned against one wall, suggesting that this restaurant owner may have taken these tools and driven out of the city to fill the baskets himself.

I was seated right away. I expected the waiter to be dressed in overalls but his attire was merely casual, jeans and a blue Oxford shirt. He was around my age, possibly a little younger, maybe a college student. He seemed unsure of himself but he managed to smile at me when I looked at him. His brilliant white teeth overlapped slightly in the front which enhanced his smile. I always notice the teeth. Sometimes imperfect teeth are more attractive than perfect ones. I don't think he realized how attractive he was when he smiled.

He brought me coffee and I scanned the menu only to find that the cheapest breakfast was a bowl of porridge for $11.50. Reading it almost caused me to spit out the two-dollar gulp of coffee I was about to swallow. Wasn't porridge historically a poor person's meal?

I ordered the porridge and gazed at the people passing by the window. I waited what seemed like an eternity for the porridge, which had probably been simmering in a huge pot in the kitchen since dawn. All they had to do was scoop it into a bowl. But they made me wait, to give me the illusion that my bowl of porridge was being cooked separately, because mine was special. Mine deserved to cost $11.50.

Or maybe the price of my porridge was exorbitant because of the price of decorating the place. Using fresh vegetables and fruit as decorations was probably expensive. This was a small restaurant. How many of the two hundred onions in the bushel basket could be used before they'd spoil? I imagined the ones at the bottom of the basket already sprouting and turning black.

Suddenly the quaint experience turned to one of disgust. How could they waste food for the sake of decoration? I studied the bushel baskets.

It occurred to me that the baskets probably weren't full. A cardboard box or some newspaper or something had to be stuffed at the bottom of each basket so that the vegetables only filled the top. Of course that's what they did. No one in their right mind would deliberately waste food. Would they? Anyway, imagining that the vegetables covered a thin layer at the top of each basket enabled me to relax, at least for a moment. But the illusion was quickly lost. As if I had x-ray eyes, I kept picturing that newspaper crumpled under the vegetables.

My attention turned to a slightly tilted painting hanging on the wall. Although most people might not have noticed that it was askew I could see that the bottom of the frame wasn't parallel to the line of the bricks behind it. Why hadn't someone straightened it? Because the staff never bothered to dust it? I looked at the other objects in the room. No dust. Everything was in order.

Maybe the painting had always been off kilter in some way or another because the staff was constantly cleaning, wiping it this way or that way and the wire hanger behind the painting was probably rubbed raw, just moments from giving way and dropping to the floor. I wanted to get out of my chair and line it up, but I knew it would only take a slight tap of my finger to get it level and

I'd probably get strange looks from the staff and the other customers. I managed to put the painting out of my mind by focusing on the people outside the window again.

I think people are generally more comfortable when they eat with someone because their mind focuses less on their surroundings and more on the person they're with. Drop me into new surroundings by myself and my mind churns like a wood chipper, sucking in everything around me and spewing out chopped up bits.

Chloe knows how I am about noticing incongruities in my surroundings. Maybe it's this kind of thinking she's looking for in her business. Maybe this is why she wanted me to come to New York, so I would work out details that others might miss.

After eating what amounted to a bowl of oatmeal soup with one sliced strawberry floating on top, I was on my way again. I decided to save the subway experience for a later time when I was with someone who could guide me through the workings of the mass transit system. My thin wallet would have loved the subway price but I went for a cab.

I stood on the corner of Broadway and studied the cab procurement procedure. I acted as though I did this all the time, just standing with my rolling bag beside me. Maybe someone would think I was a native New Yorker getting a cab to the airport for a business trip. After all I was wearing my blue business suit and two inch pumps. Two inches was my max, businesslike, not slutty. Not sexy either. Maybe even a little dowdy. Oh well.

I don't know why I was dressed up, maybe because I was meeting Chloe for business purposes. Maybe because I knew she would be dressed casually so I had to do the opposite. Suddenly I was reminded of high school insecurities.

Every couple of minutes someone would advance to the curb, stand facing the oncoming traffic and hold out their palm. Within seconds a taxi would stop and the person would get in. So with my rolling bag in my left hand I fanned the fingers of my right and extended my arm. It worked.

A rush of adrenaline shot through me. I felt a power I had never felt before. A person can actually walk onto any street and get a ride. I mentally began calculating what cab rides would cost compared to the cost of owning a car. With a car you have a monthly payment, insurance, registration fees, tune-ups, tires, gasoline, etc. And then there are parking fees and also tolls on some of the roads and bridges in this part of the country. Not to mention the stress of fighting traffic and the occasional fender bender. Why own a car when you can literally walk out of your front door and get a ride?

As we sailed through the sea of cars I thought, *this must be what rich people feel like.*

Chapter 5

The taxi pulled up to the front of the building. I paid the driver, got out and stood for a moment examining its brick facade. It was shorter than I remembered. Not that some demolition team had lopped off one of the floors or anything. Its appearance just seemed more compact than the last time I'd seen it. Of course that was years ago when I was younger, shorter and little more compact myself. I thought it would look older after all these years. But buildings like that outlived their youthful look long before I was born. The sidewalk was blanketed in a thin black film from years of taxi exhaust and I hoped I wouldn't leave black shoeprints in the lobby.

I walked inside and crammed my way into an elevator filled with business people. Not the Wall Street crowd or the Midtown bankers but the hardworking nine-to-fivers, women who toted knock-off designer purses and men who could only afford fake Rolexes.

They looked as worn as the carpet under my feet. I noticed that the seventh floor button had already been pushed, which was fortunate since my arms were pinned at my sides by the other sardines sharing this can. I got off on seven and quickly found the office. The only thing that distinguished it from all the others was the room number printed on the frosted glass door, but there was no company name.

My heart pounded as I entered. In the middle of the room sat the same empty desk with the buzzer on top. A closed door flanked each side of the desk on the back wall. This room was intended to be a reception area, but to date it had not been used for anything more than a foyer. It had the same drab linoleum floor and gray walls I remembered from the last time I'd seen it. My family had gone to the city only a few times to see Aunt Jane. She had usually come to our house for holidays and parties. She always showed up for our dance recitals and graduations too, but other than those occasions I hadn't seen her much, although I'd spoken to her on the phone a few times each year since I'd moved away, almost ninety-nine percent more than I'd spoken to Chloe.

Aunt Jane had started the event planning business a few years before Mom and Dad got divorced. She was always trying to talk Mom into going into business with her, but Mom was busy with PTA, doctor appointments and other usual mom stuff. She wasn't a soccer mom since Chloe and I weren't interested in soccer. I would call Mom a dance class/cheerleading mom who carted us to dance classes in elementary school and picked us up after cheer practice in high school.

When Mom and Dad got divorced Mom finally agreed to go into business with Aunt Jane. Once Mom began working with her, the business started to take off, or so I heard every night when Mom plopped on the couch from exhaustion. She worked so hard in those days but I could tell she loved it. She used what she learned from her years of experience planning Dad's business parties. I guess she and her sister were naturals at event planning.

In my junior year of high school I felt a new freedom. Mom was working long hours and Chloe and I had the run of the house. Chloe and I were good kids. We didn't give Mom much trouble, usual stuff, teen parties, some alcohol, no drugs. Chloe and I hung out with friends on the weekends but on weeknights we'd usually be at home waiting for her to get off work.

That last summer she offered Chloe and me some work in the business so we could earn some spending money. Chloe went into the city with her some weekends but I always liked staying home. I babysat and worked as a lifeguard at the community pool. I guess that was when I started to pull away from Mom and Chloe.

When Mom was hit by that car, everything changed. It wasn't until she was permanently gone that I wished I had seen her more often. It never occurred to me that she wouldn't be around to see us graduate from high school. It didn't seem right that she left so early. When I think of her my heart aches. And here I was, in the place where she spent most of the last year of her life. What made her want to be here? It looked like such a drab place, kind of dead. Like her.

A note taped to the desk read 'buzz for help'. A little unprofessional I'd say. Maybe this was why Chloe needed me, to point out these foibles. I pressed the button on the desk and waited. Why they hadn't hired a receptionist was a mystery to me. I assumed that the business could afford to have someone stationed at the entrance, but maybe not. The dog-eared note next to the buzzer looked ancient. It could have been written years earlier by Mom.

The door to the left of the desk opened and a young woman with curly blond hair burst into the room. "Sophie," she said loudly as she approached me with open arms. "You're really here."

She was wearing a lacey camisole and a gauze skirt that swished with a tinkling sound. The tops of her boots were covered by the calf-length hemline. I'd never seen her with blond hair, half up, pulled behind her head and secured with a chopstick. Her bracelets clanked as she flung her arms around my shoulders. I caught a whiff of a spicy fragrance in her hair.

"Hi, Chloe," I said as I flung my arms around her and squeezed. We held onto each other for a long moment, rocking back and forth. Surprisingly, the dread I had been feeling melted away as tears came to my eyes. I pulled back and looked at her face and hair. I said, "You died your hair and got a perm. It looks good."

"Yeah, it's blonde this week," she said a little too loudly, "but I didn't get a perm, I just curled it today. Come on in," she said as she guided me through the door. We entered a small office with a desk in the middle. A closed door was on the back wall to the left of the desk. Through an open door on the right wall I could see another office.

"Well, I must be seeing double," said a familiar voice coming through the back door. Aunt Jane pushed sideways through the door as she entered. Her gloved hands were raised in front of her with white goop dangling from her fingers. She wore clear goggles strapped tightly around the back of her head that pushed her hair into a bubble on top. Goop was smeared across the front of her apron, the same pink frilly apron I remembered from years earlier, slightly tattered now.

"Hi, Aunt Jane," I said with a smile. Everything about her reminded me of Mom. I had forgotten how much they looked alike. Even though the goggles distorted her hair and her eyes I could see my mother's smooth brunette hair and her blue eyes sparkling under the clear plastic.

"Well, come here and give your aunt a hug, darlin'," she said, wrinkling her nose. "You're just getting more and more beautiful."

She extended her arms toward me. Realizing that the goop was dripping, she pulled her arms to her side and bent forward to give me a cursory peck on the cheek, saying, "Let me give you a tour."

"In a while, Jane," Chloe said with a warm expression. "I need to talk to Sophie first. Is that OK with you?"

"Sure," Aunt Jane said. "I'll be in the back. But I've got some catching up of my own to do with you, Sophie."

"Of course," I said. "I'll talk to you in a while."

"Have a seat," Chloe said as she motioned for me to sit in the chair in front of her desk. "Do you want some coffee or tea?" she asked.

"No, I had coffee with breakfast," I said.

She walked to the left side of the room where a coffee maker, hot plate with steaming tea kettle, two cups and some condiments sat atop a short cabinet. She opened a cupboard on the wall and grabbed a box of assorted teas. She dropped a tea bag into a cup and poured hot water from the tea kettle.

My eyes scanned the room. Everything was fairly clean and organized. Chloe's eclectic style was prevalent throughout. A turquoise laptop computer sat on the desk. The desk looked like a table that had been salvaged from a used furniture store. It had no drawers, just a flat surface with four legs. Its fifties-style kidney shaped teak surface resembled a painter's pallet, with a hole in the top which served to guide the computer cords down one leg and over to the power strip at the wall. Two metal file cabinets stood against the left wall. On top of one was a small Buddha wearing a string of beads around its neck. The telltale smell of incense filled the room.

The window in the back wall to the left side of her desk overlooked the brick wall of an adjacent building. The window was ajar and a wispy orange curtain gently swayed to the tinkling of tiny bells dangling from its hem. Between Chloe's tinkling skirt and the curtain bells we had a symphony going on.

A bulletin board hung on the wall behind her desk. Pinned to it were overlapping papers, business cards and photos. I wanted to sort through the mess and make everything perpendicular. Positioned unobscured in the middle was a bumper sticker that read, "Women who behave themselves seldom make history." At first I thought Chloe must have cleared debris from the bumper sticker for my benefit, like a dig at me for being anal, as she had so often reminded me in the past. But I took a breath and put that thought aside. The quote was probably just a positive affirmation to remind her that her wacky way of thinking would propel her to greatness.

Chloe sat down facing me from her desk chair. "Well," she said as she leaned forward and drilled her eyes into mine, "so why didn't you want to come to my place last night?"

Her words hit me like a slap in the face. Tact was not one of her talents. There were times when she had used less direct methods of expressing herself but I could never predict which approach was coming.

"I just needed a night to myself. You know how I am, the long flight and all," I muttered, trying to avoid her eyes.

"It's been a long time, Sophie. Why couldn't we have hung out at my apartment and caught up? After all these years here we are sitting across this desk like business colleagues instead of sisters."

She had a knack for putting me on the defensive. I cleared my throat and said, "You asked me here to help with the business. Business is the reason I'm here."

"OK," she said, never taking her eyes from mine, "but you've got to chill. I know we've had our differences in the past but you're my sister. And I love you."

"OK," I said in a slightly annoyed tone. "I'm here aren't I?" I hoped she hadn't noticed that I didn't reciprocate with an "I love you too." This is what I was dreading, her immediate disapproval. Sure, she said she loved me but next would be the big sister lecture. Although she was only ten minutes older than I, she tended to treat me like a child.

"Look, here's the deal." She leaned back in her chair and took a more relaxed approach, sipping her tea between sentences. "I asked you to come here to help with the business for many reasons. I know how hard it's been for you to find a well-paying job in this economy. It's hard for all of us. Everyone I know, with or without a college degree is having trouble finding a job. Even this business has had a lull lately. Parties are not peoples' top priority when the economy is down. But there are still people in this city who have money and want to spend it on having fun. And there are still fund raisers to organize, and weddings." She paused and eyed me inquisitively.

I couldn't figure out why she had stopped. She stared as if she had asked me a question and was waiting for the answer but she hadn't asked. My eyes were darting back and forth as if I was looking for the thing that caused her to stop, maybe a hair on my clothes, or a spot or someone standing behind me.

She took a breath and opened her mouth. Then she narrowed her eyes and seemed to change gears. She said, "Now that Shannon has resigned I have no one to do the business stuff like the bookkeeping. You know how bad I am with money. You have an accounting degree. I trust you and I need you."

"I'm here because I want to help," I said.

"I know it's hard for you to give up your apartment and your car back in LA," she said sincerely. "You've made a sacrifice coming here on such short notice and I appreciate it."

"I haven't given up my apartment or my car yet," I said. "I'm subletting to my roommate's friend and my car is still there. I don't know how long I'll be able to work here, but I hope I can be here long enough to make a difference. I'll do the books until you can hire someone. Once they're trained I'll probably go back to LA."

"Um…well…there's something I haven't told you," she said with a cagey look on her face.

Mrs. Franklin 12

Mrs. Franklin was floating down the narrow corridor. The man in the white coat looked like the one who used to drive down her street in the truck that played that tune. What was that tune? She couldn't remember the melody that prompted her and her brothers to grab their pennies and race to the curb.

There he was in his clean white coat, his face hovering over hers. She remembered him handing her the popsicles with the two wooden sticks. But that was a long time ago. Her face had changed over time, but his hadn't changed at all. His face was smooth and young and blurry.

She wasn't floating now. She was rolling. The wobbly wheels of the wheelchair sunk into cracks and splashed through liquid, maybe lemonade. She and her brother had a lemonade stand one summer. Mom used to make the lemonade from real lemons and they would sell it for five cents a glass. On those days she had enough money to buy two popsicles, one to store in the freezer for later.

She couldn't move, swaddled like a baby with her arms pinned at her side. No, not like a baby, like a hamburger, so huge it's wrapped in paper so all the fixings won't squish out the bottom onto your lap when you take a bite.

A whale sat at the end of the hall, balanced on its belly with its mouth open and a smile on its face and its tail fin wagging. Sounds of growling and laughter circled around her as the man in the white coat tilted her and forced her through the gill at the whale's side. Whales didn't have gills, did they? She was now in the belly of the whale.

Ms. Fletcher? Why was Ms. Fletcher here? Dreams can be funny that way.

Mrs. Franklin said to Ms. Fletcher, "I knew you were in on it. I saw you that day. But your hair was fluffy and some other color, not like it is now. Mine was gray that day I saw you, but now it's brown like when I was a kid. Ask the man in the white coat."

Ms. Fletcher smiled and patted Mrs. Franklin's hand. "Don't worry about anything," she said.

The growling increased and Mrs. Franklin's stomach dropped. Darkness.

She drew in a sharp breath. The aroma of the pillow case against her cheek was different, not the fragrance of her detergent or her fabric softener. An annoying blade of light stabbed her eye. She turned on her back and stared at an unfamiliar ceiling. Clunking sounds and thuds banged around her. A sound gurgled around her like water cascading inside the walls. There were walls?

She snapped to a sitting position. Motionless, she panned the room, blinking repeatedly to focus through the dim light. The bed, the nightstand, the desk, the chair, the television inside the wooden cabinet…this was not her bedroom.

"I must still be dreaming," she said to herself. But the sounds of doors slamming and footsteps passing on the other side of her walls seemed real. Her dreams were never this real.

She rose and walked toward the illuminated slit in the curtains. With hesitation she touched the heavy curtain. It felt real. She gingerly moved it a couple of inches. Through the faint light of dawn, or was it dusk, she saw the familiar metal tower which she had only seen in photos.

"Paris? I'm in Paris?" she said out loud.

She jumped at the sound of a knock on the door. She spun around and froze, her eyes fixed on the thin line of light coming from under the door. Wait, something was familiar. The knock came again, like the beat of a song. She knew that knock.

Chapter 6

Of course there was something Chloe hadn't told me. It was Chloe, for God's sake. I had been gone for so long I was used to being in the non-Chloe world of the sane. I spent four years with students who aspired to learn prudent business practices and two years at a firm applying what I learned about ethics, basic accounting principles and business strategies. My innate ability to reason and think logically gave me an edge over some of the other newcomers. Then one phone call from Chloe and I jumped on a plane and flew three thousand miles to a job I knew nothing about. Had I gone temporarily insane? How could she get me to New York City with one phone call?

Now she was saying there was something she hadn't told me about the business? I forced all the muscles in my body to freeze and I reluctantly said, "Yeah, what didn't you tell me?"

"Well, I came up with an idea that will hopefully change this business and make a lot of money." She paused, searching my face for some expression of acceptance, then continued, "And it will be fun."

"Fun, huh? Well, tell me your idea," I said, crossing my arms over my chest. I sat perfectly still. I think she could sense my body squirming inside.

"It will still be an event planning business, weddings, parties and social events, but I have this idea which will expand it." She paused to read my face again. I was stone. She went on. "My idea may not bring in much income for a year or so. Like most businesses just starting out, you have to wait awhile for it to pay off. The current business may hold its own financially, but there might not be enough funds to get the new concept started."

"So what about financing?" I asked as I fidgeted with my fingers. "How would you pay for the expenses before this new concept brings in an income?" I saw the look in her eyes. The moment the words escaped from my lips I knew I had just opened a door I had worked tirelessly to keep bolted shut for the past few years.

"You're right. Financing," she said. "This might cost us some start-up money before we make a profit."

"It might cost *us* some money?" I blurted.

"You see, that's where you come in," she said with a smile.

"What do you mean?" I asked.

"I need an investor. And what better investor than someone I trust? And you must have some of your inheritance left. I mean, I even have some of mine left and you know how I am with money. You probably socked most of yours away." She paused. I didn't move a muscle in my face. "Well, you must have some of it left."

I stared at her.

"Come on, I know you." she said in a teasing way, trying to keep things light.

I stared.

She stared back. Then she leaned back in her chair and bobbed back and forth. "You have all of it, don't you?" she asked. "You have all of it and more neatly tucked into an IRA or some account you can't touch for the next fifty years. Tell me you didn't tie up your money in something you can't get to until you're eighty."

This is my sister, I said to myself. She's family, my only sibling, my twin. I took a breath and in a calm deliberate voice I said, "I like to prepare for my future."

She leaned forward and her eyes locked on mine. "Well, maybe this is it," she said. "This is your future dangling in front of you. All you have to do is grab it."

"You mean all I have to do is invest my money, don't you?" I said. "What if your idea doesn't work?"

"How could it not work? With my imagination and your business sense it's got to work," she said, lifting her arms as if she was presenting me with the entire world.

"Listen," I said, "I thought you asked me here to fill in for a while until you hire a full-time bookkeeper. Now I find out you want me to invest my money in something that you haven't even explained yet." I paused. She didn't respond. "You've got to give me something to work with here. At least tell me some details of your scheme."

"There you go calling my plan a scheme," she said, feigning hurt feelings.

"What plan?" I said trying not to raise my voice, "I haven't

24

heard anything yet."

"You mean you're interested?" she asked with an excitement that made me want to shake the marbles out of my head.

"I haven't heard anything yet," I repeated. "How can I be interested?"

"OK, time out. We've talked about this enough. The energy in here is too murky," she said as she waved her arms as if swatting at flies. "I'll get Jane. We're going to lunch."

My mouth was agape. Memories of teenage conversations with Chloe started to come back to me. I remembered why I had moved three thousand miles away. As she stood up I heard Aunt Jane's voice from behind the door say, "I'm coming."

Jane had been listening to everything we said. Was this a conspiracy? What had I gotten myself into?

Chapter 7

"The restaurant is just down the street. We can walk," Chloe said as she scooped up her purse from behind the desk. As she made her way to the door Aunt Jane burst from the backroom, apron gone and hands free of white goo. I grabbed my purse and followed.

Once out on the sidewalk Aunt Jane and I walked side by side while Chloe walked a few steps ahead of us. The walk to the restaurant promised to be uncomfortable since I was with two people who were about to entice me into raiding my bank account. Between Chloe and Aunt Jane I'd say Aunt Jane, who was childlike at times, was the more levelheaded of the two. Even though she could cut loose now and then her demeanor was usually demure. But I sensed an unfamiliar excitement oozing from her pores. This was not the Aunt Jane I knew from recent phone conversations.

"It's so good to have you back," Jane said.

"Thanks, Aunt Jane." I said. "You look wonderful. You've changed your hair. Have you been working out since I last saw you?"

"You noticed. You're so sweet. I like to stay in shape for my boyfriend, Stan," she said with a girlish excitement. "I mentioned him the last time we talked on the phone. I've been seeing him for almost a year. You'll meet him. He's great - you'll like him."

"Good, I can't wait," I said. I tapped my fingers on my purse and looked at the cars passing by. The luster of the city lights from the night before was gone and the shadows within the man-made canyons pressed around me.

"How about you?" Jane asked. "Are you still seeing…now what is his name? Don't tell me…oh yes…David?"

"We were seeing each other up until a few days ago," I said. "He and I talked briefly about marriage awhile back but now we're just OK. I don't know where we stand right now."

"Hmm, well, if you get back on track with him we'll have to

do your wedding," she said with a bounce in her step.

Yeah, just what I needed...a wedding planner three thousand miles from my wedding.

"Well, if anything changes with us you'll be the first to know," I said.

As we entered the restaurant the roar of conversations blasted us. Waitresses scurried about lifting big trays stacked with plates high into the air. Busboys bent over empty tables wiping crumbs while dirty utensils clanked into plastic bins.

Chloe shouted over the noise, "This is the best place in the area. It has good food at reasonable prices, fast service too. That's why it's always crowded at lunch, you know, because people who need to get back to their office in an hour have time to eat here."

It only took a few minutes to get a table. As we read our menus Chloe said, "They have the best Ruben sandwiches here. You've got to try one."

"I think I'll have a salad," I said.

"Salad," she said. "Anyone can make a salad. You've spent too much time in California. Are you a vegetarian now?"

"No, but I don't eat meat very often," I said.

"Yeah, me too. But when I'm here I always order the Reuben," she said.

"I used to love Reuben sandwiches. I like to eat healthier now, you know, chicken, turkey and fish mostly," I said.

Chloe closed her menu and said, "Well, I like to eat healthy too, but now and then you've got to eat something that tastes so incredibly delicious you say screw the fat and the calories. You'll have a bite of mine."

"OK, one bite," I said.

Jane closed her menu and announced, "I'm getting the BLT."

As we waited for our order to arrive I looked around. The room had no particular style. The black ceiling was high with exposed ductwork and pipes painted black to blend in. The tables and chairs were a hodge-podge of styles and colors.

"How do you like this restaurant?" Chloe asked.

I was trying to find a polite word that meant dumpy. "It's...interesting," I said.

"I really like the décor. It's eclectic, my favorite style," she said.

"Oh, it's meant to be eclectic?" I asked.

27

"Yeah," she said, "it's kind of how I decorated my apartment. You'll see it later."

Oh yeah, her apartment. I hoped it wasn't like her bedroom used to be.

The food arrived quickly. Chloe picked up half of her sandwich and lifted it toward me, "You get the first bite," she said.

I took a bite and chewed. It was surprisingly delicious. I smiled and nodded as I said with a full mouth, "You're right, it's very good."

"So, Sophie," Jane said, "how was your flight?" I think she was deliberately avoiding the subject of money.

"I forgot how awkward it is to get through airport security," I complained, "You have to take off your shoes. If I remembered that, I would have worn flip flops. And they confiscated a teeny tiny Swiss Army knife I forgot I had in my purse. All I used it for was filing my nails and clipping stuff." I was hoping the small talk would continue.

Chloe said, "That reminds me - Dad gets back from Europe in a couple days. Maybe we can all go out to dinner."

"Sounds good," I said. "You know Dad and I have kept in touch, a phone call every couple of weeks. But I haven't seen him or Jennifer since I moved away. How are the two of them doing? I mean, really doing?"

Aunt Jane blurted, "Oh, they're doing great. They do fund raisers together and they stay in shape. I really like Jennifer. If your mom was alive she would like Jennifer too. I just know it."

"So...Sophie," Chloe said.

I waited for the bomb to drop. I kept my eyes down as I speared a piece of lettuce with my fork. Suddenly I felt weak but I had been strong enough to get away from her once and I was strong enough to listen to her proposal. I looked up, hesitated for a moment and said, "Ok, tell me your plan."

She must have noticed my hesitation and replied, "Not yet, it's too loud in here. Let's talk about it when we get back to the office, OK?"

"Sure," I said.

We spent the rest of lunch reminiscing about visiting Aunt Jane's office when we were kids. We talked about Mom and Dad and cheerleading. When we got back to the office Chloe sat in her desk chair and I took the chair across from her again. Aunt Jane disappeared into the backroom. I imagined her standing with her ear pressed against the other side of the door absorbing our every word.

"Sophie," Chloe said. "I have an idea that will change our event planning business. What I mean is, we will add a feature that we've never had before."

A scraping sound coming from the other side of the door caused me to turn my head. Chloe winked at me and said over her shoulder, "Jane, if you'd like to join us you may."

From behind the door came, "Um, ah, no, that's OK. I have a lot to do back here." Chloe smiled and I heard footsteps moving away from the door.

Chloe went on. "Right now Jane and I do almost every aspect of the business. We consult with the person having the event. We get their specifics like budget, venue, theme, color scheme, menu and entertainment. Sometimes the client doesn't know what they want so we make suggestions. Sometimes we choose everything for them. We scout venues. We work with printers, florists, caterers, bands, security companies. Pretty much we plan an event from start to finish. We have part-time employees like drivers and waiters. Jane is usually the one who creates the decorations. She hires assistants to help her, mostly college students. Then we, meaning Jane or I or whoever we've hired, work the event."

"OK," I said. "So what is your new idea?"

"Some of the events we plan are surprise parties. You know, a guy takes his girlfriend out to dinner while we set up. When they return everyone jumps out and yells surprise. Or while parents take their sixteen-year-old daughter to an afternoon movie for her birthday, we set up. Just when the daughter thinks her birthday celebration is over they arrive at the party venue where all her friends are gathered. But we have never been part of the surprise process, meaning we have never planned how to deceive the person into getting to the party. That's always been taken care of by the loved one."

"OK," I said, slightly reticent, "I'm following you so far...I think."

"We've found that many people have a feeling ahead of time that they are going to be surprised. It's because they know the person they're with. They usually have an inkling that their loved one is trying to pull something over on them. So we are going to take their loved one out of the equation, when it comes to delivering the honoree to the party. We are going to offer a service, at an additional fee of course, for getting the honoree to the party. This will be a tremendous enhancement to the event. There are a lot of people with money in this city who will gladly pay to have us do this."

"So this would be a little like being 'punked'," I asked.

"A little," she said. "But the biggest difference, and possibly the most difficult part is that we have to get someone to go somewhere. Have you ever seen the movie 'The Diversion'?"

"Yeah," I said. "So we're going to scare the hell out of someone to the point of suicide in order to get them to their surprise party?"

"No. We can't scare them that much. Ooh," she said as her eyes widened and her voice dropped to a murmur, "scaring them a little would be alright."

"So give me an example of a plan you have for getting this unsuspecting person to their party," I said.

She thought for a moment. "You could tell them they won something like a car or the lottery and that they have to be in a certain place at a certain time to claim their prize. Then we would set up some place to look like a redemption center or something," she said.

"OK, but telling someone they won something doesn't take much effort. If this is going to be a paid service it should involve more than that. The first thing the person is going to do is tell their loved one about it and the loved one's facial expression is going to spill the beans. Then they're going to tell everyone who would be invited to the party, who would then have to become very good actors."

"Yeah, I thought of that but hoped it wouldn't be a stopper," she said. She got up and started pacing. She rested her fingers gently on the Buddha's belly, closed her eyes and exhaled.

I went on, "And you can't make the fake surprise better than the real surprise."

She opened her eyes wide and faced me. "What do you mean?" she said, looking a little deflated.

"You can't tell someone they won the lottery when all they get is a party. They'll be very disappointed," I said.

"Oh yeah, that did cross my mind," she said. She paused and

with a sigh she said, "You're being kind of negative."

"Please don't think my comments are negative. I think you may actually have something here," I said.

"You do?" she said wide-eyed with a faint expression of hope.

"Yes, I do…so give me another idea," I said.

"We could think of a reason to have someone arrested and when they think they are on their way to the police station they get dropped off at their party instead," she said.

"Hmm, that's a tough one," I muttered. Glancing at her disappointed expression I added, "But a possibility. I don't think you could get a real police officer to do it. So you're talking about impersonating an officer, maybe using a fake police car, embarrassing someone in public," I said. "You're talking about possibly breaking the law. I'm going to have to think that one over."

"Well, you've just shot down all of my ideas," she said.

"Those are your only ideas?" I blurted.

"Well…no. They're my worst ones," she said.

"Hey, if you really want to do this you have to think this through and take out all the kinks," I said. "You have to think of every pitfall ahead of time. You have to formulate every step of a plan and then think of all the ways in which the steps can fail. People are unpredictable. You have to create logical alternatives."

Something was happening to me. A puzzle was forming in my brain like one of those Rube Goldberg contraptions where one thing triggers another that triggers another. But some pieces were missing. Now that Chloe had opened the door to this new concept I wanted to find logical sequences to apply to these nebulous ideas as much as I wanted to rip the papers from her bulletin board and re-pin them.

I continued, "Think of my comments as pulling weeds. Once we get the weeds out we can grow a healthy garden."

"I had thought of some if the things you mentioned," she said. "I guess I've been pulling weeds too, talking about the iffy ideas first. I'm glad you think my worst ideas are the bad ones. I knew I brought you here for a reason. You're so good at figuring things out. These details baffle me." She walked to the coat rack and said, "It's getting stuffy in here again. Let's go to my place. You can meet Hasin."

"Who's that? Your latest?" I asked.

"No. He's my roommate," she said
"I thought your roommate moved out."
"She did. He's my new one."

Chapter 8

Chloe and I got in the cab. "Do you always take cabs?" I asked.

"No, I usually take the subway," she said. "It's close to my apartment and only a couple of stops to work. Sometimes when the weather is nice I walk. But today is special because you're here." She gave me a little nudge. "I'll teach you about the subway tomorrow."

"You know, I'm OK with walking," I said. "Anytime you want to walk is alright with me."

"OK, I'll remember that," she said sincerely as she patted my knee.

Unlike the taxi driver the night before, this one was silent. Strangers usually talked to me more when I was alone. I was reminded of that weekend I spent by myself in Santa Barbara.

A few months back David and I had been at odds. I just needed to get away and clear my head. I had driven north from LA on the 101 with no particular destination in mind. By the time I got to Santa Barbara I was ready to stop.

I found a single room in an old hotel on lower State Street. The carpets were splashed with huge flowers reminiscent of the décor of the 1930s. When I asked for a single room I didn't realize I would be sleeping on a single bed in a very tiny room but I imagined I was back in the early 1900s when everything was simpler and I was able to relax in a steaming bath in one of those old claw foot tubs.

I awoke thinking of David. I wanted to call him but I told myself to be strong. I would make him wait another day and hoped he would wonder where I had gone. I decided to eat breakfast at the coffee shop downstairs. I felt self-conscious about eating alone but I mustered enough courage by telling myself I was having an adventure. Whatever happened during this weekend was just part of the adventure.

I was seated in a booth big enough for four, which emphasized

33

my aloneness. The waitress was around my age, early twenties. I asked her what was happening in town and she pointed to the local newspaper on the counter. I picked it up and spread it open in front of me. When the waitress returned she asked in a bubbly tone, "Are you here alone for the weekend?"

"Yes," I said, "I just needed to get away by myself."

Her eyes widened and she said, "Shut up. That is awesome. I can't believe you're here by yourself." With uncontainable excitement she slid into the booth beside me and began flipping through the pages of the paper. She pointed out the museums, the art show at the beach and the foreign film festival at the Arlington Theater on upper State Street.

She said, "I'm Ashley. After I get off work this afternoon my sister and I are going to the foreign film festival. Maybe we'll see you there?"

"I like foreign films," I said, "I might go. I'm not sure yet." I asked her some questions and before long we were laughing. If I had been sitting with a friend she wouldn't have sat down next to me and we wouldn't have gotten to know each other. After my conversation with her I felt more comfortable spending the day by myself.

Chloe never understood my need to be alone. She would surround herself with people. I never knew a person who collected so many people. And she never missed an opportunity to criticize me for being a loner. That's why I never told her about this trip to Santa Barbara. I wouldn't want to give her the satisfaction of thinking her way of life had rubbed off on me in any way.

I went to that film festival. After sitting through two movies I saw Ashley and her sister in the restroom. Her sister was ready to go home but Ashley was just getting started. She told me about a night club on the north end of town that had a rock band and she asked me to go with her. Normally I wouldn't have gone with a stranger but she was a girl like me and I trusted her. So Ashley dropped off her sister at home and we stayed out till midnight, dancing with men, young healthy men. I was able to forget about David for a while.

That weekend I discovered that adventures come in many forms, including spending a day alone and a night on the town with a stranger. Maybe devising ways of getting honorees to their surprise parties will become my new adventure.

Chloe accuses me of being an introvert. But I love my alone time and I like being with people too. I just hadn't expressed a desire to have a relationship with her in the past few years so she must have gotten the idea that I didn't like anybody.

When I had spoken to Chloe on the phone before arriving in New York she told me her roommate, Nicole, had moved out. I assumed I would be staying in Chloe's second bedroom. But now I was about to meet her new roommate, Hasin.

Bunking with Chloe was about to be a little cozier than I had anticipated.

Chapter 9

Chloe's apartment was twelve blocks south and four blocks west of her office. I memorized the route for future excursions. The distance wouldn't be too long for a morning walk on a good weather day.

The taxi inched its way between the parked cars on the narrow streets of the West Village. Every parking space was taken. I couldn't imagine why anyone would want to struggle with having to find a parking space every day when there were so many options for public transportation. I guess having a car in this city would cause problems beyond the monetary obligations. But the looming concrete, brick and glass walls of this city might accentuate the need to escape.

I again thought of my trip to Santa Barbara and how freeing it felt to get out of a city and just drive. If I lived here I would use public transportation for everyday traveling and for under a hundred dollars I would rent a car for a day and head out to who knows where. In a couple of hours I could see my old home in Connecticut.

After Mom's passing that summer, Aunt Deb moved in with Chloe and me so we could finish our senior year without changing schools. But after graduation Dad helped us sell the house so who knows what it looked like now. Anyway, without a steady job I couldn't imagine affording a rental car anytime in the near future. Then again, the money I'd save by staying with Chloe might allow me to buy a temporary escape from her.

I stared out the cab window imagining the walls of the city folding around its inhabitants like cookie dough around chocolate chips. All the people were embedded deep within the dough of the city culture. Once entrenched within this place one might lose the desire to escape.

As Chloe sat beside me tapping her cell phone I noticed that the buildings looked alike. I wondered where the children played, if there were any children. Nothing on the outside of her building distinguished it from the others except for the three numbers on the wall next to the front steps. As she and I stepped out of the cab she warned me that her building was a six-story walk-up. No elevator.

As we walked to the fourth floor I noticed the obscured details of the antiquated architecture. The once detailed molding on the banisters and newels were covered with layers of nicked paint, hiding decades of dirt and sweat and cigarette smoke and weather.

As we walked down the hallway I noticed little doors along the wall just above the baseboards. Each one was the size of a large magazine. They were distributed evenly along the hall, one per apartment. A friend of mine had an apartment in Santa Monica with similar doors. She told me the doors used to be for milkmen to deposit the morning milk through the wall into the apartment kitchen.

Mom told us stories of having milk delivered when she was a child, how her mother would request dairy items by leaving her order in one of the empty milk bottles left on the front porch. Once, while the family was away, the newly delivered bottles sat on the porch too long and the milk curdled, popping the tops off the bottles. A river of white chunks flowed down the front steps. After that, her mother asked the milkman to place the items in an old refrigerator sitting in their garage.

Mom would say, "We didn't have cell phones or wireless anything either. The phone in our kitchen had a fifteen-foot cord so your grandmother could keep an eye on us kids while she was talking to her friend by stretching the cord around the kitchen wall. If I was going to be late getting home from the mall I'd have to use a payphone to call my parents. I would pay my brother to change the channels and the volume on the TV because remotes hadn't been invented yet. My girlfriend and I would sit in front of the air conditioning exhaust unit outside her house to straighten our hair.

I miss Mom's stories.

When we got to the end of the hall I could hear faint music. Chloe unlocked the last door on the right and we stepped into an entry hall. I caught a glimpse of the living room straight ahead. An overwhelming scent of incense hit me and I coughed.

The first door on the left looked like a cave of overlapping fabrics and trinkets.

"This is my room," she said, "just throw your bag on the floor by the window and I'll find Hasin."

Chloe walked down the hall and I placed my bag on the floor next to a futon folded under the window. I guessed this was to be my bed for the next few weeks. I looked around the room. The double bed was neatly made and strewn with pillows of different patterns. I recognized some of the velvet and satin pillows Chloe had sewn when she was in high school. I was surprised that they still looked fresh and new.

A large piece of fabric with a Celtic knot pattern was pinned to the wall above her bed. The night stands were covered with a variety of art deco figurines and one Barbie doll dressed like Jackie Kennedy with an a-line dress and a pillbox hat. I didn't remember that doll from our childhood.

Next to the dresser was a pattern of nails pounded into a wooden slab on the wall with at least fifty necklaces draped over the nails. Cascading over the dresser mirror was a piece of wide lace with an assortment of earrings poked into the netting. Next to the door a hat rack held knitted scarves of various lengths and colors. I recognized some of them from Chloe's knitting kick in high school. Every hook on the coat rack was topped with hats of different types and colors.

Out the window I noticed the narrow side street bustling with people coming home from work. Chloe popped her head in the doorway. "Hey," she said, "Hasin is in the shower. I'll give you the tour."

"I like your room," I said trying to be polite. "It's so you."

"Yes, creatively functional…that's me. This is the bathroom," she said pointing to the left. I could hear the sound of water spraying behind the closed door. She continued, "I cleared a drawer for your things to the left of the sink."

She stopped where the hallway ended at the living room, pointed to the left and said, "That is Hasin's room," then turned to the right and said, "This is the kitchen."

I looked around the corner and gazed at the small kitchen with a counter dividing it from the living room, an opening at the right. She spun in a circle and said, "So that's the tour."

With the hallway behind me, bedroom-bathroom-bedroom to my left, the living room straight ahead and the kitchen on my right I could see the entire apartment.

As I walked into the living room she made her way into the kitchen. "Sit down. How about a glass of wine? Is Merlot OK?"

she said as she pulled a bottle from a cupboard.

"I'd love one," I said, scanning the room.

She opened the freezer and grabbed a box of something. She reached down and turned the oven knob, removed an aluminum tray from the box and shoved it into the oven. She set a timer and placed it on the counter. As she twisted the corkscrew she said, "What do you think of my place? It is small but it's home."

"This must be expensive. How do you afford this?" I asked.

"It was Dad's, remember?" she said.

"Oh yeah, he still owns it," I said. "Does he charge you rent?"

"Yeah, he does. No free ride, but it's a good deal. I get a better rate than if I'd rented any of the other ones in the building. And since it has two bedrooms I can rent one and save money."

"Great," I said.

"How do you like our decorating?" she asked.

"This décor is…interesting." I said hesitantly. I had to come up with another word to compliment things that I didn't particularly like. How many times could I get away with using the word interesting?

I sunk down into the couch which faced the open door to Hasin's room. I was looking at clean white walls. His bed, which had a plain wooden headboard, was neatly made with a black comforter and matching pillow shams. Atop each white pedestal night stand was a contemporary lamp. His alarm clock had an old fashioned version of a digital clock. The numbers flipped vertically on rollers like the dial of an odometer. There was a round yellow rug was on the floor between the bed and the door.

The décor of the living room seemed to be a mixture of Chloe's taste and Hasin's taste, neo-hippy and mid-century modern. Beyond interesting - more like yard sale.

Chloe handed me a glass of wine and sunk into the armchair next to the couch. As I took a sip, the bathroom door opened and a dark-skinned young man emerged wearing a white towel around his waist which accentuated his bronzed chest and muscular legs. His hair, almost shoulder length, was black, wavy and wet. My eyes were fixed on a drop of water that made its way down his chest and over the ripples of his stomach.

He was looking down adjusting his towel and humming along with the tune playing on the stereo when he looked up and jumped slightly. As his electric green-brown eyes met mine I think I jumped too.

Mrs. Franklin 11

Mrs. Franklin sashayed through the front door bellowing a show tune. With one motion of her arm she tossed her bag on the floor and scooped Nibbles into her arms. Cradling Nibbles like a baby she swayed back and forth to the rhythm of her song.

She tossed Nibbles onto the armchair and raised her arms up into the air. With one hand behind her head and the index finger of the other hand pointing at her stunned cat she vamped her way to the chair, step touch, step touch, as Nibbles ran for his life and hid behind the curtains. She bounced to the curtains and in one quick motion, flung them open as her song made its crescendo. Nibbles dashed behind the couch and Mrs. Franklin collapsed on the floor in laughter. She rolled on her back and laid flat with her arms and legs splayed. Her breathing was strong. Her chuckles were intermingled with sighs of relief.

"Nibbles, Mommy isn't crazy," she said as her breathing began to slow, "Mommy is just happy. His name is Jeff and tomorrow night will be our third date. That's right. Three dates, Mr. Nibbles. I'll turn fifty-three next month and I have a third date with a wonderful man. In fact you met him earlier tonight when he picked me up for dance class."

She patted the floor beside her and said, "Come here, little one. Come on." She closed her eyes and heard his faint purr coming closer. When she felt Nibbles' tiny body rub against her thigh, she turned on her side and stroked his soft fur.

"Well, Nibbles, I am going to take a shower and if I can possibly slow down I am going to sit in my chair."

When Mrs. Franklin came back into the living room she was wearing the new robe and satin nightgown she bought the week earlier. She usually lounged in a sweatshirt and old stretched out sweatpants, the ones dotted with paint spots from when she painted the bathroom. Who cared what she looked like when she was alone in her own home? When she recently realized she was the one who cared, she stuffed her sweats into a drawer to await the next paint

41

job and went shopping.

She ran her fingers through her silky brunette hair, reminding herself that getting off the subway a few weeks ago and seeing her shabby reflection in the store window had led to her not only dressing better but looking younger.

Within minutes Mrs. Franklin was in her chair. She closed her eyes and felt her silent breath rise and fall in her chest. Her aching muscles were beginning to relax and a rhythmic purr came from her lap. Exhaustion had finally set in. But this was a new kind of exhaustion she hadn't known since adolescence. An evening of vigorous dance was her reward for working hard at her job every day. Lounging in her chair, even if only for a few minutes, was her reward for staying healthy.

Her serenity was jolted by a knock at the door. Nibbles flew to the floor as she stood up. "OK, Nibbles, you wait here, I'll get the door," she said as she tightened the belt of her robe and padded toward the front door. She pressed her eye to the peephole and saw two young men dressed in uniforms standing side by side. She opened the door.

"Can I help you?" she asked.

"Did you call for a paramedic?" one of the men asked.

"No, I didn't."

He lifted a sheet on his clipboard and asked, "Is your name Arlene Franklin?"

"Yes…it is," she said with a puzzled look on her face.

"We were dispatched to a 911 call originating from this address ten minutes ago," the man said.

"That can't be," she said.

He looked toward her feet and pointed to the ground. Nibbles was poking his head between her ankles. She stooped down and picked him up. "Hold on a moment. He's always trying to escape. I'll just put him in the bathroom."

As she turned her back to the door she heard something behind her and felt a sharp stab at the base of her neck. The room started to stretch and spin around her. She opened her mouth but no sound came out. As her body started to sag and her knees began to buckle she felt Nibbles being lifted from her arms. As she went down she could feel strong hands around her waist, gently lowering her to the floor.

Chapter 10

"Hasin, this is my sister Sophie," Chloe said.

He walked toward me with an outstretched hand, his other hand holding his towel against his side. "It's very nice to finally meet you," he said looking at me with those eyes. Chloe hadn't told me how handsome he was. She hadn't said anything about him. I felt my heart flutter as I reached out and touched his hand. He had a firm handshake and as he smiled his perfect white teeth matched the brilliance of his towel. Yeah…perfect teeth…not my favorite…usually.

I don't know exactly what I said to him. I may have spewed a mass of gibberish. But I hope it was something like, "It's nice to meet you too."

"I'll put on some clothes," he said as he smiled. He didn't say it to both of us. He said it to me, looking directly at me. Then he kept looking at me as if he was waiting for me to say something. For a moment I couldn't take my eyes off of him and then I felt small and vulnerable so I looked away. As he turned and closed his bedroom door behind him I noticed a drop of water fall from his hair and trickle slowly down his back. I turned my head to see Chloe staring at me over her wine glass. I had seen that impish smile before. When we were kids she would get that smile just before leaping on me and tickling me until I peed in my pants.

"What?" I asked, knowing exactly why she was staring.

"You have a crush on my roommate," she said with a sideways smile. "You luuuuv him."

"Well, you could have warned me," I said. "I mean how often does a tall, dark, handsome, half-naked man walk into a room where you're sitting?"

"For me, in the last month or so, every day," she said. "But forget it. He's gay."

"Shut up," I blurted. "He doesn't seem gay. You're making it up."

"He's really gay, baby sister," she said.

She could have been making it up. She used to tell little fibs when she was in a mischievous mood. I could imagine her letting me get real comfortable around this guy. Then I'd be coming out of the shower half-dressed sometime in the near future to have Chloe inform me that he's not gay. It would be her practical joke on me.

She continued, "Of course he doesn't seem gay in the five seconds you've known him, but he is. However, sometimes I think he hasn't made up his mind about which gender he prefers. Surprisingly he doesn't date much. He talks about guys but he rarely brings them here. He has some girlfriends too. Just friends, he says. But they look at him the way you looked at him just now. You know the type of girl who hopes she'll be the one to change him, convert him to heterosexuality with the capability of siring super babies." She spewed the last two words like she was announcing the prize behind the curtain.

"You got all that from the look on my face? And anyway, shhh, he'll hear you," I whispered.

"You know I'm very intuitive. You just don't like the things I intuit about you. Anyway, living with a gay guy or a bi guy, whatever he is, is much easier than living with a straight guy, less complicated."

"Is he Arab?" I asked. "He looks dangerous."

"Ooh…stereotyping," she said playfully. "Is that a slur that just came out of your mouth, little sister?" she asked.

"No. I didn't mean it that way. You know what I mean. That look on his face," I said.

"Well, he's not Arab. His family moved here from India when he was a boy. He puts on that dangerous look just to mess with you. That look gets to women and he knows it. He uses it as much as possible. He's kind of a dick that way. But when you get to know him he's really a good guy. And as for being dangerous…if you try hanging a piece art on the wall at a height other than sixty-five inches from the floor, which, according to him is interior design eye level, he may kick your ass. He's been trying to wean me from my interior design deficiency, as he calls it. You may have noticed the combo living room décor. He's in the process of teaching me the decorating principles he learned from some 101 class in college. But I'm resistant."

"Yes, the living room décor is…..ah….."

44

"Interesting?" she said.

"Yeah…interesting," I said with an apologetic cringe.

"You've got to stop using that word," she said. "It's me. If you don't like something you can tell me."

"Well, let me put it this way," I said, "I wouldn't choose this décor, yours or his, but it's growing on me. Your bedroom reminds me of you when we were younger and I like it. I can see that the living room is a work in progress. It may be the wine but I'm starting to feel comfortable. Is that better than saying interesting?

"Yeah," she said with a smile. "It's a start."

Chapter 11

Hasin emerged from his bedroom wearing jeans and a fitted tee shirt. I could see the impression of his chest under the fabric, the chest that mesmerized me only moments earlier. Straight guys usually didn't wear their shirts so tight. And it was tucked into his jeans, a little too neat for a manly man.

He walked to the kitchen and poured himself a glass of wine. He brought the bottle with him and topped off our glasses before setting it on the coffee table. As he turned around to take the chair leaning against the opposite wall, I got a glimpse of the jeans stretched over his muscular thighs. I sighed and glanced at Chloe who was almost snickering.

"So, you're Chloe's little sister. Five minutes younger by her account," he said with a flirtatious but warm smile. What was he doing? Teasing me? Making fun of me?

"Ten minutes," Chloe corrected. She never missed an opportunity to remind me that she was the older sister.

"Yes, Chloe and I are twins," I said. I couldn't get the smile off my face. I wanted to look away but I couldn't take my eyes off of him.

"You know they say that personalities of identical twins who are raised together are often less alike than those who are raised apart," he said. "It's something to do with people needing to feel unique or special. When they're around their twin they can consciously be different. When they're apart they can't observe the other and revert to their natural personality, which is similar to their twin's."

"Well, the evidence of that theory is sitting right here in front of you," said Chloe raising her glass. "Sophie and I couldn't be more different."

"And we like it that way, right?" I said as I raised my glass to Chloe.

"Yep," she said, taking a gulp.

"Oh, I don't know," he said in Chloe's direction. "Just last week you were wearing your hair exactly the way Sophie is wearing hers right now, which would support my theory, so why the extreme hair change just before Sophie's arrival? Maybe you're trying too hard to be different."

"Oh, so now you're a psychologist?" Chloe said, turning to me with a wink and then back to Hasin. "Why don't we talk about you, Mr.-Know-It-All. Sophie would like to get to know you."

I winced, hoping he hadn't taken her comment to mean that I was interested in him romantically. He looked at me now. "You mean Chloe hasn't told you about me?" he asked.

"No, until today I didn't know she had a roommate," I said.

He gasped, turning to Chloe, "Shame on you, girlfriend."

"OK, let me see if I have this right," Chloe said. "You are twenty-eight. Your family moved here from India when you were twelve. That's why you have a faint accent. Your parents both work for the Indian Consulate. You have two older sisters so you're comfortable living with women. Everyone in your family is a U.S. citizen now. You majored in theater arts and now that you've graduated you get acting gigs here and there. But they don't pay the bills so you work at Nufani's as a waiter and sometimes you work for me. How did I do?"

"Kind of cliché, I know, wannabe-actor - but really a waiter," he said as he rolled his eyes, "You got most of it right. But she left out the part about me being intelligent, compassionate, handsome and modest."

I smiled. "How did you and Chloe meet?" I asked.

"Chloe and I were going to NYU at the same time," he said. "She saw me on campus and wanted my body and..." There was something playful about his banter, not obnoxious like some overly flirtatious men. I think he was making fun of himself, not me. I like men who have the confidence to do that.

"No, it wasn't like that," Chloe interrupted. "He and I had a mutual friend and when I needed someone to work at one of the events I offered him some hours. He's worked for me off and on ever since."

"She still wants my body, she just won't admit it," he said with a smile.

Was it the wine causing me to fanaticize about this gay man? I wanted to grab his tee shirt and pull it from his jeans and reach up under it and run my hand over his chest. It had to be the wine. I didn't get thoughts like that very often. And anyway, I had a boyfriend waiting in L.A.

"That reminds me," I said, "I need to call David." I set my glass on the coffee table and walked down the hall to Chloe's bedroom.

"OK, Sophie, but you're next," he said from behind me. "I want to find out everything about you."

As I walked toward Chloe's bedroom I raised my hand in an acknowledging gesture. I entered her bedroom and closed the door. I took my phone from my purse and dialed David's number. It was late afternoon on the west coast so he wouldn't be home from work yet. I thought of texting but I wanted him to hear my voice. I needed to make some kind of contact. I sat on the bed with the phone to my ear. It rang four times before his message came on. His voice had always given me a warm feeling I hadn't felt with other boyfriends. He and I hadn't talked in days and I wanted his message to go on and on, but it finished too soon and I left a message asking him to call me back. Then I hung up, put my hands in my lap and just stared.

I don't know how long I had been sitting when I decided to go to the window. My eyes followed the people walking down the street. Were they like me? I mean, did New York City people think differently than LA people? They all walked fast like they had somewhere to go. I didn't have anywhere to go. I just stood and looked and missed David. I must have been in there a long time because when I came out Chloe was making a salad in the kitchen and Hasin was gone.

"Where is he?" I asked.

"He had to go to work," she said. "You and David must have had a lot to talk about."

"No, I left a message," I said. "I was just relaxing, you know, just thinking about things."

The timer dinged and Chloe removed the meal from the oven. She poured us another glass of wine and we ate at the kitchen counter.

"Sorry for the frozen dinner," she said. "It's been a long week and I wanted to do something easy. But the fresh salad should make up for it, Ms. California health child."

"It's all good," I said. It seemed that with Chloe's interest in Buddhism, gypsy clothing and incense she would be more into health food. I got a look at the frozen dinner carton and saw the word organic. I think she just needed something to tease me about. She had always been an enigma to me. Maybe Hasin was right when he said she may have been trying too hard to be different.

As we ate dinner Chloe caught me up on Aunt Jane's boyfriend and the business. She and I talked about Dad, who was due to come home soon from his European vacation with Jennifer. After my parents divorced Dad had lived in what was now Chloe's apartment. It wasn't until after Mom passed away that Dad met Jennifer and they bought a place on the Upper East Side. I guess my moving almost three thousand miles away had put a crimp in Chloe's and my already stressed relationship. She suggested talking about the new developments in the business and I told her I wanted to wait until another time when my head was clear.

"No, let's not wait," she said. "I think we might come up with some creative ideas tonight *because* we've had a couple glasses of wine. Let's try it."

"OK, but you can't make fun of me," I said.

"Sure I can. If you deserve it," she said with a mischievous look on her face.

We both laughed.

"OK," I said, "how would you tell people about this new service? How would you get your first customer?"

"First of all you've got to stop saying you and your," she said, "It's us doing it. Please say we."

"OK, how would *we* tell people about this new service?" I asked.

"We could advertise," she said. "You know, intriguing crazy ads that will get people's attention."

"Hmm...too much advertising might ruin it," I said. "You might...*we* might do better with word of mouth. If the whole idea of this new concept is secrecy and surprise then we might not want to draw too much attention to ourselves."

"Well, we don't need to advertise just yet anyway because we already have our first customer."

"Who?" I asked.

"Shannon's fiancé, Wade," she said. "Shannon quit her bookkeeping job with us because she's marrying this rich man and doesn't need to work. He is such a regular guy, not snobby or anything. He can afford Armani but I think most of his clothes

49

come from The Gap. We're already doing their wedding next September and he asked if we can do a surprise engagement party for her. When he told me how nervous he was about getting her to the party I asked him to let me handle it. I explained that I wouldn't just get her there. I'd make a day out of it. My suggestion sparked something in him. He asked me to make sure she would be so utterly thrown off track that she'd have no idea what was really happening. He told me if I came up with something that cost money he would pay whatever it took. That gave me the idea to add this service to our business. Once this first assignment is done, Wade might spread the word to his friends about our business."

"I recall you mentioning something about me investing money. Why do you need me to invest if you already have a rich client?" I asked.

"Like I said, I'm not sure if the business will be steady. I don't know how expensive these new projects will be. I don't know how to budget. We might need to rent another office, you know, one we can manipulate for a project. You should know about these things, Ms. Business Major. With Shannon gone I need someone who is savvy about money," she said. "Look, I don't need your investment yet. Let's just see how it goes. What I need most is your business sense."

"OK, you've got it," I said as I raised my glass.

Chloe raised her glass. To accentuate the toast she let out a dainty burp and we both laughed. That was the end of our business talk.

We moved to her bedroom where we flopped across the bed and talked for an hour, staring up at the ceiling. She and I grabbed scarves and hats from the rack and put on dances for each other like we did when we were kids. We even tried doing a couple of cheers which got us a clunk on the floor from the tenant below.

By the time we were ready for bed we had laughed so hard and so long we could barely stand. We just lay on the bed, collapsed into fetal positions, groaning in pain. We thought we might have gotten food poisoning and considered taking ourselves to an emergency room. But then the pain subsided just long enough for me to unfold my futon and collapse on top of it.

She finally turned out the light and we talked for another hour. When we were kids we had our own rooms but every once in a while Mom and Dad would let us both crowd into one bed for the night. She and I would laugh and shriek until Mom was at the door demanding we settle down and go to sleep. We'd be quiet at first but within minutes we were tickling each other and laughing again. Usually Mom's third warning was a threat to send us to our separate beds. So we would finally succumb to sleep. I missed those days when I still wanted to be like my sister.

Our words floated across the dark room softer with each passing minute. The silences grew longer between our questions and answers. I don't know what our last words were but the futon turned out to be more comfortable than expected.

I fell into a peaceful sleep that made up for the night before on the skimpy hotel bed. I woke up once during the night and lay there wide awake, smacked with the reality that I was in business with Chloe, but soon drifted back into dreamland.

Chapter 12

Chloe and I rose with the sun. She said to shower first while she made coffee. I opened the drawer which Chloe had cleared for me and began tucking my ablutions neatly in a row, managing to get everything in the drawer except for my hair brush, which I placed on the counter. My things were somewhat crammed in the tiny space but at least they had a home and I immediately felt more settled.

During my shower I thought I heard the bathroom door open. After showering I flung the curtain open to see "coffee's ready" written on the steamed mirror. I opened the window to relieve the room of mist and used my towel to clear the mirror. After doing my hair I went to Chloe's bedroom to dress. She popped her head into the room before taking a shower and said, "I moved a few things in the closet so there's some room and a couple of empty hangers if you need them."

I grabbed the empty hangers and was about to hang up my blouses when I noticed something out of the corner of my eye. Pressed near the left wall, flattened between other garments was a periwinkle sweater.

I moved the garments aside and raised the sweater on its hanger. I turned it, gazing at the front as well as the back, noticing that it looked brand new. But it wasn't brand new. Chloe had worn it in high school. She'd kept it all this time, almost ten years. It seemed weird. Did she love the sweater? If so, why didn't it look more worn? Or did she keep it to remind herself of something? I hung it up, taking the time to stuff every inch of it between two other sweaters, making sure I wouldn't get a glimpse of it later.

I walked to the kitchen and poured myself a cup of coffee and leaned against the kitchen counter. Hasin's door was closed. He must have gotten home very late because we never heard the front door open.

When Chloe emerged from the bathroom I felt a twinge of disgust, but I stuffed the feeling down like I'd stuffed the sweater between the clothes in the closet. My feelings would become as hidden as that sweater.

Chloe and I grabbed a quick bite, bagels with cream cheese, and headed for the subway. We descended the stairs and she directed me to a vending machine mounted on a wall. I deposited money into a slot and indicated the amount to be loaded on a card. When the transaction was complete a card about the size of a credit card popped out of the machine. I was to swipe the card each time I entered the turnstile and the cost of one ride would be deducted from the card. I had the choice of purchasing cards as I needed them or purchasing a monthly pass. I didn't know how much I would be using the subway so, for the time being, I encoded ten dollars on the card. That amount would cover approximately four rides.

I thought the subway station would be grimy with strange people lurking in dark corners, but all areas were well-lit. There was no trash on the ground and the walls looked clean and well-maintained. Most of the people looked like students and ordinary commuters. As a group I'd say they looked complacent, settled into their daily routine. They walked as though they knew exactly where they were going.

Once on the subway, people mostly kept to themselves. The seats were filled so Chloe and I stood, our fingers wrapped around the same pole. Some teenagers were wearing earbuds. They stared straight ahead, oblivious of their surroundings. I wondered if they knew that they might be easy targets for pick-pockets or muggers since their attention was distracted by music blasting in their ears. But I suppose experienced pick-pockets would know students don't have money so they wouldn't waste their time.

The woman reading the Wall Street Journal seemed normal. A young man seated next to me with the pack on his back looked like someone I might be friends with. Two women wearing sweat pants and walking shoes perused a tourist map. Mother and daughter, I guessed, since the younger of the two looked like a young version of the older one.

A man sitting across from me stared straight ahead, his gaze fixed on nothing. His inattention to his surroundings gave me the opportunity to study him. He was a slender light-skinned African-American around forty years old. His wire rimmed glasses were perched on top of his closely shaved head. Only the tips of the nose

53

guards touched the top of his polished surface while the thin wire ear pieces curved around his ears and pressed firmly against the side of his head, making a slight circular indentation in his skin. He wore a navy blue pin striped suit. The black satchel on his lap must have been filled with important papers because his arms were wrapped around it in a death grip.

On closer inspection I noticed that the shoulders of his coat were too wide, the seams drooping down his arms. His slender twig arms swam in his sleeves. His pant legs bunched at his ankles. The enormous size of his black patent leather wingtips were like dressy clown shoes. His bony fingers peaked out of the sleeves revealing neatly cut fingernails, except for one. The pinky fingernail of his left hand was a half inch long. And it was painted iridescent royal blue. I stared at that fingernail for a minute hoping he wouldn't notice me looking. Then my gaze rose to his lonely, fearful eyes fixed on nothing. He did not waver.

When Chloe and I got to the street I asked if she had seen the man in the business suit with the blue fingernail. She shrugged it off as if it was an everyday occurrence. I filed the experience away in my mental library of unusual people, New York subway people.

Chapter 13

Today was to be my orientation. The morning would be dedicated to touring the office and learning about the business. I would be spending the rest of the day with Shannon, learning about financial aspects of the business. She would arrive around ten.

Chloe and I entered her office. She dropped her purse on the desk and motioned me toward the door of the adjacent office, the one I had caught a glimpse of the day before. It mirrored Chloe's office without the window. An ordinary rectangular wooden desk sat in the middle of the room topped with a computer screen and keyboard. Great! I could leave my laptop at the apartment and save it for emails, and personal things. A bulletin board hung on the wall behind the desk, empty except for a bunch of push pins poked into the lower corner and a calendar still flipped to the previous month.

"This will be your office," Chloe said as she made a sweeping motion with her arm. "As you can see our offices have a connecting door and here's a door to the front reception area as well as a door to the creativity room in the back. Shannon sometimes closed the door between our offices when she was crunching numbers. I think my music was distracting to her."

"Your music?" I asked.

"Yeah, sometimes I play music. I usually play new age music because it seems to effectively align my thoughts with the current tasks, but my music was not her cup of tea, so to speak. Not that she liked hard rock or gangsta rap. She and I just had different tastes. But most of the time the connecting door stayed open and the doors to the reception area stayed closed. You can leave your door open or closed. It's up to you, but I think it's better to keep it open so we can communicate without getting out of our chairs. Sometimes the sounds coming from Jane's projects in the backroom can be distracting. When her assistants are helping her it can get pretty loud back there, you know...the pounding and sawing. So put your purse in your desk and I'll show you the backroom where Jane creates decorations for the events."

I had seen the room twice, once when Mom and Dad brought Chloe and me to the city and we dropped by the office to pick up Aunt Jane for lunch, and another time when I was in high school just after Mom started working with Aunt Jane. I remembered the room looking like one of those old black and white photos with rows of women in turn-of-the-century dresses sitting at sewing machines. It had been dark and dingy and I wondered how Aunt Jane could work in such a depressing place.

The room we entered was brighter and roomier than I remembered. The front wall was all windows that opened to a brick building across the alley. The walls were painted white and the light through the windows gave the room a natural glow. Sitting in front of the windows were two white drawing tables, side by side. Each table had a utility lamp clamped to it. Next to each table was a utility table with a computer screen and keyboard on top. Beside them was an upright bin filled with rolled papers. Extending the length of the left wall were floor-to-ceiling cupboards. A ladder with wheels at its base was connected to a horizontal rod on the ceiling above the cupboards. It was resting about half way down the length of the wall.

As I scanned the right wall I saw a half dozen metal lockers. In the corner against the back wall was a small room next to the door that led to my office. I could see a toilet and a sink inside. I turned further and noticed that the back wall, the one dividing the offices from this room, was covered with a colorful conglomeration of art supplies hanging from hooks. A very large table, which was as big as a room itself, sat in the middle of the room where Aunt Jane created decorations for the events. The table was cluttered with half-made sculptures and bits of ribbons and silk flowers. Besides the things on the table, the room was fairly neat. The cabinets were labeled, the doors were secured and it looked as though everything was in its place.

I turned to Chloe and said, "The last time I was here this room looked like a sweat shop. You've done a lot with this place. I'm impressed."

"Thank you," she said. "I made some changes, but Mom did most of it. She really turned this business around. She believed that a positive working environment was essential for success and she was a stickler for organization. You remember how she was, kind of like you."

I nodded. I couldn't tell whether she had just given me a complement or a criticism. I knew that while she viewed many of my attributes as assets, the dial on her judgment meter was usually teetering toward annoyance. Chloe paused and said, "There's one more thing I want to show you. Do you remember Mom talking about wanting to have a secret door or a secret room?"

"It sounds familiar," I said. "I remember her talking about wanting to have a secret room at home. She sometimes walked through the house eyeing the walls and closets. She'd get the measuring tape and make notes. But she never built a secret room."

"Well, she never built a secret room at home," Chloe said. A slight smile formed on her face and she continued, "Come over here. I want to show you something."

Chapter 14

Chloe led me toward the left front corner of the room where the cupboards met the windowed wall. She grabbed the handles of two cupboard doors and pulled them apart revealing a small room behind them. Chloe and I stepped inside and she flipped on a light.

The walls were painted like a dark forest with ferns and trees. A green velvet couch sat against the left wall. It had a curved back and a slanted armrest on one end like the fainting couches in Victorian times. Against the right wall was a window blacked out by dark velvet curtains. Straight ahead was a gnarled tree painted from floor to ceiling with branches spread to the side walls and up over our heads. I couldn't make up my mind whether this forest scene was more appropriate as a home for a speckled fawn or a decrepit witch.

The bark of the tree was painted to look old and crusty, like the surface would scratch your fingers if you touched it. Something was there on the wall, like a door or a frame of some sort, but it blended into the shape of the tree so well I couldn't tell what it was.

"What's this?" I asked.

Chloe moved to the far wall and touched a point on the tree trunk. With a humming sound the trunk parted revealing an elevator behind it.

"It's the service elevator. It's how we get the supplies and the finished decorations in and out of this room. Mom painted the walls and the ceiling. Then she hired a company to install the cupboards with the rolling ladder. Instead of ending the cupboards at the elevator alcove she had cupboards doors installed in front of it."

"This is incredible. All the cupboards look alike. I can't tell the difference between the real cupboards and this one."

"Yeah, Mom did a good job at hiding this room," Chloe said.

"She got her secret room after all. Why didn't I ever know about this?" I said with a tear in my eye.

"The construction was being done that last spring before Mom died. I worked here occasionally but you stayed home and worked at the pool. You were never here. For a few weeks I'd come to work and see building supplies stacked in front of the elevator room. The construction was complete a few days before she died. It wasn't until after she died that Jane told me Mom had intentionally hidden it from us because she wanted to surprise us," Chloe said as a melancholy smile formed on her face. "Surprises are usually nice, aren't they?"

"Yeah, usually," I said, thinking about Mom's death.

Chloe wouldn't look at me. She looked at the tree painted on the elevator doors as if she had never seen it before. Then she spoke, "Mom was building the couch when she died. The pieces were up on the table for weeks. I had seen her working on it but I didn't know what it was. After she was gone I figured out what to do and finished building it."

"So why didn't you ever tell me about this?" I asked.

"Why? Would it have mattered?" she said still looking straight ahead. "You never came to the city. You didn't care about the business. Then you were gone."

I was glad that she left out what she really wanted to say, that she thought I didn't care about Mom or her. I felt a burning anger rise in my chest. I wanted to tell her what I thought of her hints of disapproval but I didn't want to start a fight so I kept quiet.

She closed the elevator doors, turned to me and said matter-of-factly, "So, this elevator goes to a loading area at the side of the building. I'll give you a key. But don't use it to come in and out of the building because it's kind of creepy down there at certain times of the day. Keep using the regular elevator in the lobby to come in and out."

I said, "What do you mean by creepy?"

"Well, the elevator drops you in a hallway on the ground floor that leads to a loading dock in the alley. It's kind of dark and dirty and sometimes stinky. Once I saw a guy peeing on the alley wall in the middle of the day. I never go down there unless I'm with someone like Jane or one of our other employees."

"Is this elevator exclusively for our use?" I asked.

"No. The tenants on this side of the building have use of this elevator, so sometimes when you need it, it may be in use. You have to wait," she said.

"Can the other tenants get off at our floor and walk into our office?" I asked.

"No. Every tenant has a key that gets them into the elevator. But each key only allows them to go to their floor and the ground floor. So once someone gets in they can't get off at our floor."

"That sounds weird," I said.

"Yeah, well, it was set up years ago when the building was built and has stayed the same ever since. Most of the companies don't use the elevator much. We probably use it more than anyone with all the large decorations we have to transport."

As she walked out of the elevator room she turned off the light. Something made me look up and I saw fluorescent stars dotting the ceiling.

"OK," I said. I couldn't stop thinking about Chloe's comment, implying that this secret room wouldn't have mattered to me, that I had abandoned her. She and I would definitely talk about it another time.

Chloe turned to me and said, "By the way, we call this room the rabbit hole."

As we moved back to Chloe's office the door to the reception room opened and Jane entered carrying two large bags against her chest.

"Hi, girls," she said.

We both said hello as she walked through the office to the backroom. We had just taken our seats when the office door opened again and Shannon walked in. She was tall, average weight, late twenties, with straight blond hair to her shoulders. She wore jeans and a translucent, billowy flowered blouse over a turquoise camisole. She wore tall, wedged sandals made of turquoise leather with straps that tied at the ankle. Her face was soft and relaxed.

Chloe rose from her seat. She walked across the room and gave Shannon a hug and said, "Sophie, this is Shannon. Shannon, this is my sister Sophie."

As Shannon extended her hand to shake mine I noticed the iridescent polish on her nails and the jingling bracelets on her wrist. Then my eyes were drawn to the chunk of rock shining like a beacon on her left hand. Further down I saw turquoise stones and silver beads embedded around the open toes of her shoes and the same iridescent polish on her toenails.

Chloe said, "Shannon is going to explain about the accounting and the business in general. I'm going to talk to Jane."

As Chloe disappeared into the backroom Shannon and I moved into her old office, my new one. She sat at the desk, motioned for me to pull up a chair beside her and turned on the computer.

As she began to speak I noticed that the flamboyance of her attire did not reflect her personality. She spoke in a soothing voice, with a patience that was the opposite of Chloe's raw temperament. I understood why their personalities were compatible and why Shannon had gotten close enough to Chloe to ask her to be a bridesmaid. They were flip sides of the same coin.

But Chloe and I were flip sides of the same coin as well. So why had Chloe and I had such difficult times in the past? Why had Chloe and I held so much resentment toward each other? I would have to put that thought aside and concentrate on business for the time being.

Shannon and I went over the computer programs which facilitated the payroll, accounting, accounts payable and accounts receivable functions. She pulled files and ledgers from the cabinets and showed me every step in her accounting process. She went over steps of event planning from the customer's initial consultation to hiring vendors, scheduling staff and tracking expenses. During my short time in the business world I found that the accounting principles I learned in school were the tip of the iceberg. Companies used a variety of accounting software, but these programs were merely tools for accomplishing the basic tasks.

By the end of the day I learned that eight projects were currently in the process of being planned and six were in the initial consultation stage. I was happy to find that the business was not in need of advertising. The current projects included a mix of events such as a sweet sixteen party which might draw the paparazzi, an anniversary event for a large wholesale business, weddings, charity auctions and more.

Chloe was primarily the liaison between the customers and the vendors, including caterers, entertainers and rental agencies. Aunt Jane was the artistic director, designing decorations and supervising staff. In addition to scheduling event staff Jane would work the events, pouring drinks and supervising servers. A pool of ten part-time employees, mostly college students, helped with preparation, delivery and events, including Hasin.

With my education and Shannon's clear explanation, I was able to grasp my responsibilities by late afternoon. Putting them into practice without Shannon sitting beside me was going to be a challenge though, but I was up for the task and I felt that as I acquired a greater understanding of the business, I would be able to find ways to enhance the accounting system.

Before leaving, Shannon made it clear that I could pick up the phone anytime and ask her for advice. As she and I said our goodbyes I thought of the one thing I could not reveal to her, which was that I was here to change the business, starting with a surprise for her that she would hopefully never forget.

Mrs. Franklin 10

The subway rattled south toward home. When Mrs. Franklin heard the announcer say, "Thirty-Fourth Street," she remembered something that had been flitting in and out of her head for days. She could have been home in less than an hour without even changing trains. That was the predictable thing to do. But her body felt like a tightly wound spring. She couldn't sit any longer, so when the subway stopped she was out the door.

She hadn't shopped for clothes in over a year and Macy's was only a short walk. She looked at passers-by, every one of them. She smiled at them all. A few smiled back. It occurred to her that any of them could be the one. But getting off at Thirty-Fourth was unusual for her. How could anyone have anticipated her doing it? Maybe they could have been riding in the same subway car. They could have gotten off when she did and they could have been behind her at this very moment.

She abruptly stopped, spun around and faced the oncoming crowd. The people flowed around her as she studied their faces. Most of them, preoccupied with their thoughts or conversations, passed without acknowledging her. She held tightly to her purse as they brushed up against her. A couple of people bumped into her and she apologized. She noticed a man who stopped and faced a store window. Maybe he was stalling, waiting for her to continue down the street. She wanted to wait long enough for him to give up and look in her direction. But suddenly she didn't care. For the first time in a long time, she didn't care.

She turned and continued down the busy sidewalk. Her feet bounced with anticipation of buying new shoes. Her arms swung through the air like they were already draped in new silk. She had dropped a couple more pounds in the last week and she felt breezy and almost giddy.

She came to a beauty supply store and stopped. Superimposed over the items on the other side of the glass was her reflection. She saw a gray-haired woman looking back at her, her mother or possibly her grandmother. Not her. It had been five years since she had stopped dying her hair. She had been proud of her salt and pepper hair and enjoyed compliments. Yes, it was beautiful hair. But only women who had complimented her, women who wished they had the nerve to look this old. She had succumbed to middle age, hadn't she? She opened the door and walked inside.

In a couple hours she was back on the subway with armloads of shopping bags. Nibbles had been waiting in the empty house long enough. Tonight the living room would be turned into a fashion runway and Nibbles, her audience of one, was going to get a show. Her hair would have to wait until the weekend. On Monday her coworkers would be saying good morning to a brunette.

Chapter 15

Chloe and I sat in her office same as we did the day before, she in her desk chair and I in the seat across from her.

"Well, where do we start?" she asked. As she spoke she looked down at her blouse and brushed off a hair. She touched a piece of paper on her desk and slid it a couple of inches. She scanned it like she was preoccupied with something written on the page, as if to trivialize her request.

I didn't recall Chloe ever asking me to take the lead before. She usually dove head first into everything she did. Maybe that's why she wouldn't look at me. For one second I noticed vulnerability in her I had never seen before. I knew that inside her were oceans of ideas and a sincere desire to make her new concept work. But she needed me to organize it all and prove their validity.

"I thought about this while I was in the shower this morning," I said. "First I have to tell you what I will do and what I won't do. I will do research and help plan the projects. If I have to, I'll plan every detail of every project. But I'm uncomfortable with performing the projects. Actually, the word uncomfortable is too mild. I am terrified of taking on a role in which I am lying to someone's face and pretending to be someone I'm not. So you and I must first agree that I won't be the one luring the clients to their events."

"OK, I agree. I have no problem luring the unsuspecting clients. I welcome the challenge. I'll perform the projects," she said.

"Good. I think we need to brainstorm, you know, just start throwing out ideas. I need a chalkboard or a large tablet of paper, something we can post on the wall."

"We have a chalkboard in the back but we can't use it because it has planning info that can't be erased right now," she said. "We have a roll of butcher paper. We could pull off a piece and tape it to the wall."

"Perfect," I said. "Go get Aunt Jane. She can join us. We need all the perspectives we can get."

Chloe opened the door to the backroom and yelled for Aunt Jane. She came out holding her gloved hands in the air like a surgeon who had just scrubbed for surgery, except they were dripping with something red, like blood.

"What's up?" Jane asked.

Chloe and I stared at her with questioning expressions. "What?" Jane said, "Oh, this?"

Chloe and I nodded.

"It's corn syrup and red dye. I'm trying something, decorations for a zombie theme party."

"Oh, yeah, that's right...the zombie party." Chloe said. "Aren't you jumping the gun, Jane? We haven't signed the contract yet."

"I know. But I talked to a make-up artist friend of mine this morning and I googled some info and I couldn't wait," Jane said as she scrunched up her face and formed her hands into claws.

Chloe came back with, "It looks like fun but are you at a point where you can stop what you're doing? We need your help with planning some strategies."

Her eyes widened. "Yeah, I'll just wash up and get these gloves off," Jane said.

"And please tear off a large piece of butcher paper and bring it with you," Chloe said.

"And some felt pens too," I added.

"Ooh, I'll be right back," she said as she turned with childlike excitement. While we waited for Aunt Jane, I poured myself a cup of coffee and stretched my legs. She returned without the gloves and was dragging a long piece of butcher paper behind her.

Chloe took the paper from Jane and pulled two pieces of tape from the dispenser on the desk. She motioned for Jane to take the other end of the paper and the two of them taped it to the wall. Then I picked up a felt pen and walked to the paper. Jane took my seat and Chloe sat back in her seat behind the desk.

I said, "OK, before we think of specific scenarios we first need to set an objective. Even though we'll be talking about Shannon's project we'll be applying this concept to all future projects. So, what's our objective?"

Chloe replied, "In this case our objective is to get Shannon to her surprise engagement party without her suspecting and without her fiancé being involved in getting her there."

"Well said," I blurted as I quickly wrote her words at the top of the paper. "So, is the only objective to get her to the party? Do we just want to get her there or do we want to create an experience for her on the way?" I asked.

Chloe's eyes widened as she said, "We definitely want to create an experience for her."

"OK, so her loved ones can't be part of the process of getting her to the party but they must be part of the process before party day, meaning that they need to fill us in on Shannon's habits, her likes and dislikes. And they need to create ironclad alibis of why they won't be available on that day." I began to pace. "For instance, her fiancé needs to tell her ahead of time that he has business plans or something that he can't get out of, some reason why he can't be with her that day. Prepping the loved ones ahead of time must be part of our service."

Aunt Jane looked confused. She said, "So we're talking about pulling a prank on Shannon to get her to her party?" Jane asked.

"Yes, I guess you could put it that way," Chloe said.

"Are the pranks going to be pleasant or horrible?" Jane asked. "Because I've seen TV shows where they pull a prank on someone and sometimes they are pretty bad. Some people look like they're going to have heart attacks from the stress."

"Hopefully they won't be horrible, Jane. But they can be edgy, confusing, exciting and a little scary," Chloe said. "That's what I'd want."

"Something memorable," I added.

"Yes," Chloe said, "the prank has to be as memorable as the event we're taking them to." She stood up and began to move. Her eyes changed as if something palpable was forming in front of her face. She said, "Hmm, the word prank is overused. It's too mischievous for what I envision."

She sat down and began plunking the computer's keyboard. She motioned for me to look at the screen. Standing next to her I noticed that she googled some synonyms for the word prank, like baffle, dupe, fool, snow, snooker, none of which seemed to have a more positive connotation than the word prank. We both looked on with disapproval. As we perused the list she stopped at a word I would have never associated with the act of fooling someone.

Chapter 16

"Squeeze?" I asked. "That's an odd choice."

"Maybe not," she said as she quickly found some definitions of the word. "Look at this one," she said, pointing to one of the definitions. She recited, "Put pressure on somebody to act in a particular way." She raised her face with an inquisitive look, to ask for my approval. The twinge of my curling lip told her she already had it.

"OK," she announced with conviction. "We'll refer to the execution of the surprise delivery as 'The Squeeze'. One syllable...that's good." I nodded in agreement. She continued, "And we'll refer to the person to whom the squeeze is being done as..."

"The mark," Jane shouted, raising her arms like an Olympic gymnast sticking the dismount. "They always call the person on TV the mark."

"Good. The mark it is," I said as I took my seat and wrote frantically. Then I turned to Chloe and asked, "So, have you thought of any..." I hesitated, "squeezes yet?"

"No, not specifically," Chloe said. "I've known Shannon for a couple of years so I already know a few things about her personal life. But our relationship has mostly been professional. I get smidges of ideas but I haven't been able to come up with anything that's complete. I get crazy ideas but I think most of them are impossible or illegal."

"Let's form some ideas about the squeeze business in general," I said. "Why don't we make a list of things we can and can't do? We'll start with the most extreme thing and go backwards until we find things that are viable. For instance...here's the most extreme thing I can think of." I turned to the paper and divided it into two columns with the felt pen. I titled the left column Can't Do and the right column Can Do. In the left column I wrote "Kill someone." In the right column I wrote

"Pretend to kill someone."

"Oh, I see," said Chloe. "We could have a fake dead body or pose someone as a dead body or tell someone that a person is dead. Hey, we could get the mark to go somewhere if we tell them that someone they know is dead."

Before Chloe could think about what she'd said, Jane raised her hand like an awkward school child.

"Yes, Aunt Jane," I said, turning to see tears filling her eyes.

Chapter 17

"Aunt Jane, what's the matter?" I asked.

Jane sucked in a jagged breath and said, "Having the two of you in my life is the closest I've come to being a mother, especially now that your mother is gone. Chloe, Sophie, I know how hard you both took you mother's death. So did I. She was my only sister. I just have to say that you can't tell the mark that their loved one is dead. It's not funny. You do not want to cause anyone to experience the grief that comes with thinking that a loved one is gone. It goes too far. You just can't go there."

Chloe blurted, "I shouldn't have said it. I wasn't thinking." She wrapped her arms around Jane. Tears welled up in my eyes and I joined them in a bear hug. After a long minute we pulled apart. Jane put her hand against Chloe's cheek and gave her a nod. Then she turned to me and stroked my hair. She straightened and took a cleansing breath saying, "OK, my darlin's. Now that we've got that straight, let's go on."

"OK," I said. "We will not tell the mark that a loved one is dead. But we can fake a dead body and we can convince the mark that someone they don't know is dead. Or how about this? It's along the same lines. We can't do real bodily harm to the mark or anyone else."

"But we can threaten bodily harm," Chloe interrupted. "We can pretend to do bodily harm to someone in the vicinity of the mark. We might convince the mark that bodily harm has been done to them. And...we might convince the mark that if they do a particular thing it will cause bodily harm to someone else."

"If I hear the words bodily harm one more time I'm gonna scream," I said. "Hopefully we'll think of things that are more pleasant than...you know," I whispered, "bodily harm. So, next idea please."

The paper was filling up fast.

Jane raised her hand and said, "We can't hurt the mark's feelings. That might make their party day very distressing. You know, people remember getting their feelings hurt long after it happens. Some people remember hurt feelings for life," she said. She took a beat, like she was remembering some elementary school incident. Then with an impish look on her face she said, "But we can embarrass them."

"Yeah, embarrass them. That's good," Chloe said. She thought for a moment. "Um, we can't steal something from the mark, but we can take something if we return it to them later."

I wrote furiously.

I said, "We can't pretend to give them something they would love to have. And like I said before, we can't pretend to give them something that's better than their party. For instance, we can't say they won a car and that they have to be somewhere at certain time to claim it, because finding out that they only get a party might be disappointing."

"Yeah, you're right about that," Jane said. "Hey, I'm worried about breaking the law. We can't break the law."

Chloe stopped, turned abruptly and said, "Of course we can break the law."

"What?" Jane and I said simultaneously.

"Sure we can break the law now and then. They do it all the time in the movies and nothing happens to them. You know, like a car chase," Chloe said. "We just have to be careful."

Jane and I looked at each other, then at Chloe. I said, "Wait a minute, movies aren't realistic. Movies don't tell you what happens to the hero whose ten-minute car chase has just demolished twenty cars. Movies don't explain that in saving the beautiful woman he has just caused millions of dollars in damage and killed or crippled innocent people in the process."

I looked at Chloe for an inkling of awareness. Her head was down and her lips were pursed. She looked up with a smile and said, "Just kidding." She looked at me for approval. When she noticed the puzzled look on my face she went on, "Of course I was kidding."

I didn't believe her. Then with a flourish she rose and grabbed her coat from the back of her chair, exclaiming, "It time for a break. I'll be back in fifteen." She left, closing the door behind her.

I turned to Jane. "Aunt Jane, does she always leave when things get meaty?"

"Yes, she always does," Jane said with a nod of her head. "But she'll be fine when she gets back, like it never happened."

When Chloe returned, Jane and I were in the backroom. Chloe popped her head in the door and with a smile she said, "Hey, slackers, get out here, break time is over."

While Chloe was gone I thought about how I could convince her that breaking the law was a bad idea. I slowly began to talk. "We've been talking about extreme scenarios which I don't envision for Shannon's project. I think we need to talk about these extreme possibilities because we may need to use them in the future. But we need to start small and work our way up. Shannon's project is our prototype and it should be solid and doable."

"Yes, I agree," Chloe said.

I went on. "I wasn't trying to criticize your ideas, Chloe. What I meant to say is that a movie has an ending. The consequences after the movie ends are not part of the story. But this is real life and there are consequences we have to consider. We have an ongoing business. We have to think of ways to get someone to a destination without causing devastating consequences for them or for us. We have to think of projects that can be repeated. We can't deliberately break the law unless we are prepared to accept the consequences."

Chloe thought for a moment and carefully said, "So if we commit a misdemeanor like parking too long in a loading zone, paying the ticket might be a reasonable expense if we must park there to accomplish the squeeze."

"Yes," I said. "And to further complicate that scenario of parking in a loading zone, we would have to know ahead of time how long we could park there before the car might get towed. Having the car towed might be devastating to the squeeze and the budget. Unless, of course, having a car towed is part of a squeeze."

The three of us were now smiling.

Chloe thought for a moment. "So you're saying that we can break the law as long as we agree in advance that the consequences are worth it."

"Yes, I suppose I am," I said.

Jane interrupted with, "What about restrictions with places and things? What restrictions would we encounter in different places?"

"Give me an example, Aunt Jane," I said.

"Um..." She thought for a moment. "Well, it might be impossible to do anything at an airport. You know, Homeland

Security."

"At this point in our fledgling business we might want to stay away from jetting someone out of the city on a hijacked plane. But let's go ahead and brainstorm about places and things," I said.

We all thought for a moment. Then Chloe said, "We can't manipulate the subway system. But we can have a fake cab and a cab driver if we have enough money in the budget to either rent a cab or borrow a cab or turn a regular car into a cab. It sounds expensive though. I don't know if it would be possible this early in our business."

"We can use other cars," Jane said. "Hey, people walk so much in this city, if we need to divert someone we can do something simple like block a sidewalk so they have to walk in another direction. But we could only do it for a few minutes, or we'd get into trouble."

"How about a fake ambulance?" Chloe said. "We'd have to either fake the vehicle or convince an ambulance company to let us use an out-of-service vehicle. Again, expensive but possible."

"We could hire a limo and driver," I said. "Oh…we could hire a helicopter."

"I just happen to know a guy who flies a helicopter for City Tours. We could hire him for something," Chloe said. "And I know a guy who has a private plane at Teterboro. Not as many security issues there."

Jane smiled. And said, "Stan told me you can't fly an airplane or helicopter in restricted space and New York City is restricted space. The helicopter tour companies can do it because they have permits."

I said, "If your helicopter guy does something for us it would probably have to be within the guidelines of his license. I don't think we'll get anyone to put their pilot's license on the line for one of our projects."

"The same holds true for a boat," Chloe said. "We can't navigate a boat into restricted water."

Jane interrupted, "I did that once, when I was in school. A few friends went out on this guy's sailboat. He sort of knew how to sail but the rest of us didn't know what we were doing. Between the wind and the swells and the beers we ended up in restricted water. The Coast Guard cited him and I think he just got a ticket."

"So we could sail a boat into a restricted space and pretend we did it by accident. It might work once," Chloe said.

"We could crash a car," Jane said, "if the car belongs to us, but only a fender-bender, because we don't want to injure a driver or a passenger…or a pedestrian. And we don't want to spend too much money replacing cars, do we? Hmm, maybe crashing a car isn't such a good idea."

"We could pull a gun. I mean a fake gun," Chloe shouted.

"We can't pull a gun or a fake gun in a public place though," I said, "because there might be a cop or even an off-duty cop who would shoot us. And onlookers would be calling 911. We can't tie up the 911 lines. That wouldn't be right."

"Yeah, we don't want to do anything that would cause people to call 911," Chloe said. "Bad karma. I hadn't thought of that. We wouldn't want the 911 lines tied up if there was a real emergency."

"But we could pull a fake gun in a private place," Jane said.

I thought for a moment. "It's easy to pull a prank, excuse me, put a squeeze on someone. But I think our most difficult task will be to get someone to go somewhere. For instance, how would we get a stranger to leave a building?"

"We could pull the fire alarm," Jane said. "No, it's a felony to pull a false alarm. If we were caught we'd get arrested. And like the 911 calling, we wouldn't want the fire department to be called out on a bogus fire."

"But we could rig something that sounds like a fire alarm, that is, if it was in a controlled environment," I said. "By the way, we will probably need to rent a controlled environment, like an office or a warehouse, which will be expensive. Then we can manipulate it, you know, redecorate it to be anything, a store, office or studio."

Chloe said, "As for rigging something, I know a guy who works for the phone company. I bet he could rig all kinds of equipment. And as for the controlled space, Dad might be able to help us with that."

The energy was shooting around us like fireworks. We would take the ideas and hurl them into the room like cars racing around the track at the Indi 500. Then we'd pluck one idea and bring it in for a pit stop, tweak it slightly and send it back on the track. Of course, in my attempt to bring us back to reality, I had to put on the brakes.

"What if we meticulously plan and the whole thing goes wrong?" I asked. "How would we get the mark to the event?"

"We'd go to Plan B," Chloe said.

"And what is Plan B?" I asked.

"Drugging and kidnapping," she said with a smile.

Jane and I laughed.

"I'm serious," Chloe said.

"Plan B? That plan doesn't deserve to be called plan B, C or D," I said. "I think we'll call it Plan Z. Anyway, who would we get to drug our mark?"

"I know a guy," Chloe said.

I turned to Chloe and folded my arms across my chest. "You know a lot of guys. All ex-boyfriends I presume. I've never known anyone who stays friends with so many ex-boyfriends."

"Some are ex-boyfriends and some are just friends," she said.

"So you think this drug dealer friend of yours will be willing to drug our mark and manage to keep us out of jail too?" I asked.

"No, not a drug dealer. Dr. Bob. I've known him for years. He'd do it," she said.

"Great. Dr. Bob sounds like a DJ. So DJ Bob somehow drugs our mark and now we have an unconscious person arriving at their party. Surprise! Yeah, that'll work," I said.

"Oh…OK…you're right, I hadn't thought it through. Hopefully we'll come up with a better Plan B before we have to resort to Plan Z," Chloe said.

The three of us sat silently with mouths open. Jane broke the silence with, "I'm hungry."

"Me too," Chloe said.

"My brain is exhausted. Let's go to lunch," I said. "By the way, Dad gets back today, right?

"He and Jennifer got back last night," Chloe said.

"OK, I'm going to call him this afternoon and find out if he's available for dinner. Are either of you interested?"

Chloe and Aunt Jane simultaneously said, "Yes."

Chapter 18

Dad and Jennifer had met just after Mom and Dad divorced. I met Jennifer a couple of times. She was alright, a former hippy like Dad, hippies-turned-entrepreneurs. Dad always said the hippy thing had its time and place. The social problems of the sixties were specific to the times - the Viet Nam war, the draft, the racial equality issues, the gender equality issues. He would say the problems of the sixties could not be duplicated in today's economic atmosphere. Once the bras were burned, the pot was smoked by everyone including your grandmother and the races and homosexuals were on the road to being recognized as equals. At least now in the thriving metropolises, the fight was won.

I grew up in a family where race and homosexuality were not issues. I chose my friends according to the things they believed, what they did and how they treated me. My parents didn't care about the color of my boyfriend's skin or his culture as long as he was honorable. The matter of my boyfriends didn't come up too often though while Chloe was around because she managed to date most of the guys I was interested in anyway.

After college, graduates like my dad started wearing closed-toed shoes and suits and ties. The intelligence that had been focused on challenging government from the streets shifted to using government through political influence, status and money.

For many years Dad had a well-paying job and our family was financially stable. But when I was a teenager he invented and patented this tiny thingamagig that has to do with traffic control. I guess when you invent something that's used on virtually every traffic light on every street corner in every city in America you get rich.

Now Dad and Jennifer are comfortable in a multimillion dollar apartment overlooking Central Park. As a hobby Dad flips real estate and Jennifer has her own natural cosmetics line.

Dad's wealth hasn't changed him much. He likes playing basketball with his buddies at the gym. He likes to buy fresh food at the market and he and Jennifer often cook together. In the evenings he likes sitting at home in his sweats watching TV. He and Jennifer get up early on Sunday mornings and take a jog around the park, stopping for a latte at Starbucks along the way. They enjoy seeing movies, particularly the ones at the independent film festivals that come to the city. And occasionally they help raise money for the American Cancer Society. When Dad met Jennifer she had already had a successful mastectomy. The two of them began participating in events that promoted fund raising for cancer research.

I called Dad's cell phone number. He answered, "Frank Hopper."

"Hi, Dad," I said.

"Hi, Sophie, are you here?" he asked.

"Yeah, I got here a few days ago. I'm staying with Chloe," I said.

"When are we getting together? I miss you," he said.

"How about dinner tonight?" I asked.

"Hmm, I may have to move some things around but I think tonight is alright," he said.

"Can Chloe and Aunt Jane come too? And of course, Jennifer will come, right?" I asked.

"Yeah, the more the merrier," he said. "Hey, I've gotta go. I have a meeting in two minutes. I'll call you around five," he said.

"OK. Bye, Dad."

Dad and Jennifer were already waiting in the foyer of the restaurant when Chloe, Jane and I arrived. Everyone hugged.

Dinner was somewhat casual. We were all talking at the same time. Dad and Jennifer talked about their vacation, which included a bicycle tour along some back roads in Italy. They took the trip with a couple they've known for years who lived in their apartment building. The four of them ended up buying a small villa on the west coast of Italy, a place both families will take turns using.

Chloe and I talked about our brainstorming session with Dad while Jennifer and Aunt Jane talked about herbs and fragrances. I was hoping Dad would get the hint that his financial support would be appreciated, but the subject didn't come up. I noticed him glancing at Chloe a couple of times as if he was deliberately holding something back. He finally said that he would be glad to help us in a pinch. I didn't know what that meant but I got the idea that he was not about to fund the entire business. He had a lot of resources available to him and he assured us that we could call him anytime if we needed help.

When we got back to the apartment Hasin was watching TV with a guy, a boyfriend I presumed. The guy's chiseled chin and concrete hair was too perfect. Just after we arrived Hasin said goodbye to his friend in the hallway and Chloe went to her bedroom to make a phone call. When Hasin returned I was in the kitchen heating water for tea. He came into the kitchen and playfully bumped me with his hip. I smiled and asked if he wanted tea. He said yes and flung himself on the couch.

I handed him the tea and took the armchair, propping my feet on the coffee table and leaning against the soft leather. He and I watched some reality show that took place here in New York, something to do with designers. When it was finished he gave my foot a tap with his outstretched toe and announced that he was going to bed. I think he may have lifted his eyebrows when he said the word bed as if he was inviting me to join him, probably just wishful thinking on my part.

I sat for a moment in silence. I noticed a book on the coffee table - a novel, I thought. I saw that it was the latest James Patterson crime thriller. I had been reading a lot of mysteries and crime novels lately. There was something about the structure of the plots, like puzzles, that attracted me. I picked up the book and began to read but because of the wine at dinner and the busy day, my eyelids were sagging.

When I got into the bedroom Chloe was already asleep. I sunk into the futon, pulled the covers over me and listened to the rhythm of the city sounds wafting through the open window.

Chapter 19

It had only been a month since Shannon had quit her administrative position with PJ Enterprises to marry entrepreneur Wade Farrington, and PJ Enterprises was planning their wedding. Ironically she had met Wade while filling in as a bartender for a reception his firm had booked with our company.

Wade was from a wealthy family. He was thirty-two and not only handsome but one of the nicest guys you'd ever want to meet. While attending college Wade had worked part time at his father's firm in an entry-level position. He quickly proved that he was competent as well as innovative. After he graduated from college his part-time job became full time. His father relied on his subordinates to grant promotions based on merit rather than family ties. By age thirty-two Wade had been promoted several times. His father was confident that after retiring, his son would run the company with integrity.

Wade was a powerhouse when it came to his career but when it came to meeting women he didn't have a knack for flirtatious banter. He didn't want to be one of those guys who flaunted his career and his monetary status to lure women. He had been looking for a woman who loved him in spite of his money.

The night Wade met Shannon he had repeatedly returned to the bartending station even though he had only ordered two drinks and had been nursing the second one for hours. That evening Shannon and Wade learned that they had some things in common: going to museums, bike riding and dancing.

Shannon had mentioned to him that she was always keeping her eye out for a better paying job in her field, but she was surprised when he had handed her his card and told her to send her resume to his firm. He had also mentioned that he would keep her in mind if a position became available. That night's conversation with Wade seemed superficial and polite to Shannon. She hadn't expected him to follow through on his offer, but she had hoped he would call her.

Shannon was surprised when Wade called her at the office the next Monday and asked her out to lunch. The relationship quickly turned to romance after he suggested they take salsa dance lessons together. During the first dance class their bodies were pressed dangerously close to each other and they realized the inappropriateness of her working for his company.

She hadn't expected to fall in love so quickly. Before meeting him she had envisioned eventually meeting a man, getting married and working full time until they were financially able for her to stay home and raise children. After dating Wade for almost a year he invited her to move in with him. A couple months later he proposed. But because of Wade's ability to support a family and her lifelong desire to have children they concurred that she would quit working and they would start a family as soon as they got married.

That our company would plan their wedding was a given, but when Wade's parents told him they wanted to give the two of them an engagement party, he asked them to keep it a secret from Shannon. And he got them to agree to use our company to plan the affair. That's when he called PJ Enterprises.

In his initial phone call he expressed to Chloe that he was fearful about being able to pull off an effective ruse to get Shannon to the party. That's when Chloe came up with the idea that PJ Enterprises would get her to the party, for an additional fee of course. While his parents were footing the bill for the party, he would be funding the delivery of his unsuspecting fiancée. And he would be giving PJ Enterprises carte blanche to do anything necessary to give Shannon an interesting experience on the way to her destination.

Invitations went out stating that Wade and Shannon's engagement party was to be a surprise for the bride-to-be. And while the party planning was in full swing, Chloe had not yet formulated how she would get Shannon there.

This is where I came in. Chloe was the idea person as well as the person to deliver Shannon to the party. I was the one to plan the details of the project. I would research particulars and anticipate potential pitfalls. Not only did I have to create every step of the plan, I had to think of every way in which each step of the plan might go wrong. I had to either come up with an ironclad plan that wouldn't be affected by variables or create alternatives. Today was not intended to merely be a brainstorming session. We intended to specify every detail of the plan and formulate as many alternatives as we could think of.

The workday would be long.

I only knew three things about Shannon. One, she had worked for Chloe. Two, she was a lightweight when it came to drinking alcohol. Three, she chose Chloe to be one of her bridesmaids. It wasn't much to work with, but Wade had given us a list of her likes and dislikes which would be somewhat helpful.

I taped the butcher paper to the wall and said to Chloe, "I need to know some things about the venue of the party. You talk and I'll write. By the way, we have to get a permanent board. Taping butcher paper to the wall isn't going to cut it for long."

Chloe looked around the room as she thought. "OK, I'll just start talking. The party is going to be at Wade's uncle's house on Long Island. His aunt and uncle have a beautiful home on an acre with a boat dock in the back. There will be a hundred people or so. The party will be in the backyard. The weather should be good and the flat green lawn is perfect for the canopies. There will be appetizers and cocktails, no sit-down dinner. We're setting up a dance floor for a live band. Shannon has never been there but she has been to Wade's parents' house which is only a few miles away."

"So we need to get Shannon from Manhattan to a house on Long Island and make her believe she has a logical reason for going there. Is that right?" I said.

"Yes," Chloe said.

"Let's see, how can we get her to go to a house that she's never been to?" I said. "Have the two of them thought about buying a house?"

"Shannon mentioned to me that Wade wants to buy a house somewhere outside the city," Chloe said. "They haven't decided yet but I know Shannon prefers the city."

"Maybe he could tell her they are going to look at houses. But Wade can't be a part of this." I thought for a moment. "But you can. I've got it!"

"Already…that was easy," Chloe said.

"Not so fast. This is going to take some research and a lot of coordination but I think I may have an idea. You go on the internet and look up realtors on Long Island. Have you seen the venue?" I asked.

"Yeah, Jane and I were there last week," she said.

"OK, go on the internet and print out some photos of houses similar to Wade's aunt and uncle's house. Then we can get comparable prices. Is our car in the parking garage?"

"Yeah but Hasin is using it tonight for the Montgomery affair," Chloe said.

"OK, how about tomorrow? Is the car free tomorrow?" I asked.

Just then Jane came from the backroom. She was holding her hands out in front of her chest like claws. She stopped and looked at each of us then at the scribbled butcher paper on the wall. "What's going on?" she asked.

"We're starting to plan Shannon's party, particularly the part about delivering her. Want to stay and add your two cents?" Chloe said.

"What do you have so far?" Jane asked.

"Sophie assigned me to get realtor's names and phone numbers on Long Island," Chloe said.

"How about Diane, my sister-in-law? She's been selling Long Island real estate for years."

"Do you still keep in touch with her?" I asked.

"Of course I do, she's family," Jane said. "Joe's death doesn't mean I stop talking to his sister. By the way, everything for the Montgomery affair tonight is done and the staff is scheduled."

Chloe gazed at Jane's fingers curled in front of her like hawk talons. "What's with the hands, Jane?" she asked.

"Oh...yes...do either of you have tweezers? I seem to have gotten a few splinters in my hands."

Chloe and I both shook our heads.

"Come here. I'm a whiz with a needle. There are some in the back," Chloe said as she followed her through the door.

"Chloe, get me that info and you and I are driving to Long Island tomorrow. We're going to scout out some houses. I've got some research to do today," I said as I walked to my computer. "And Aunt Jane, please call your sister-in-law."

"OK, sounds like fun," Jane said over her shoulder.

"Wait," Chloe said as she leaned back through the open door. "I have an event tomorrow afternoon, a small affair."

"Can one of the temps take your place?" I asked.

"I don't think so. It's pretty much Jane and me doing it. And it's for some friends of mine so I need to be there," Chloe said.

"Is anyone using the car tomorrow?" I asked.

"No. The car will be in the garage all day," she said.

"Alright, I'll drive to Long Island tomorrow. Once you get a hold of the realtor, whether it's Jane's sister-in-law or someone else, please google directions and print them out."

"Will do, Sis," she said.

"Is Sis my official title?" I asked.

"No, your official title is Sista Life Saver," she said with a wink. "I'm so glad you're here."

Mrs. Franklin 9

Standing on the sidewalk Mrs. Franklin could see the lights emanating from the second floor window. She hesitated, exhaling a long breath before opening the door and climbing the stairs. She felt the low beat of the music vibrating the stairwell walls.

As she entered the foyer she noticed a young woman wearing a tee shirt and a short skirt. The woman was leaning against the wall with her arms folded across her chest and a gym bag over one shoulder. She was looking through the glass door at the dancers inside the studio. A slender man wearing a leotard, tights and leg warmers leaned against the opposite wall. He held his mouth tightly as he texted something on his cell phone. Two middle-aged women in sweat suits sat on a bench. They were engrossed in conversation about playing bridge.

When the music stopped the instructor said something to the class and the dancers clapped their hands. They filed out of the door and past the people waiting in the foyer and those waiting entered the studio. Two girls, maybe in their early twenties, ran into the room laughing as they dropped their bags next to a wall. Three others came through the door, including two women and an attractive middle-aged man.

The instructor slipped a CD into the player as she welcomed everyone and instructed them to put on their tap shoes. The others sat on the floor at the perimeter of the room, taking their shoes from their bags. Mrs. Franklin found a spot at the back of the room and removed the new leather character shoes she had recently purchased from the Capezio store. The shiny new taps nailed into the heels and toes of each shoe had never touched a hard floor.

As she began to buckle the strap of her shoe she looked across the room into the mirrored wall at her gray-haired reflection dressed in sweat pants and sweatshirt looking back at her. Even though she had lost weight in the past few weeks, the oversized sweats hid the new curves that were beginning to emerge.

The instructor said, "This is beginning tap for adults. We'll be taking this slowly. First we are going to go around the room and briefly introduce ourselves. I would like to know what dance experience you've had and why you've chosen this class."

The students walked to the middle of the room and positioned themselves evenly into two rows. Mrs. Franklin chose a spot in the back row. When her turn came around she said, "My name is Arlene Franklin. I took a tap class when I was seven but I don't remember it much. I took ballroom dancing in junior high and some jazz in college. But I haven't danced in years."

"Why did you choose this class?" the instructor asked.

"I just needed to get out of the house and get some exercise. You know, something healthy and fun," she said.

"Great, and how about you?" she said motioning to the attractive middle-aged man. "Last but not least."

He cleared his throat and said, "My name is Jeff Sterling. I've line danced and I've done the two step and the swing, sort of. I'm here because I got a role in the local community theater play "Stepping Out" and I need to learn to tap. Fortunately the play is about adults who can't tap very well."

Everyone chuckled but Mrs. Franklin's stomach turned as her eyes widened with shock. He went on. "The play's choreographer is teaching us the two dances for the play but I thought I might learn the basics here."

"Yes," said the instructor, "you will. So let's get started."

Mrs. Franklin's began to shake. Was this ever going to end? She didn't know what to think. This class was supposed to get her going in a new direction, to get her mind off of the elusive impending what-ever-it-was. She wanted to run out of the room but she felt compelled to stay. She had to confront Mr. Sterling after class or she would go crazy.

When class was over the students went to their respective spots at the perimeter of the room and changed into their street shoes. Mrs. Franklin kept an eye on the man as she quickly changed her shoes. When he was finished changing he stood up and began to walk toward the exit. She quickly grabbed her bag and followed him. She mustered all her courage and said from behind him, "Mr. Sterling."

"Yes," he said as he turned to face her.

"You said you are in "Stepping Out"?" she asked.

"Yes," he said.

Of course he was in that exact play, she thought. Why couldn't they have thought of something more original? Is this why Courtney had suggested this tap class?

"Where and when is the play? I'd love to see it," she lied, knowing she had him, since there was no play.

"It's at the Gazebo in the park about six weeks from now," he said. "I can't remember the exact dates."

Of course he couldn't remember the exact dates of an imaginary play.

"Wait, I think a poster is here in the studio." He moved to a bulletin board next to the door and lifted a flyer revealing a poster with the headline, "Stepping Out". "Here it is, June seventeenth, eighteenth, nineteenth, twenty-fourth and twenty-fifth, two weekends."

Her mouth dropped. She watched as he began to remove the push pins and reposition the poster on top of the other papers on the board.

"This is better," he said. "How will anyone know about our play if it's buried under all these papers?"

Mrs. Franklin caught a glimpse of some writing on one of the flyers he was about to cover. "Wait," she said, "let me see that one."

He handed her the flyer entitled 'Give Someone the Joy of Dance, Sponsor a Disadvantaged Child'. "This sounds like a good cause. I might want to do this. Let's not bury this one. I think we can hang it on the bottom of the board so it's not covered. Just take these two pins like this. There. Now we can see your poster and this one."

She dug a pen out of her purse and wrote the phone number from the flyer on a scrap of paper. As she was writing Mr. Sterling said, "Look at this one. Ballroom dancing, Tuesday nights, here in this studio. I've wanted to try ballroom dancing but I don't have a partner."

Absentmindedly she said, "Yeah, me too, same problem."

"Well, if you ever want to take the ballroom class, let me know," he said.

Her brow furrowed and she did a double take as she said, "Sure." She turned and headed for the exit.

Mr. Sterling said from behind her, "Hey, would you like to get a cup of coffee or something?"

Her face flushed. She was sure she would be embarrassed when she turned around to see him talking to someone behind her? But no one was behind her. She stared at him in bewilderment. She wasn't sure if she'd heard him correctly. Wasn't an invitation to coffee code for I think you're attractive and I want to get to know you better? How could that be? No one had shown an interest in her in years.

He hesitated when he noticed her look of amazement, then said, "Ah, I'm on my way to the coffee shop on the corner. Since we're classmates and…community mates, would you like to join me? That is, if you have time."

"Um…yeah…I have time. OK, I guess," she said in a fog. She still wasn't convinced.

Chapter 20

Once out of Manhattan the roads were clear and the drive to the real estate office was relatively quick, an hour or so. Aunt Jane had contacted Diane, her sister-in-law, who was originally hesitant to help. The bottom had dropped out of the real estate market and she was concentrating on sales rather than doing sisters-in-law favors. But Aunt Jane had encouraged her to listen to the details before declining. After some convincing Jane had appealed to Diane's adventurous side.

I met Diane at the realty office and explained about our plan in detail. She showed me the homes Chloe had found on the internet. When I explained about some of the additional information we got on Shannon, her likes and dislikes, Diane was able to find other potential properties.

After seeing eight houses I decided on two foreclosures because they were vacant and sometimes damaged. Whether Diane would agree to us making changes was iffy, but with a little persuasion and some compromises she agreed. Next I needed to schedule the modifications, which would be cosmetic and not too pricy. She and I agreed on having the workmen meet her the next week.

There was one variable I hadn't worked out yet. I timed the drive from Manhattan to the real estate office and added a predictable amount of time for Chloe and Shannon to see two houses. But if seeing the two houses turned out to take less time than I anticipated, they would arrive at the party too early. I would have to create something for the two of them to do as a buffer between house hunting and party. Any lag time might cause Shannon to suggest going back to the city.

The driving time from the real estate office to Wade's aunt and uncle's house had not been tested. After saying goodbye to Diane I drove north toward Montauk. The mileage had been googled and the printed information was on the seat next to me. Now it just needed to be timed.

I remembered something on Shannon's information list so I stopped at a small harbor. I parked the car and started walking along a causeway that led to the slips where the boats were docked. Power boats with flying bridges were intermingled with sailboats of all sizes. The docks were enclosed with a chain-link fence and I could see a few people on their boats, sanding, painting, and some just kicking back drinking beer.

I noticed an open gate so I took the ramp down and walked between the slips. My stomach felt a little queasy from the motion of the surrounding boats, and the fishy smell made me feel a little nauseated. One bright light is that the unpleasant feeling in my stomach gave me the perfect idea for the project. As I turned to leave the slip area a young man came from below the deck of a sailboat. When he saw me he raised his forearm to shield the sun from his eyes and said, "Hello."

"Hello," I said. He was shirtless, tanned and gorgeous. His dark brown hair was slightly bleached by the sun. His tanned face made his wide smile look fluorescent. But even from a distance I could tell his front teeth slightly overlapped. Umm, perfect.

"You look lost. Do you need some help?" he asked.

"Oh, I'm just a little queasy from the motion of the dock and the boats and the sea air," I said.

"Yeah, that's something you get used to after a while," he said.

I couldn't take my eyes off him. He was so beautiful. I was trying to think of a way to prolong our conversation so I said, "Do you know of any restaurants in the area, some place good for lunch? But not a fast food place...a nice place...but not too expensive, something cozy or classy...on the main road? Near the main road is OK too. I mean I'm not sure where the main roads are but..."

My ramblings were beginning to annoy me. The words floated out of my mouth aimlessly like thousands of feathers released from a pillow which I had just stabbed repeatedly.

He smiled with a confidence that said he knew I was nervous. "I'd recommend the Roadhouse Grill," he said as he grabbed a shirt that was draped over a rail and jumped to the dock.

Up close he was even better looking. I couldn't look at him. He was like the sun and I couldn't stare right at him for fear of going blind. So I began rummaging through my purse and talking.

"Uh, where is it? I mean, I don't know this area, or how far it is or anything. I think I have a paper in here somewhere. I'm usually so organized. Let's see, where is it? I think it's in one of these compartments. If you give me the address I could jot a note. Oh…I forgot…I can maybe get it on my phone. This place is sort of remote. Does GPS work here?"

He just stood there next to me. I sensed that he was smiling. "I'm going there now," he said. "Why don't you follow me?"

"Oh, I don't need it now. I need it for someone else. I mean I just need a suggestion for some friends…who are coming next…um, no, I should see it now, and…ah…sure, OK I'll follow you."

As we walked to our cars I pondered the relationship between having someone of the opposite sex in close proximity to my body and my temporary loss of brain function, but in a few minutes my car was behind his and we were pulling into the restaurant parking lot. He took a parking space at the side of the restaurant and I parked near the front. We met just outside the entrance.

"This place has good food, a comfortable atmosphere and reasonable prices. The bar has a signature drink if you like rum, and the chef specializes in shrimp. What more could you ask for?" he said shrugging his shoulders.

"This does look like a comfortable place," I said, glancing in the window. "Thanks for showing it to me."

"Are you staying for lunch?" he asked.

"Oh, no, I'm working. I have a couple more things to do this afternoon and then I'm back to Manhattan," I said.

Why couldn't I have said yes? Just yes. It would have been easy. He asks, are you staying for lunch and I say yes. Maybe he would have asked me to have lunch with him. But no, I had to say…what did I say anyway?

"You live in Manhattan?" he asked.

"Yeah. I live with my sister and I work there. I'm here to scout out some ideas for our business."

"What business?" he asked.

Maybe I could get him back on the subject of lunch if I could sort out the jumbled words in my head. "Well, our new concept is just getting off the ground," I said. "The business has an element of secrecy. So I can't talk too much about it."

"I get it," he said. "If you tell me then you'll have to kill me, right?"

I laughed. "It's hard to explain." Sure it's hard for me to explain when I know nothing about flirting. And I know nothing about having a conversation with a gorgeous man.

I extended my hand to shake his. As his hand touched mine I swear I could feel electricity shooting up my arm. I said, "Thank you for your help. If you're ever in Manhattan look me up. I mean it. Next time you're there, give me a call." Oh my God. Where did that come from? Was I being too forward? Maybe he was just being polite and I just invited him to come visit me. How creepy was that?

He said, "And how will I do that?"

"Do what?" I asked, feeling his hand in mine as my tongue thickened and a bead of sweat trickled down my neck. I needed more practice at this. I felt like I was on the brink of having some kind of seizure.

"Call you," he said with an adorable snicker.

"Oh, I'm sorry. My brain must be somewhere else. Here's my card," I released my grip on his hand, took a business card from my purse and handed it to him.

"Sophie Hopper, PJ Enterprises," he said out loud as he read the words. "Sophie is a beautiful name. What does PJ stand for?"

"It originally stood for my mother and my aunt's initials, Phyllis and Jane. And that's what we tell everyone." I lowered my voice and murmured, "But now it stands for something else. That's the secrecy part. It's an inside thing." I feared I had said too much.

He looked me in the eye and squinted, saying, "Hmm, PJ...pajamas...peanut butter and jelly?" Then he shot me a sly expression and said, "Practical joke."

My mouth was agape and my eyes widened in surprise. I smiled and said, "You're the first person to ask. But I'm not going to tell you if you're right or wrong. Not until I know you better."

I extended my hand again and as we shook hands he said, "It was nice to meet you, Sophie. I'm Chris. If you're ever in this area, look me up."

"And how will I do that?" I asked.

"I don't have a card but I just started working here and you know where I live," he said.

"Where?"

"My boat," he said.

"OK, sure. I wouldn't want to bother you at home. But if I'm in the area I may stop by the restaurant. Nice to meet you, Chris," I said.

He went inside.

I drove north from the restaurant to Wade's uncle's house, noting the mileage and the time. On the way back to the city I thought of David and how we had recently drifted apart. He hadn't returned my calls. I didn't know if it was because he was angry with me or hurt or done with our relationship. I felt like phoning him from the car but I didn't have a Bluetooth. I knew that was just an excuse. If I wanted to call him I could have pulled to the side of the road and made a call. But I needed to stay strong. He would call me when he was ready.

After talking to Chris I felt sad, like something was missing. I missed having a boyfriend. As I passed the restaurant I saw Chris' car parked in the lot. My hands wanted to turn the steering wheel but I forced myself to continue south. I was on assignment, working for my new employer. We only had a week to plan all the details of the project and alter the houses. The sooner I got the information back to the office, the better.

I wouldn't be there on event day. Only Chloe and Shannon would experience the things my research and planning accomplished. I would be waiting and wondering if my plan worked, starting with their breakfast.

Chapter 21

On her way to a late breakfast with Chloe, Shannon recalled only getting together with Chloe twice since quitting her job, once to settle on the band for her reception and once for lunch. She missed spending time with Chloe, being able to glean from her a unique energy she hadn't experienced around anyone else.

She was hoping they would catch up on all the things that had happened since the last time they'd seen each other, but there was one thing she didn't want to talk about. She wouldn't allow herself to talk about it yet. Of all the people she knew, Chloe was the one in whom she could confide, even more than her mother and her sister, but Shannon wasn't ready to speak the words because she wasn't sure yet.

The taxi stopped at a light and she took her compact from her purse and gazed into the mirror. Her lips were pinkish mauve, a color she often chose for daytime. She felt fresh and beautiful. Chloe would particularly notice that she was wearing lipstick. She flipped the compact closed and slipped it back into her purse.

Until she met Chloe she'd never worn lipstick and she hadn't cared about wearing makeup or fashionable clothes. She had preferred playing down her appearance so as not to attract anyone who might distract her from her studies. It wasn't until she was working at PJ Enterprises that she began to look at herself differently. Even though Shannon was a few years older than Chloe, it was Chloe who had taken Shannon under her wing and mentored her about the more flamboyant possibilities of life.

The first time Shannon wore lipstick she realized she had been hiding in plain sight. The day she walked down the street with her new red lips she noticed people looking at her. And for the first time in her life she liked being noticed.

With Chloe's help the simple act of putting on lipstick had opened up her life to new possibilities. She had become less fearful about standing out in a crowd. She was able to engage more easily in conversations with strangers. She attributed her ability to attract and meet Wade to Chloe's mentoring.

As the taxi moved forward she heard the papers rustle on her lap and she thought of Wade. Wade was occasionally required to meet with colleagues on Saturday and today was no exception. His meeting was expected to last until noon. After the meeting she and Wade were to drive to Long Island and look at three houses Wade had found for sale.

With all the foreclosures on the market he thought it was a good time to buy a house at a relatively reasonable price. For less than a million five they would be able to purchase a house that had been appraised at over four million just a couple years earlier. He had printed information from the internet and made appointments with a realtor. He had asked her to take a few minutes to look at the photos and prepare herself for the appointments but she hadn't done it yet. When the taxi stopped in front of Café Bernaise in the Village, Shannon stuffed the papers into her purse and got out.

Chloe was waiting inside the restaurant. She was happy that Shannon had agreed to have breakfast with her, not only because it was part of the plan but because Chloe enjoyed Shannon's company. Chloe missed their working relationship and she had been ecstatic when Shannon asked her to be a bridesmaid. Chloe felt privileged that the first experiment in her new business concept involved someone who was so dear to her.

But right now none of that mattered. Today's outcome would test their extensive planning. This was the prototype for all the projects to follow. After this project was complete Chloe was counting on Wade to make referrals to colleagues and friends. She whispered positive affirmations that every engagement party attendee, all of them, would want to use her service.

But the entire day could go wrong. A disastrous chain of events could be waiting to happen. Would she and Sophie have to rethink the entire squeeze concept? Could they be interpreted as mean-spirited? Would their concept be shelved forever? Chloe attempted to push the negative thoughts aside and focus on the current task.

As she stood alone in the foyer of the restaurant with her arms folded over her chest, she felt perspiration gathering under her blouse. She unfolded her arms and shook out her hands, stiff from the pressure against her body. She closed her eyes and cocked her head back and forth and around in a circular motion. She could hear cracking sounds as her neck released the tension it had been holding since her arrival. She loosened her jaw and stretched her mouth, drew in a long breath and let it out slowly.

She took a step forward, then turned and stepped in the opposite direction. She began pivoting in circles and then forced herself to stop for fear that someone in the restaurant would think she was a nut case. When did she start caring about what people thought? Is this what insecurity felt like? The feeling was foreign and frightening. The word terror came to mind.

Sophie had said she wouldn't do a squeeze because it terrified her but Chloe thought Sophie had exaggerated. The word terror was reserved for situations like falling off a cliff, being held at gunpoint and watching a semi bearing down on you at ninety miles an hour. The word terror was not meant for pulling a practical joke on a friend. But all her rational thinking could not make the feeling go away. For one second Chloe knew what Sophie had meant about terror.

When she saw Shannon through the restaurant window she realized that one second was all she would allow herself to feel this ridiculous feeling. The word terror was not meant to apply to this situation. Sophie was wrong. Chloe would never succumb to Sophie's fear.

Shannon entered the front door and caught a glimpse of Chloe near the hostess station. Chloe lifted her hand in acknowledgment and Shannon walked toward her. Had she ever lifted her hand into the air to acknowledge someone's presence? Was it something she would do on any other day? She wondered if she was acting normal. At this moment she didn't know.

Shannon walked with open arms toward Chloe. Chloe kept reminding herself to act normal. What was normal? She usually took pride in being abnormal. She didn't know what to do. She opened her arms and took a long breath. When Shannon hugged her she let out her breath and repeated a silent mantra to release all fear. She drew back and looked into Shannon's eyes and felt a calmness wash over her like a protective veil. By the time they got to the table Chloe was herself again.

The two of them spent an hour catching up. They talked about the wedding dress and the bridesmaid's dresses and incidentals. Shannon asked how the business was doing and Chloe carefully left out the part about the new business concept of fooling people into getting to their parties.

As the waiter cleared the plates he placed the bill on the table. Chloe removed her credit card from her purse and slipped it into the leather folder, then excused herself and went to the restroom. Her call to Wade from the restroom didn't delay her in the least.

When Chloe returned to the table Shannon's phone was ringing. Shannon picked it up and said, "Hi, honey. Are you finished?" A moment passed and she said, "Oh, no, I was looking forward to our afternoon together. Yes, I have them. Well, I don't know. I'm with Chloe right now."

"What?" Chloe whispered. "What is it?"

Shannon covered the phone with her hand and said, "His meeting is running over. He won't be able to go to the realtor appointments. He's asking me to keep the appointments but I don't want to go alone. I have the realtors' phone number. I could call her and cancel the appointments and you and I could go shopping."

"No," Chloe said, "you and I can shop anytime. Let's see the houses. It sounds like fun. We can go get your car and make an afternoon of it. And I know a great little restaurant south of Montauk where we can have a late lunch. It'll be girl's day out. You know Ms. Bride-To-Be, we won't be able to do this too often when you're weighed down with babies and puppies and tuna casseroles."

Shannon smiled and put the phone to her ear. "Wade…Chloe is going with me. I'll tell you what I find out tonight when I get home. Love you, too."

Chloe looked at her watch. "I think we have time for dessert."

"No dessert for me. I want to fit comfortably into my size eight wedding dress. I'm not going to blow it over a dessert."

"But you hardly ate anything. Come on, just one dessert?" Chloe said.

"One dessert now, one next week. I have two months to go," Shannon said. "Don't tempt me when I'm feeling so good. I have the most wonderful fiancé on earth and when I walk down that aisle I want him to look at me and think the same about me."

Chloe signed the tab and slipped her credit card into her wallet. She felt a flutter in her gut as she thought about what the day's events might hold. "Good. Let's go," she said.

Chapter 22

Wade had googled directions to a realty office near Massapequa, or so Shannon thought. Chloe had actually googled and printed the information and had given the flyers to Wade which he in turn had given to Shannon to take with her to the restaurant. Handing her the flyers so that she could prepare for an afternoon of house hunting, talking up the houses and telling her he had a meeting, was the extent of his involvement in the setup - that is, besides paying for the entire thing.

Once Chloe and Shannon were on their way to Massapequa, Wade's part was done. All he had to do was to wait for her to arrive at the party. It's a good thing he wasn't in on the details because when Chloe had handed him the flyers, he was already wringing his hands with nervous anticipation. Now that Chloe had her own bout with fear, she understood his trepidation, but she had gotten through it and was now solid as a rock.

Massapequa was a hamlet about thirty-five miles north of New York City, about an hour's drive. Many of the properties were priced at over a million dollars and boasted private boat docks in the backyards. Shannon had been to Massapequa a few times and thought it was quaint. She understood why some people would want to get out of the city and live the rural life, but she preferred living in the city and couldn't understand why Wade insisted on looking at homes so far from his job. She could picture herself living there later with their children, the ones who weren't born yet, and she understood they would need an outside play area. But that was a few years away.

She guessed that he may have wanted to be closer to his parents since they lived further north in East Hampton. Whatever the reason, this seemed to be important to Wade and she was happy to accommodate his wishes. She didn't think anything would come of the day's excursion except for a delightful visit with her friend Chloe.

When they arrived at the realty office it was early afternoon. The realtor, Diane Hunter, introduced herself to Chloe and shook her hand as if they had no prior knowledge of each other. Even though they had never met, Chloe had spoken with Diane twice on the phone during the finalization of plans.

Both houses had been vacant for some time and Diane, the agent for the bank-owned properties, had been hesitant when asked to allow temporary changes to be made to them. While Sophie had scouted the properties, it was Chloe who agreed not only to return the houses to their original state but add at least one enhancement to each. This promise satisfied Diane and solidified the plan. Sophie, putting on her bookkeeping hat, had originally balked at the additional expense, but after thinking it over she knew they were fortunate to get any realtor to agree to their unusual request. The changes they made were relatively inexpensive and when they presented the expenses to Wade, he agreed to pay the costs. Immediately after meeting with Wade, Sophie had made arrangements for crews to be sent to both houses to spruce them up, so to speak.

The third house to be shown, the final destination and party venue, was Wade's uncle's house. This house had not been altered in any way - besides having a stage, canopies, tables, chairs and decorations set up in the backyard.

Shannon was never given photos of the inside of the houses, only the outsides. But Wade had been instructed to talk them up, saying he'd seen photos of the insides and that he wanted Shannon's honest opinion of these 'gems', as he called them. The details of the project, the selected houses and the specific redecoration plans had not been disclosed to Wade. The effect of the redecorations had not yet been tested. The test would be Shannon's response.

Diane, forgetting the details of the day's events, reverted to her usual mode of doing business by suggesting that she drive them to see the three houses. Chloe had to surreptitiously remind Diane that she wanted to take Shannon to a late lunch at a favorite restaurant of hers which was farther north and that they wanted to see the first two houses before lunch and the third house after lunch.

Chloe's intent was to stretch the day's schedule so that Shannon would not get to the venue too early and would also not suggest going back to the city before seeing the third house. With lunch scheduled after seeing the second house they were almost guaranteed that they would get to the party on time.

Diane's facial expression told Chloe that she now remembered her part of the plan. She said, "Alright, why don't you follow me to the first two houses? Then you can go to lunch from there and I'll meet you at the third house at five."

"How does that sound?" Chloe asked Shannon. "I'll get to take you out to lunch and we'll be back in the city by six-thirty."

"Sounds good," Shannon said. "I'll leave a message for Wade so he knows what time I'll be home."

Chapter 23

As Shannon and Chloe followed Diane's car to the first house, Chloe picked up the flyer and read some of the features to Shannon.

"This one has a boat dock in the back," Chloe said. "Does Wade have a boat?"

"No, but he wants one," Shannon said. "That's why he chose these houses to look at. They all have boat docks in the back."

"That sounds fun...having a boat," Chloe said.

"Not to me," Shannon said with annoyed defiance in her voice. "The only time I was on a boat was when I was twelve. I went fishing with my cousins off the coast for an entire afternoon. The water was choppy and my stomach didn't do well. Besides having a dull headache from the moment I stepped onto the boat, I threw up...twice."

"Well, the water in these communities is calm," Chloe said. "Maybe you'll get a new perspective on boating."

"I don't think so. I get queasy just thinking about boats," Shannon said.

Chloe mentally crossed her fingers. She could see the driveway of the first house just up ahead. Shannon pulled into the driveway and parked behind Diane's car.

The house was a one-story ranch style, white with white trim. The front yard had been well kept. The lawn was wide and flat. A few bushes adorned the base of the front porch. Next to the porch was what looked like a tall wooden mast from a ship. It was secured to the post of the porch and it reached into the sky well above the roof of the house.

Shannon and Chloe got out of the car and began to walk up the steps. Shannon's gaze started at the base of the mast and traveled up to the crow's nest at the top. Her head tilted so extremely that her equilibrium faltered. She grabbed the handrail of the stairway to steady herself. She noticed a small flag at the top of the mast which said "Brennan," probably the name of the family who owned the property prior to foreclosure. She pursed her lips and puckered as if she had eaten something sour. She didn't say a word.

Instead of a door knocker or a peep hole in the front door there was a port hole. It had a brass frame with clear class. Diane opened the front door and they stepped into the foyer. An unpleasant odor wafted past their noses.

"What is that smell?" Shannon asked as she put her hand over her mouth.

"Yeah, it's terrible," Chloe said, knowing exactly what it was.

"It's from the previous owner's business," Diane said. "I was told they grew some kind of spores for cosmetic labs, something to do with organic cosmetics. They moved out without taking their trash. We get that kind of behavior with foreclosures. We haven't been able to get the smell out yet, but we're working on it. That's one reason why this place is cheap."

"Cheap! It's over a million dollars," Shannon said as she clamped her thumb and forefinger over her nose.

"The bank thinks it's worth the price," Diane said. "But you can always make a lower offer."

Chloe wished she could have commended Diane for her quick thinking. Diane seemed to be enjoying the story Chloe and Sophie had fabricated about this house. Chloe, on the other hand, couldn't say anything about the house. She had to pretend she didn't know what was coming next.

Shannon noticed something on the left wall near the front door that looked like half of a wooden steering wheel embedded horizontally into the wall. She turned to Chloe and said, "A coat rack I presume?"

Chloe shrugged, "Yeah, I guess so."

Through her fingers Shannon's lips spoke muffled words, "This house is very nautical. I hate to say it, but if he really likes this stuff maybe he should rent a boat dock somewhere far away from me and we should buy a normal house to live in."

They stepped into the living room. Shannon looked around at the walls and said, "What would you call this color? Navy blue?"

"Yes, I'd say navy blue," Diane said.

"Who paints such a small room navy blue?" Shannon said. "It's like standing outside alone on a moonless night, dark and creepy. No, it's more like being in a cave. And that rope framing

101

the fireplace mantel? That's the thickest rope I've ever seen."

"I believe it's a mooring rope, if that's the right term," Chloe chimed in. "It's used to tie up large ships to a dock, I think."

"It's as thick as my wrist," Shannon said as she inspected the rope. "I think it's glued to the wall around the mantle. So what's it doing here?"

"Decoration, I guess," Diane said.

"Yeah, very unattractive decoration," Shannon gave Chloe a sideways smile and stuck out her tongue in disapproval.

They walked into the kitchen. Shannon caught sight of the powder pink walls and the pumpkin orange cupboards. A dining area was enclosed in a fence-like structure that looked like more wooden steering wheels. Her face lost its color and her mouth formed a sickened look like she might throw up. She said, "Did Wade see interior photos of this house?"

"Yes, he did," Diane said.

Shannon said nothing. They walked down a long hall leading to a master bedroom. The odor was stronger in this room. The walls were painted lime green and a ceiling fan was spinning. Shannon covered her mouth and nose with her hand hoping to get a whiff of the perfume she had dabbed on her wrist before leaving her apartment. Diane noticed Shannon eyeing the green walls and said, "The master bath is where they grew the smelly stuff. Just look past the wall color and the smell. Picture this place with a fresh coat of paint and fresh air.

Shannon was conspicuously silent. A French door led from the bedroom to a covered patio in the backyard. She opened the door, stepped onto the patio and released the breath she had been holding. Chloe followed.

The backyard was small and flat with closely pruned bushes scattered around its perimeter. The patio continued toward the far left back corner of the yard where a power boat bobbed next to a small wooden dock. Shannon felt something rise in her throat when she saw the bobbing boat. Then her attention turned to the waterway. She walked to the back edge of the yard and stood looking at the water. She noticed that the dirt between the bushes dropped off about three feet to the water. No fence, no barrier of any kind. She turned to Chloe and said, "Is it all men or just my fiancé who doesn't think of anyone but himself?"

Chloe hadn't expected this kind of reaction...yet. "What do

you mean?" she asked.

"He and I have already agreed to start a family right away. If we were to buy this house our babies would live here. They'd need a place to play outside. There's no fence, no wall. If they weren't watched constantly they'd end up falling in the water. But I guess his precious boat is more important."

Chloe had never heard Shannon speak about Wade in this derogatory manner. Shannon had always thought of Wade as a selfless, caring person. Had the plan already gone too far? Shannon hadn't even seen the second house yet. And they still had a few hours to go before Shannon would be delivered to the party.

Shannon went on. "The colors in this house are atrocious. I know I have to look past the colors. Painting is cheap. But did you notice that every bedroom we passed in the hallway has a door to the backyard? I wouldn't be able to sleep at night knowing that my toddler might open the door and wander to the water's edge. And all the built-in nautical crap, what's with that? And that smell? I don't know what Wade was thinking."

Chloe said, "He only saw photos. He didn't know about the smell. Give him a break. And this is only the first house. Maybe the other ones are better."

"Maybe. It's a mystery why he wanted me to see this house. But you're right. The next one has to be better than this."

Chloe's body contorted into an imperceptible cringe as she thought of the next house.

Chapter 24

Chloe and Shannon followed Diane to the second house and parked in the driveway behind Diane's car. The style was New Victorian, two stories, gray with white trim. Shannon's eyes widened as she closed the car door behind her. She turned to Chloe and said, "This is a beautiful house."

The limbs of a sprawling oak tree shaded the entire front yard. Lush greenery surrounded its perimeter. Everything was immaculate: the painted siding, the leafless driveway, the spotless front porch. As Diane opened the lock box dangling from the door knob Chloe noticed the red front door.

"Good Feng Shui," Chloe said.

"What?" Diane said as she pushed the door inward.

"A red door is good Feng Shui," Shannon added. "So let's see how the chi is flowing inside this house. Hopefully better than the last."

Diane walked through the door into the foyer and Shannon and Chloe followed. The walls were white and the ceilings were high. An arched doorway on the left wall opened onto a formal step-down living room. Shannon looked through the doorway at a brick fireplace on the far wall. As they entered the living room Shannon's focus was on the fireplace.

"This is cozy," she said.

Shannon turned slightly to the right and noticed French doors at the far end of the room that opened onto a patio with a fountain. The room had a pleasant serene feel. Out of the corner of her eye she saw something brownish red on the right wall. She turned suddenly and saw the entire wall, floor to ceiling, spattered with what looked like blood and ground-in dirt.

Shannon gasped. "Oh my God, what is this? Was someone murdered here?"

"It's art," Diane said. "It was painted on the wall by a well-known artist from Germany. See the artist's signature over there in the bottom right corner? Gunter somebody."

"I've heard of him," Chloe lied. "His work is very expensive. I think having this painting on the wall adds value to the house."

Shannon turned to Chloe with a look of disbelief. Before Shannon could open her mouth Chloe blurted, "Or you could paint over it."

"Painting over it wouldn't do any good," Shannon said, "because the thought of this bloody murder scene would haunt my dreams as long as I lived here."

Diane said, "It's clear that you don't like this wall but people in certain circles would pay a lot of money for this house because of the painting. The bank sees it as an asset. That's why they're trying to sell the house with it intact. If it's not sold within a month we'll paint over it."

Diane's ad-libs were flying like fireworks. She continued, "I guess there are people who like this artist's work because a photo of this room was on our website and, believe it or not, two people wanted to look at this house because of the painting."

"Was my fiancé one of them?" Shannon asked.

"I believe so," Diane said.

Shannon turned to Chloe with a perplexed look. Her mouth was open but no words came out. She looked down as if she was contemplating what to say and then she hesitantly said, "Let's see the rest of this house."

Diane led them through a doorway to the kitchen. Shannon stopped in the doorway and steadied herself against the door jamb. The kitchen was large with an island that separated it from a spacious family room. A sink was on the far counter under a window that looked onto the backyard. The island stood in the middle with a second sink, a cook top and a grill.

Under other circumstances she would have liked the design of this kitchen, but it was the colors that stopped her dead in her tracks. The walls were painted deep purple throughout the entire kitchen as well as the family room. The cabinets were fire engine red and the counter tops were black. It wasn't until she was in the room that she noticed the knives.

Above the island, hanging from the ceiling, was what looked like a large knife rack, but on closer inspection Shannon noticed that razor-sharp knives and cleavers were dangling from a twisted metal grid by thin chains. All blades pointed downward, leaving the sharp tips dangling just above their heads. As they walked under the contraption, the knives swayed with a slight clanking sound. Diane pressed a button on the wall and the grid lit up. It was a chandelier. The light shining through the knives cast gruesome shadows on the wall. Seeing the look on Shannon's face Diane said, "That can be changed out."

"What kind of sick people lived here?" Shannon said. Without waiting for an answer she said, "I suppose Wade saw a photo of this room too."

"Yes," Diane said. "I believe this is more of der artist's design work."

"Those knives are sickening. And the colors are obnoxious. Wade has never mentioned liking extreme colors or macabre décor." Shannon turned to Diane and asked, "Does this mean the entire house was decorated by the artist?"

"Not the entire house. Only the master bedroom, oh yes, and the master bath," Diane said.

Shannon turned to Chloe again with a look that said, *Help*!

Chloe raised both shoulders indicating that she didn't know what to say. The color drained from Shannon's face and Chloe said, "Maybe Wade's color blind."

"He's not color blind. And even if he was, anyone could see in a photo that this room looks like a torture chamber. I'd be claustrophobic and sick every day if I lived here."

"You could ...," Chloe said.

"Yes, I know. I could paint. That's not the point. The point is that my fiancé actually likes this hideous house with its built-in crime scene and gruesome kitchen. And he actually likes the other one, the smelly nautical death trap of his future offspring. And he sent me here because he thinks I'd like them. He called them gems. Does he even know me? Do I know him?" Shannon started to breathe deeply. She turned to Diane and said, "I'm sorry. I have to get out of here."

Chloe almost laughed when Diane said, "But you haven't seen the rest of the house. There's a boat dock in the back."

"I've seen enough. I think I have to throw up," Shannon said as she galloped to the front door.

Chloe turned to Diane with a look that said, *Maybe we've gone too far*.

Chapter 25

When Chloe got outside Shannon was draped over the porch rail, one hand clutching her stomach. Chloe looked over the rail to the flower bed below. Apparently Shannon had contained her urge to throw up. Chloe patted her on the back and stroked her hair. Shannon straightened and took a couple of deep breaths.

Chloe said, "I'm sorry these two houses were so upsetting to you. I'm sure the third one is better."

"Yes," Diane said as she locked the door behind her, "the third one is better. I don't think you'll find any extreme decorating in the third one."

"I don't know if I want to see the third one," Shannon said. "Maybe we should just go home."

"No, we can't go home yet," Chloe blurted. She managed to compose herself and say, "It's our girls' day out. Let's forget about houses for now. I'll drive us to the restaurant. You just relax. When we get there we'll sit and have a glass of wine and a bite. There is a logical explanation for why he chose these houses. Maybe he was testing you, maybe he was joking. That's it…he must have been joking."

"He doesn't joke like that," Shannon said. "And I feel sick. I don't know if I want to go to the restaurant."

"Well, I'm not taking you home in this condition. And we are not going to end our day like this. We're going to go to the restaurant and we're going to relax and forget about these stupid houses. By the time we see the third house we'll either be laughing at its horror or marveling at its grandeur."

"OK, I'll go," Shannon said. "But only because it's our day."

Diane left for her office. She would meet them at the third house at five o'clock.

Chloe pulled into the parking lot of the Roadhouse Grill on the main road near the edge of town, a casual place with only a few tables and a bar. Outside the front door was a brick patio with four tables shaded by green umbrellas. A young couple was seated at a far table, their plates spattered with bits of lettuce and bread crumbs, piled at the far side of their table. Their chairs were pushed together and the two of them sipped coffee as they looked at a map spread in front of them.

The restaurant's façade was made of rustic wood siding. Flanking each side of the door was a window with a flower box filled with spring flowers draping gently over the side. Chloe noted that Sophie had found a charming place, one that would hopefully calm Shannon's nerves.

Chloe entered the front door with Shannon closely behind. Only two of the small round tables were taken, and the bar along the left wall was empty except for one couple seated at the far end. As Chloe turned to suggest they get a table outside, Shannon brushed past her, making a beeline for the bar.

Shannon took a barstool in the middle and motioned for the bartender. As he walked toward her she asked if they served lunch at the bar. He said they did and she motioned for Chloe to join her. As Chloe approached the bar Shannon said, "Is the bar alright with you? They'll serve us lunch here and we can ogle the cute bartender."

Chloe was taken aback by her bartender comment, but took a seat beside Shannon. The bartender slid two menus in front of them. He smiled and asked, "Can I start you off with something to drink?"

Shannon blurted, "I'll have a Bloody Mary, no celery, two olives."

Chloe shot her a sideways glance and said to the bartender, "Iced tea for me, please."

"No, not iced tea," Shannon whined. "You have to get a real drink. House hunting is done and now the rest of the day is ours." She turned to the bartender and said, "Two Bloody Mary's."

"Alright, one drink," Chloe said. "And please bring me an iced tea also." She would figure out how to get Shannon to the party later.

Shannon's eyes were fixed on the bartender as he made the drinks. She turned to Chloe, raised her eyebrows and said, "Cute, huh?" As the bartender slid the drink toward Shannon, he smiled politely. Shannon picked up the toothpick with two olives, set them on a napkin and began to suck on the straw. As he slid the drink toward Chloe he paused, holding the glass just out of her reach.

She looked up to see him smiling at her in a way that was much too smolderingly sexy to be polite. She felt herself blush for a moment, then she smiled and waited for him to place the glass in front of her. Her eyes followed him as he went to help the couple at the end of the bar.

Shannon didn't notice their silent exchange since she was too busy guzzling her drink. She paused and said, "What a hearty drink this is. It's like food. This could be my lunch."

Chloe thought their coming to a bar may have been a mistake. Shannon might do better if she drank more slowly, but Chloe felt that voicing her opinion would be inappropriate since it wasn't something she would normally do. Instead she'd have to keep Shannon talking instead of drinking. She didn't want to deliver an intoxicated guest of honor.

Chloe took a dainty sip of her Bloody Mary and a gulp of iced tea.

Chapter 26

Chloe checked her watch. It was four-fifteen. It would take them at least twenty minutes to get to the party. So for the next twenty minutes Chloe would have to engage Shannon in conversation to make sure they wouldn't arrive too early.

They had each ordered a salad but Shannon had hardly touched hers. She spent most of the time talking and drinking. They had talked briefly about wedding plans and Wade's job and Shannon's new life in the world of the unemployed, but Chloe had steered her away from talking about the houses. She wanted Shannon to arrive at the party in an upbeat mood. Now Chloe noticed that Shannon seemed to have something on her mind.

Shannon had downed her first drink and was well into her second. Chloe, on the other hand, had only sipped at her drink. Her glass still looked full. She kept reminding herself that she was working and that Wade was waiting for his fiancé to be delivered to him safely and in a timely manner. He was paying a sizeable sum to insure that Shannon's day was interesting as well as enjoyable. Chloe regretted that the time spent at the two houses was disturbing to Shannon. The only enjoyable part of her day might be after she arrived at the party.

Chloe had tried to dissuade her from having a second drink, with no luck. She had thought that pulling this practical joke on her friend would have been easier than pulling one on a stranger, but Chloe was beginning to realize that their familiarity caused Shannon to express herself with ease. Shannon would have probably been less open with a stranger. If Shannon had spent the day with the realtor, perhaps she would have been more demure, less apt to express her true feelings about the houses. If the realtor had taken her out to lunch Shannon probably wouldn't have ordered an alcoholic drink. But because Shannon felt comfortable with Chloe and because she felt that this might be their last girls-day-out, she was acting and talking with an unexpected abandon.

The bartender leaned his palms on the counter and said,

"Anything else I can get you?" He winked in Chloe's direction. She smiled and winked back.

Shannon leaned forward and motioned with her index finger for him to come closer. He leaned in, his face just inches from hers. She thought she was whispering but what came out was a shout, "What is..." She put her finger to her mouth to shush herself and continued in a loud whisper, "What is there to do in this sleepy little town?"

His gaze went to Shannon's mouth then back to her eyes. He glanced at Chloe and smiled as if to say, *Your friend is drunk.* Then he turned back to Shannon and said, "You mean tonight?"

"Yeah," Shannon said, "What are you doing when you get off work?"

Chloe's eyes widened. Shannon was flirting, an engaged woman for God's sake flirting with a stranger. For the first time Chloe thought she might not get the bride-to-be to the party. Or she might have to reveal everything to get her there.

The bartender could sense Chloe's disapproval. With a playful smile in Chloe's direction he said to Shannon, "Well, sometimes I go to O'Reilly's, but when I get off work tonight O'Reilly's will be dead. So I'm going home. I'll watch some TV and go to bed." He emphasized the word bed in a teasing way that Chloe and Shannon both noticed.

With Shannon's gaze locked on his, she lifted her eyebrows and said, "Sounds fun. Need any company?"

Chloe cleared her throat and said, "We're just here for a short time. We have an appointment in a while. Then it's back to the city."

"Nooooooo," Shannon whined as she leaned back in her chair. Like a child who had just been asked by her mother to turn off the television and wash the dishes, "Not back to the city."

The bartender patted Shannon's hand and turned to walk to the end of the bar. As he passed Chloe the two of them exchanged a smile. He stopped and said, "You look familiar. Have I met you before?"

"What a line," Shannon said under her breath.

Chloe realized he must have seen Sophie just days before. She lifted her hand to her cheek to block her face from Shannon and looked directly at him. She motioned with her eyes in Shannon's direction, gave her head a quick tilt and said, "I don't think so."

His facial expression indicated that he got Chloe's meaning. "Oh, my mistake," he said as he made his way to the end of the bar.

Shannon leaned her forearms on the counter and focused on his butt as he walked away. She said, "Ooh I wish I'd had that for lunch."

Chloe turned to Shannon and said, "Hey, what's going on with you?"

"What do you mean?" she asked, still following the bartender's path with her eyes.

"Two drinks in the middle of the day? Flirting?" Chloe said.

"What's the big deal, Mom?" she groaned.

"Shannon. It's not like you. Are you OK?" Chloe asked.

"I'm upset. Chloe, I don't understand why Wade wanted me to see those houses," Shannon said with a slight slur in her speech.

"You can ask him when you see him," Chloe said. "Maybe he didn't notice the colors in the photos."

"Oh, please. Don't make excuses for him," she said, picking up her glass and slurping air from the bottom. "Anyone could see in a photo that those houses were weird."

Chloe was scrambling to say the right thing. "Look, interior decorating is obviously not his thing. Talk to him. The two of you will find a place that suits you both."

"He knows what suits me. Manhattan suits me. I don't want to move away from the city. I love our apartment," she said.

"I'm sure the two of you can work it out."

Chloe watched Shannon twist her glass in circles on the wet cocktail napkin. With her head dropped Shannon said, "There's something I have to tell you." She paused, searching for words, "Wade has been acting…strange in the past few days.

"What do you mean?" Chloe asked.

Shannon opened her mouth. A couple of high-pitched squeaks came out and she burst into tears.

The bartender looked up from his conversation with the couple at the end of the bar. He walked toward Shannon and Chloe, grabbed a pile of cocktail napkins and handed it to Shannon. As she pressed the entire pile to her wet eyes the bartender gave Chloe a look that said, *Yeah, she's had enough,* and went back to his conversation with the couple at the end of the bar.

Chloe put her hand on Shannon's shoulder and said, "What do

you mean he's acting strange?"

Shannon dabbed her eyes and said, "He's been distant, like he's nervous about something, like he's hiding something."

Chloe had to distract her from what was obvious to her, that Wade had been nervous about the party. "What could he be hiding? You don't think he's cheating, do you? He doesn't seem like the kind of guy who would cheat," Chloe said, immediately regretting her choice of subject.

"I don't think so. But even non-cheaters can lose interest." She blubbered into what was now a ball of soggy paper.

"I'm sure you two will be fine. You just need to talk to him," Chloe said.

"Talk to him. How can I talk to him when he has this stupid all-day meeting on a Saturday? He sometimes has Saturday meetings, but never all day. He's avoiding me."

"When you get back tonight the two of you can sit down and talk. Everything will be fine," Chloe said. "I'm sure of it."

"No, he's getting cold feet. I know it. I mean… his ridiculous request for me to see these houses. He must be planning to move out here by himself because he sure wasn't thinking of me when he chose these two idiotic places," she shouted.

"Why would he have asked you to look at these places if he was planning to move here by himself?"

She paused, searching for an answer. "Because he wants to throw me off track so he can make a clean getaway."

"Clean getaway? What kind of crap are you watching on TV? You're upset right now, but think about it. He wouldn't go to all this trouble if he were planning to move here by himself. He just wouldn't do it. Would he?" Chloe said.

"Oh, uh…no…I guess not," Shannon said as she blew her nose and bounced the liquid paper wad on the counter.

"No, he wouldn't," Chloe said. "If he were planning to move here by himself, he would have hidden it from you. Because that's what normal guys do. Nobody, except maybe a sociopath, would go through such an elaborate plan to deceive someone." Chloe paused to evaluate what she had just said. Just then her phone rang. She saw that it was a text from Wade. She said to Shannon, "Excuse me…business." As she turned to text him back, Shannon sniffed and sucked air from her empty glass. Then she grabbed Chloe's drink and drained it.

Chloe ended her phone call, turned, and noticed Shannon now sucking air from the bottom of her third drink. Chloe said, "I think what we have here is a man who loves you, a man who would do anything for you, a man with a slight interior design deficiency."

Shannon laughed. "Slight deficiency?" she cried. "I'd call it an extreme deficiency."

"Tell me," Chloe said, "would it be so terrible if his only faults were that he wants a boat and he likes obnoxious colors?"

"No, I guess not," Shannon admitted. "He really is a wonderful person. He's kind of a nerd, but that's what I love about him. He's not pretentious. He isn't cool. He's honest and down to earth."

"Yes, he is," Chloe replied.

Shannon sniffed and said, "Maybe I can convince him to leave the decorating to me."

"Yes. Of course you can. You'll be the decorator," Chloe assured her.

"Yeah, I like decorating," Shannon said.

"Being with you is the most important thing to him. You know he adores you."

"And I adore him," she said, tearing up again. She leaned over the counter, grabbed more napkins from under the bar and pressed them to her eyes.

Chloe went on, "I don't think he's getting cold feet. But for argument's sake let's say he is. Would he be worth fighting for?"

"I've never believed in fighting for a man. If he wants to be with me he will. I would never force someone to be with me," Shannon said.

"But think about all those weddings we did while you worked for me. Every bride, with the exception of only a few, had second thoughts at one time or another. It's normal to have doubts. But every one of those brides had a wedding day that was the happiest day of her life. Remember?"

"Yeah, I remember," Shannon said.

"The only reason why we weren't aware of the grooms' doubts was because men don't talk about their feelings, especially with the wedding planners. The grooms probably had their doubts at one time or another, but they didn't tell us."

"So you think what he's feeling is normal," Shannon said.

"I don't know what he's feeling," Chloe said, thinking about him waiting at this moment to impress his bride-to-be. "You could be imagining this because you're having doubts."

"Oh, no, don't put this on me," Shannon said. She paused and pushed away the empty glass. "OMG, I've doubted him in the last few days. I've been so worried about him having cold feet I didn't notice that I was having doubts."

"Are those doubts going to stop you from being with him?" Chloe asked.

Shannon straightened in her seat and said emphatically, "No. Nothing will stop me from being with him as long as he wants to be with me."

"Then you'll be fine, because I am sure he wants to be with you," Chloe said as she patted Shannon's arm. Chloe continued, "We're going to see that third house because Diane has already scheduled her day around us. And who knows, maybe you'll like it. If not, we'll get a laugh out of it."

"Yes, I need a laugh," Shannon said as she grabbed her purse, jumped from the stool and danced toward the door.

Chloe said, "If you're alright I'm going to the restroom before we leave. Do you need to go?"

Shannon shook her head back and forth in an exaggerated manner as she swayed her hips. As Chloe stepped from the barstool she noticed the bartender heading in her direction. He stopped in front of her and made eye contact. He said, "You're visit was thoroughly enjoyable. I hope you come back soon."

Chloe smiled and as she turned into the hallway she saw Shannon wave at the bartender. He made a cursory wave in Shannon's direction and a deliberate smile in Chloe's. As Chloe opened the restroom door she heard Shannon singing, "Weeee're off to see the wizard…"

Inside the bathroom Chloe made two calls, one to Diane and one to Wade.

Chapter 27

Chloe drove. Shannon sat in the passenger seat with her eyes closed. She quickly opened them and said, "Whew, I'm a little dizzy. I think I need some air." Shannon rolled down the window and leaned her head against the window frame.

Chloe said, "We're almost there. I think it's only a few blocks away."

The clock on the dashboard said five. They would arrive at the house in a few minutes. Chloe slowed down, checking the addresses to make sure she was going in the right direction. As they turned into the driveway Shannon raised her head and remarked, "Look at all those cars parked down the street. There must be some kind of event going on down there."

Chloe ignored the comment and parked the car. Diane's car pulled in behind theirs and parked. Diane got out of the car and said, "OK, girls. Last but not least. I think you'll like this one."

Shannon said, "I hope so. But first I have to pee. Do you think I can use the bathroom when I get inside?"

"Why didn't you go at the restaurant?" Chloe asked.

"Because I didn't have to go then. I have to go now."

"Well, this is not a foreclosure," Diane said. "The people live here. We'll ask them when we get inside."

They climbed some steps to the front door. Diane rang the bell and a middle-aged woman answered the door. The woman said, "You're right on time, come with me."

Chloe's heart began to race. She held the door and ushered Shannon in ahead of her. She shot Diane a glance that said, *We're almost there*.

As the woman led them through the living room, Shannon's eyes were drawn to the tasteful décor. The woman opened a sliding glass door leading to the backyard. As soon as Shannon stepped onto the patio a blur of people yelled surprise and a barrage of live music filled the air.

Shannon jumped. She turned to Chloe and said, "Oh, this is

116

where the event is." Shannon turned back to the crowd and yelled, "Sorry to bother you. We're just here to look at the house. We'll only be a few minutes."

Chloe moved close to Shannon and whispered in her ear, "Shannon, this party is for you."

Wade, who was standing at the front of the crowd walked toward her. Shannon ran to him and threw her arms around him. She said, "What are you doing here? Oh, it doesn't matter. Everything will be alright. Wait."

She released her hold, took a few steps back and lifted her right foot. She teetered to one side and slammed her foot down to catch her balance, then she slowly lifted her foot again and loosened the heel of her shoe. With one motion she kicked her foot into the air, hurling the shoe haphazardly, sending it toward a blue dolphin ice sculpture sitting atop a table dotted with stemmed glasses. Those standing nearby ducked as the flying shoe poked the dolphin in the eye and bounced into a punch bowl. The crowd gasped as the dolphin began to lean to one side and Aunt Jane, who was standing by, lunged to steady it.

Before Wade could stop her, Shannon loosened the heel of her left shoe and kicked a line drive toward a waiter holding a tray of appetizers. As the shoe shot past him he swung out his free arm, caught the shoe and folded his arm behind his back as if nothing had happened, simultaneously holding the tray motionless.

Shannon said to Wade as she spun in a circle, "It's alright if you have cold feet. See, now I have cold feet and it doesn't matter, because I loooooove you. We can work out any problems. Chloe said so. And Chloe is always right.

He walked toward her and placed his hands on her shoulders. "Shannon," he said in a sobering tone, "I love you and I am going to marry you. And this is our engagement party."

"Shuuut up," she gasped, "Why didn't you tell me?"

"Because I wanted it to be a surprise," he said.

"You're so sweet. You're the sweetest man in the world. I love you so much," she said as tears filled her eyes. Then she flung her arms around him and kissed him with a loud smack on his mouth.

He gently pulled away and said, "Your family and friends are here. Let's sit down." He guided her toward a chair. He gave Chloe an inquisitive look. Chloe angled her head toward Shannon and made a motion with her cupped hand as if she was tipping an invisible glass. He nodded in acknowledgment.

Shannon looked up at him and said, "Do you really like those houses we saw today, because they're terrible. I hate them. I'm sorry but I do. I really hate them. This one is beautiful though. Are we buying this one?"

"We're going to sit down and then I'll explain the whole thing to you," he said.

"Oh, I forgot. I have to pee first," Shannon said.

Wade motioned to Shannon's sister and said to her, "Can you please take her to the bathroom. I'll be at this table. Just bring her back here and I'll get her some coffee."

Shannon's sister took her by the shoulders and aimed her toward the sliding doors. As they walked away Wade heard Shannon say to her sister, "Is this your engagement party?"

Her sister said, "No, honey, this is your engagement party. I got married last year, remember? You were my maid of honor."

"Oh, yes. I'm so happy for you."

Chloe walked to Wade's table and sat beside him. "I'm sorry," she said. "She had three drinks on a virtually empty stomach. I couldn't stop her."

"That's unusual for her. The important thing is, did she have fun?" he asked.

"I wouldn't call it fun. Although I think this is a day she won't forget," Chloe said. "Let's just say she was reminded that she loves you dearly, and I believe the two of you will make it through any problems that come your way. And she was truly surprised. In fact, I think she still is."

"Thank you, Chloe," he said.

"Wait awhile to ask her about today's details. None of this is sinking in right now. A cup of coffee and a little time will help her." Chloe rose from the chair and said, "I am sure the two of you will look back on this day and laugh."

"Thanks again, Chloe. I couldn't have done it without you."

Mrs. Franklin 8

"Hello," said the voice on the phone.

"May I speak to Courtney?" Mrs. Franklin said. Her body was shaking. She knew it wasn't the coffee. She had been drinking decaf in the office for months.

"Speaking," Courtney said.

"Courtney, this is Arlene Franklin."

"Hello, Mrs. Franklin. How are you doing?" she asked.

"Terrible," she said, "I'm a mess. And since I'm calling you by your first name, please call me Arlene.

"Alright, Arlene. What can I do for you?"

Her polite tone was beginning to get on Mrs. Franklin's nerves.

She said, "I don't know if I can do this anymore." Her speech was jagged and fast. "I mean…the waiting. I see weird people everywhere. I've gotten knocks on my front door in the middle of the night and hang up calls at home and at work. What's going on?"

"I'm not sure what you mean," Courtney said with polite indifference.

"You know what I mean. Someone is going to do something and there's nothing I can do about it. I just have to wait and wonder. It's the wondering that I can't take. I don't think I can do this. It's too stressful. I can't sleep at night."

"Where are you right now?" Courtney asked.

"I'm at work," she said. "I shouldn't be calling you right now. I don't have time. I'm due in a meeting in a five minutes but I just can't take this anymore."

"When do you take lunch?" Courtney asked.

"Eleven-thirty," she said.

"You work near Fifty-First and Third, right?" she asked.

"Yes, but…"

"Arlene, I'll meet you at the Oxford Deli on Lexington at eleven-forty-five. Do you know where it is?" Courtney asked.

"Yes, eleven forty-five. But I just don't ..."

"Arlene," Courtney said in a condescending tone, "everything is going to be alright."

"But..."

"Arlene," Courtney repeated in a sobering tone, "I'll see you in a couple hours."

"OK, I'll be there."

Courtney was already seated at a table when Mrs. Franklin arrived. When she sat down she noticed that Courtney had already ordered two soups and two salads. "Hope you like soup and salad," Courtney said. "I thought we would have more time to talk if I got here first and got the ordering out of the way. This place has the best homemade soup. Have you ever eaten here?"

"Yes, I have. It's great food, very fresh." Mrs. Franklin was not in the mood for small talk. She continued, "Thanks for seeing me on such short notice. I have to talk to you." She let out a sigh that expelled every bit of air, deflating her tense body.

"Arlene," Courtney said as she loaded her fork with lettuce, "I hate to tell you this but what you're feeling is normal. Everyday occurrences can get blown out of proportion when you let your imagination run away with you."

"But the hang up calls, the knocks at my door," she said, "I'm not imagining those. It's creeping me out. I can't sleep. I can't eat." Her soup and salad sat untouched on the table.

"Well, I don't know what the calls and knocks are about but I must say you've lost a few pounds and you look awesome," Courtney said as she stabbed a tomato.

"What? I don't need a compliment. I'm serious. I need help."

"What you need is to get your mind on other things. You need to get out of your house and do something new," Courtney said.

"Get out of my house?" Mrs. Franklin shouted then lowered her voice to a whisper, "You're not listening to me. I'm afraid to go out of my house. Even on the way to work a creepy guy followed me."

"What did he look like?" Courtney asked as she chewed.

"He was dressed in a suit. He was tall, nice looking..."

"Sounds like someone who could follow me any day," Courtney said.

Mrs. Franklin's jaw dropped. "He was creepy," she said.

"Like how? What did he do?" Courtney asked.

"Well, he stood next to me and he took my same subway and he looked at me," Mrs. Franklin said.

"He looked at you?" Courtney asked. "Could it be that he liked what he saw?"

"Oh please, no one looks at me that way," she said, "and what are you doing? You're not getting what I'm saying. I'm scared. You said I could call you anytime, so I called. But you're acting like what I'm saying doesn't even matter. Can't you see I'm a wreck?"

Courtney thought for a moment. She put her fork on the table and said, "Arlene, I am going to ask you some questions. You probably won't understand why I am asking them. But for the next few minutes just go with it, alright?"

"OK," Mrs. Franklin said hesitantly.

"I think you need to find a hobby, something to keep you busy outside of your career." She paused to pick up her fork. "Do you have any interests?"

"Not really," Mrs. Franklin said as her body deflated even further.

"OK, let's try this. Is there anything in your life you haven't done that you wish you could do. Something fun, like bike riding or singing or dancing?" Courtney loaded her fork and took a bite.

Mrs. Franklin stared at the floor. Courtney had time to chew, take another fork-full and chew it. Finally Mrs. Franklin said, "Dance." She looked up at Courtney. "My husband never danced. I always wanted to take a dance class."

"Like ballroom dancing?" Courtney asked as she picked up her bottled water and took a swig.

"Well, I think ballroom dancing would be fun if I had a partner. But, no…tap dancing," she said. "I've always wanted to take a tap class. I took one tap class when I was seven. But tap is for kids. I'm too old to take a tap class, right?"

"Oh, I don't know. I don't think anyone should say they're too old for anything. I've heard of adult tap classes," she said with her mouth full.

"Really," said Mrs. Franklin, picking up her fork.

Courtney gulped. "Sure, adult tap classes. Have you ever seen "Stepping Out"?" Courtney asked as she noticed the puzzled look on Mrs. Franklin's face. She went on. "It was made in the eighties, a TV movie I think, starring Liza Minnelli. I saw it on video a few years ago. It's about regular everyday people, all adults, taking a tap class."

"Really?" Mrs. Franklin said as she poked her fork into the mound of lettuce.

Courtney could see Mrs. Franklin's facial muscles relax. She finished chewing and said, "Yes, and if I remember the movie correctly, most of the adults taking the class didn't tap very well but they really enjoyed themselves."

"But that was just a movie," Mrs. Franklin said.

"A movie about everyday people like you. I want you to promise me something. Arlene, I want you to promise me that you will enroll in the next available tap class you can find. Will you do that?" Courtney put the fork down and gazed into Mrs. Franklin's eyes.

"What about the hang up calls and the weird people?" Mrs. Franklin asked.

"Arlene, I listened to every word you said. It's not that I'm ignoring you. I just know more about this than you do. It's my job. Promise me that you'll stop suspecting every stranger you see and you'll enroll in a tap class, OK? If you need help finding a class I'll be glad to find one in your area."

"OK...tap class." Mrs. Franklin said, taking a bite and chewing.

Chapter 28

Now that Shannon had been safely delivered into Wade's open arms, Chloe was free to enjoy the party. After all she was a bridesmaid and an invited guest. But Chloe wasn't ready to deal with the people at the party. The day's outcome could be loosely labeled as a success. She knew that staying at the party and discussing this new business concept with guests was a good idea, but the thought of explaining anything to those who hadn't a clue about the project was unthinkable to her. Shannon was safe with her man and when the time was right he would do the explaining. Chloe would call Shannon later to find out if she had experienced any enjoyment at all.

Chloe quickly found Aunt Jane who was pouring champagne into stemmed glasses. "Hi, Jane, how is it going?" Chloe asked, noticing that the front of her dress was covered in blue liquid, obviously the result of using her entire torso to move the dolphin sculpture back into place.

Jane, who was oblivious of her fashion foible, said, "Hey, girl, it's going great. How did your day go?"

"Well, I got her here. And she was surprised. So I guess today went alright. But we've got some serious debriefing to do on Monday."

"Good," Jane said. She filled a glass and handed it to Chloe. "Here, you're done for the day. You deserve it."

"I think I'll decline. But thanks," Chloe said.

"You look restless. Are you staying for the party?" Jane asked.

"For a short time," Chloe said, eyeing the stack of business cards on the table. "Could you make sure people see the business cards and that they know about the surprise delivery service as well as the event planning service?"

"Will do," Jane said.

"I see the band is taking a break so I'm going to talk to them. By the way, your dress has some blue stuff on it," Chloe said.

"Oh, yeah. See the blue dolphin ice sculpture over there? I had

123

to maneuver it back into place after Shannon whacked it with her shoe. It's a wonder it didn't fall over. Pretty good structural design on my part, huh?"

"Yes, I can always count on you to design the most imaginative decorations. I just wish you hadn't gotten it all over your dress. A little unprofessional, don't you think?" Once the words came out of her mouth Chloe cringed at the thought of hurting Jane's feelings. But Jane's energy level was high.

"Yes, you're right. I have a change of clothes in the house," Jane said as she motioned for her assistant to take over. Jane bent down and picked up Shannon's shoe from under the table. As she jogged toward the house she wielded the shoe like a flag. She spotted Shannon sitting next to Wade, and as she passed the table she plopped the shoe on the lawn next to her foot, saying, "Here you go, darlin'."

Chloe walked toward the stage where musicians were strapping on guitars and twisting amplifier knobs. Diane had suggested the band. She knew Long Island like the back of her hand had seen them play at several local events. After checking references it was decided that their repertoire was mild enough for the outdoor venue and diverse enough for the varying ages of the guests. Chloe stopped at the stage and asked who was in charge. A young man raised his hand. Chloe asked him, "Hi, how's it going?"

"Good. We're about to start the second set," the man said.

Chloe went on. "Are you familiar with the bartender at the Roadhouse Grill?"

"Which one?" he asked.

"A guy, late twenties, tanned, tall, dark hair, nice smile, brown eyes," Chloe said, surprised that she remembered so many details.

"You probably mean Chris. He's a good guy," he said.

"Kind of flirty though, right? A lady's man?" she asked.

"Not really," he said, shaking his head, "If he flirts, especially with a customer, he probably likes them. He's pretty selective...more than me."

"So...is he single? I mean, does he have a wife or a girlfriend?" she asked.

"He must not be married 'cause I'm pretty sure he would have asked us to play at his wedding. I don't know if he has a girlfriend right now, but I don't think so."

"Thanks," Chloe said.

She turned and made her way to the table where Wade and Shannon were sitting. As much as she loved Shannon, she couldn't stay. She needed to go. It had been a long day and she was sure that with so many friends and family members surrounding her, Shannon wouldn't notice her bailing early. But she felt she had to at least say goodbye. She knelt beside Shannon and tapped her on the knee. Shannon turned and gave a yelp of joy when she saw Chloe.

"Hey, honey, I've gotta go," Chloe said. "Have fun."

"No, you can't leave yet," Shannon said.

"Look, you've got a hundred people to talk to tonight. We can see each other any time. I'll talk to you when I drop off the car."

"Thank you, Chloe," she said. "I love you."

"Love you, too," Chloe said. As she turned to go she paused to notice Shannon wrapping her arms around Wade's shoulders. He embraced her and gently kissed her lips. Chloe sighed.

She made her way through the house, picked up her purse and car keys and walked out the front door to the driveway. It was her job to get Shannon's car back to the city since Shannon would be riding home with Wade. Diane had left after making contact with Jane, leaving the driveway clear behind her.

Chloe turned on the engine and stared out the windshield. She recalled Shannon leaning into Wade as he held her in his arms. They were surrounded by in-laws and future in-laws and cousins and nieces and nephews and siblings and friends. Shannon had been transformed from surprisee to guest of honor. Chloe hadn't remembered ever turning down the opportunity to be at a party, but she was about to make her escape. This was something Sophie would do - leave when things were just getting fun. She shuddered to think Sophie's short stay with her may have already had a negative influence on her.

Chloe could hardly remember the last time she was in a man's arms, and even then she hadn't felt the tenderness she saw in Shannon and Wade. She didn't want to stay at the party but she wasn't ready to go home either. She was about to do something she was sure Sophie would never do. The car didn't have to be in Shannon's parking lot until the next afternoon. Chloe could take her time. She could make one stop before heading home.

Chapter 29

Chloe pulled into the parking lot of the Roadhouse Grill around seven. The sun was low in the sky, casting a pink glow at the horizon. She noticed a smoky haze wafting from a vent on top of the roof. When she opened the car door the aroma of grilled steaks swirled around her. Warmth washed over her as she recalled those special dinners back in high school with Mom, Dad and Sophie. She inhaled deeply and savored the aroma. With the late lunch still settling in her stomach the aroma of grilled food was the closest she was going to get to having dinner tonight.

The air was cool and crisp, and the outside tables were full. Tall metal heaters glowed red between the umbrellas. She opened the front door to a crowded room of people conversing, wrapped in soft dinner music and candlelight. There seemed to be standing room only but she spotted one open seat at the bar. She took the seat between a couple of young guys with beers in their hands and a nondescript middle-aged woman with what looked like a margarita in front of her. The woman stared straight ahead. Chloe hoped she didn't look as desperate as this faded flower next to her. She turned to the woman and asked, "Hi, do you know the bartender who was working earlier today?"

The woman's face lit up. When she opened her mouth her bright white smile took ten years off her age. She said in a friendly tone, "Yes, his name is Chris. But his shift is finished. I think he left." As the words came out of her mouth the woman became more attractive. Chloe smiled, trying to think of something else to say to her.

Just then a young woman carrying two bottles of vodka came from the backroom. The woman walked behind the bar and placed one bottle alongside the other bottles on the counter, then removed the cap from the bottle in her hand, inserted a pourer into the top and dropped the bottle in the well. The woman picked up a towel and wiped her hands. When she noticed Chloe she asked if she wanted to order a drink.

126

Chloe said, "I'm not sure yet. I wanted to ask you if the bartender who was working around four-thirty is still working."

"Well, he's not working but he's still here." She turned and pointed to three guys at the far end of the bar. "That's him with his back to us. I'll get him."

Before Chloe could stop her the woman was leaning at the end of the counter saying something to Chris. He focused on her mouth, trying to decipher her words over the din of the crowd, then he raised his gaze to Chloe, who was now getting out of her seat. Chloe made a gesture of acknowledgement and began to walk in Chris' direction. He said something to the bartender and began walking in Chloe's direction. They wove between the people until they met in the middle.

"Hello," Chloe said.

"Hello. You came back," he said.

"I wanted to thank you for being so nice to my friend this afternoon. She was going through a hard time."

"I hate to admit I was eavesdropping, but with so few people here, the conversation was hard to ignore. And you may not have noticed but she was loud. I take it she's getting married?" he said.

"She's at her engagement party right now," Chloe said.

"And why aren't you there?" he asked.

"It's a very long story," Chloe said. "Not a bad story, but long."

"I've got time," he said with a smile.

"I thought you were going home to bed tonight," she said.

"That's what I tell drunk women who are coming on to me. I was planning to leave right after this beer," he said.

"Well, it was nice seeing you again. I just wanted to say thank you," she said with a smile. She stood there gazing into his eyes. Then she made a motion as if she was about to turn around and leave.

"Wait...you came all the way back here just to say thank you?" he asked.

"Um, not exactly," she said. She felt a slightly alluring smile form on her face.

He looked at her and said, "If you have time maybe we could sit down and talk."

Chloe scanned the room. "It looks like all the chairs are taken," she said.

"Well, I know another place with some comfortable chairs," he said with a grin. "Well, not exactly chairs. More like cushioned booths."

"What do you mean? Another restaurant?" she asked.

"No, not a restaurant, but it does have a galley. Do you like sail boats?" he asked.

"I've sailed a couple of times," she said.

"Well, we wouldn't be sailing, just sitting at the dock. And since you don't know me, if it makes you feel more comfortable, the couple who has the slip next to mine is having a party tonight on their boat. Kind of like a block party. I've met most of the people who'll be there. They're interesting people, some our age, some older. How about it?" he said.

"Sounds good," she said.

He took a swig of beer and set the bottle on the bar. "I'm stopping at the store on the way home to pick up a couple steaks. Why don't you follow me?" he said. "If you don't like steak you can pick up something else to throw on the grill."

"Steak sounds good," she said.

If the party turned out to be boring she hoped the two of them would have their own private party.

Chapter 30

When the sun came up I was awake, eager to find out how the project went. Chloe's bed was the same as the night before. She could have slipped in during the night and left early in the morning without waking me, but I knew she hadn't because I had taken the pillows she had haphazardly tossed on the bed and arranged them in an orderly fashion, turning the patterns upright and placing them at either ninety or forty-five degree angles. My perfect angles were still intact. Even if she hadn't slept in her bed but had just popped in for a moment, let's say to change her clothes, she would have noticed the change in the pillows and would have jumbled them up just to annoy me.

Last night's assignment was our first and I was nervous about the outcome. I was curious to find out if my instincts and preparation had been successful. I had done most of the planning and supervision of the redecoration of the two houses and created the time schedule. Chloe was up to the task of luring Shannon to the party and I knew she would stick to the schedule. If the project was a failure the blame would have to go to me.

I had called her cell phone twice after seven p.m., knowing that Shannon had been delivered to the party prior to that time. But Chloe hadn't answered either of my calls or returned my messages. I also sent her two texts with no response.

Now at noon on Sunday she was still incommunicado. I resented that I had been sitting at home waiting for her call while she was obviously having a great time at the party. She would say her actions are those of an independent woman who doesn't have to answer to anyone. I call it rude.

On the other hand her car could be lying in a ditch off the side of the road. If that was true I would be the most evil person on the planet, thinking my sister is rude while she is lying dead, draped over a steering wheel, possibly the last words uttered from her mouth, "Sophie, I love you." But that can't be. I would have gotten word from the police by now. She wouldn't have strayed far from the main highway when she knew I was waiting. I think.

I never know with Chloe.

How can I possibly do business with a woman who obviously has no regard for others' feelings? She was the one who lured me to this big, fat city to save her business. She should have had the decency to return my calls. I stayed home on a Saturday night while everyone in the world was out having fun. And now it was Sunday afternoon, not the best day to go out and have a wild time. But I would think of something. I would make sure I wasn't in the apartment when she got home. She could wonder where I was for a change.

After showering I dressed, did my hair, grabbed my coat and purse and was out the door. I started walking up the street. The air was cool and a few billowy clouds were scattered across the blue sky. The Empire State Building was just ahead to the north. In the short time I'd been in the city I hadn't seen any tourist attractions except the outsides of those I passed on the street while riding in a cab, like Radio City Music Hall, The Met and Madison Square Garden.

I entered the lobby with its art deco décor. Ushers dressed in what looked like high school band uniforms and pillbox hats guided the tourists into an elevator. Upon exiting the elevator I noticed lines painted on the floor directing tourists to their next stop on the way to the observation deck. Room after room of roped waiting lines turned back and forth, but it must have been an off day because all the waiting lines were empty. I was able to walk briskly to the ticket counter.

I had a choice of going to the first observation level or the upper level for an additional cost. What the hell, this might be the only time in my life I would be at the top of the Empire State Building. Why not go all the way?

The first observation level had a three-hundred-sixty degree view of the city. I managed to jam in between some people to get a clear view, sandwiched between families speaking various languages. Central Park lay to the north, the Villages with their low profile buildings to the south and the financial district along the southern rim with its towering buildings. I could see the ocean and the rivers and the bridges crossing over to Brooklyn and New Jersey. I think I saw the lower tip of Connecticut and of course the lower end of Long Island, where the party took place the night before.

Next was my ascent to the top observation deck. Only a couple of small elevators led to the upper deck and I was the only one in line. As the elevator doors opened I saw an elderly, gaunt man who seemed old enough to have worked there since the day the building opened. I entered and the door creaked as it closed. The man was so wrinkled that when he grabbed a handle on the metal gate and slid it closed in front of the outer door, I think I could see the bones in his hands.

He was dressed in a red uniform with epaulets on the shoulders and wore what looked like a bellboy cap from my grandparents' era. He eyed me with fiendish delight as if I wasn't the first young lady he had eaten today and he was getting hungry.

A circular brass device with a lever was attached to the side wall. He rested his hand on the lever and as he moved it forward the elevator began to rise, creaking and clanking along the way. He looked at me as if he wanted to say something so I said, "Have you worked here long?"

He smiled and said, "Oh, yes. I've worked here since I was twenty-five. This is the only job I've ever had. I'm almost as old as this building."

"You must have seen a lot of interesting people during your employment here," I said.

"I must have. I can't remember any of them though," he cackled. He pulled on the handle, stopping the elevator. Then he moved the handle in the other direction and we descended. Then, with a look on his face of sheer geriatric mania, he moved the lever back and forth, making the elevator bounce up and down.

I involuntarily blurt out a nervous laugh, wondering if my phone would dial 911 from this moving coffin. It reminded me of the Tower of Terror at Disney's California Adventure, that time after finals when a group of friends took off for the day. The creaking elevator, the old man in red uniform, the up and down motion - the terror was all too familiar. Even though this was presumably safe, I knew the ancient equipment and the ancient man could fail at any moment.

I stepped onto the upper observation deck, a small circular room wedged into the trusses of the metal tower on top of the building, enclosed with windows. From any point in the room one could catch a three-hundred-sixty degree view of the world. I had to duck under the diagonal metal beams to maneuver around the perimeter. Except for the thought of having to ride the soon-to-be condemned elevator navigated by the geriatric cannibal, I was generally relaxed.

Once I was back on the street I had to find something to do. I couldn't get home too early. I wanted to make Chloe wait like she made me wait. I remembered that Hasin was in an Off-Broadway play, a very Off-Off-Broadway play. I could grab a bite to eat and be there before it started. From what he had told me, the play usually wasn't sold out and I could get a ticket at the door.

In the second act Hasin had a love scene with a woman. I couldn't take my eyes off his lips saying the words to her. I imagined what it would feel like having him say those words to me. I felt my face flush. What a ridiculous thought. I snapped out of my trance and turned my head slightly, looking at the audience members on either side of me. They were still, riveted on the scene. I swear this conundrum of the man standing on the stage was either the greatest actor on the face of the earth or he wasn't very gay.

When the play was over, some of the actors mingled with the crowd. When Hasin saw me he came toward me with open arms and wrapped them around me saying, "Hey, why didn't you tell me you were coming? I could have comped your ticket."

"I didn't plan on it," I said, feeling his strong arms around me and his face pressed against mine. Was his touch different now than it had been before, or had he ever touched me? Yes, the handshake that first day. The teasing nudges in the kitchen. But unlike his playful teasing, this embrace was from the electrifying, half-naked stranger who had walked into the living room the first day I met him.

He pulled back and said, "Hey, are you alright? Was the play OK? Did you like it?"

"Yes, the play was good. And you were fantastic. You're really a good actor," I said.

"Thanks. Hey, a couple of cast members are getting a bite to eat. Why don't you join us?"

It was a little late for me to eat since I'd already eaten dinner earlier, but still early as New York night life goes. "Sure, I'd love to," I said.

Hasin, the woman from the love scene and a young man and I

132

walked to a small restaurant around the corner. We sat at a booth, the woman and the man next to each other and Hasin and I across from them. During the conversation I got the idea that the woman had no interest in men and she didn't seem to have any interest in me either...I mean that way. The man, who was quite effeminate, seemed to have an interest in Hasin. It was questionable whether Hasin had an interest in him but they seemed to get along well. It was the first time I saw Hasin acting effeminately. The three of them acted like they had known each other for a long time and enjoyed each other's company.

After dinner Hasin and I walked back to the apartment, arriving around one a.m. When we got there Chloe was already asleep. I quietly tiptoed into the bedroom. I thought of stomping into the room but my anger had subsided and all I wanted to do was get to sleep.

She must have had an exhausting weekend. I was curious about what had kept her away for so long. In the morning we were scheduled to debrief Saturday night's event and possibly start a new assignment. I could hardly wait to hear what she had to tell me.

Chapter 31

Like a sixteen-year-old boy in the back seat of a car at lover's lane, morning came too soon. I had been too tired to even wash my face the night before. My raccoon eyes felt like two bags of rocks as I sat upright and blinked at the dresser mirror. My head looked like it had been clamped in a vice. Some of my hair was shooting straight up on top of my head and some was pressed flat against my ears.

Chloe must have been in the shower. Her bed was empty and I could hear water running in the bathroom.

I stood and walked to the door with zombie-like determination, my goal, to devour a hot cup of coffee. I opened the door and padded down the hall to see Hasin and some guy I'd never met before sitting on the couch. One of his boyfriends I presumed. Where had he come from? Hasin and I had gotten back around one and he hadn't been here then. Of course one in the morning isn't late for New York City. He could have arrived after I fell asleep and I wouldn't have heard a thing.

"Hey, sleepy head," Hasin said in a sing-song way. "Was last night too much for you?"

"You can tell?" I said making my zombie path to the kitchen. "I'm not awake yet. Did you make coffee?"

"Yeah, it's in the carafe," he said. "Hey, I want you to meet my friend Jarrod."

I paused and turned toward the stranger. As I reached out my hand to shake his I mechanically said, "Nice to meet you, Jarrod. Please excuse the tee shirt and panties. I'm not quite human yet."

Jarrod reached out and took my hand, but instead of shaking it in the usual up and down manner he held it longer than I would have expected. He looked me in the eye and smiled. "Nice to meet you," he said flirtatiously. "You look lovely." He meant it.

Why was Hasin's boyfriend flirting with me? He had probably been one of Hasin's classmates at the school of hetero-acting gay men. For a moment I was taken aback and almost popped out of

134

my stupor. Then I remembered that most of Hasin's boyfriends were handsome and charming. Why did the cute charming ones always have to be gay?

I turned like a robot and resumed my path. In the kitchen I heard them say their goodbyes and the front door closed. Hasin came into the kitchen, opened the refrigerator door and began scanning the shelves.

"Well, what do you think?" he said.

"About what?" I said as I poured half and half into my cup.

"Jarrod," he said lifting a carton of orange juice and sniffed the spout.

With shameless indifference I said, "You two make a lovely couple. I think you can stop looking for Mr. Right."

He poured some juice into a glass and leaned back against the counter. As he lifted his glass to take a sip he said, "Oh, he's not gay."

"What?" I said. The sound of my own voice jolted me out of my stupor. I leaned forward and held the coffee cup away from my body as drops splashed over the rim and dotted the floor. I gave Hasin a sideways look and set the cup on the sink. I grabbed a paper towel, tossed it on the floor, curled my toes around it and mopped the up the coffee.

With a deliberate yawn he said, "No, he's not gay. He's my sister's old boyfriend. We grew up together. He just came by this morning on his way to work to pick up something. And I wanted him to meet you. So…what do you think?"

I lifted my foot, pulled the paper towel from my toes and tossed it into the sink. "So let me get this straight. You bring a cute straight guy over at this god-awful hour to meet me. You let me parade in front of him in my underpants and you're asking me what I think of him? I think you better ask him what he thinks of me."

"Oh, he's interested. I can tell. He gave me the look," he said.

"Is that the look that says thanks for introducing me to the half-naked girl?" I asked. "I can see how a man might overlook the mascara-encrusted eyes and the tornado hair because of the translucent panties, but will he be interested in me when I'm actually, you know, fully clothed?"

"Oh, maybe I was insensitive. I'm sorry for blindsiding you," he said. "I'll do better next time."

Chloe, already dressed for work, bounced into the kitchen. "So, did you meet Jarrod?" she asked.

"You knew?" I said disgustedly. I crossed my arms over my chest and said, "You both knew ahead of time and didn't tell me? If the two of you really want me to meet someone you have to let me know so I can prepare myself. With the exception of you, Hasin, and your gay friends, the only man who gets to see my bed-head is the one who deserves to be in bed with me."

As Chloe took a sip of coffee she said, "So that thing you did with your hair the other day was intentional?"

I paused and shook my head as an uncontrollable laugh eked out. "Do you really want to open that door, Miss Color-of-the-Week-Hair?" I asked.

She eyed me over the rim of her cup and said, "You love my hair. Admit it. You wish you had the nerve to change your hair. Anyway, I wasn't criticizing, just commenting."

I stared at her and asked, "By the way, when did you have time to add that ghastly pink streak to your hair?"

"Last night, while you were out on the town. And…ghastly?" she said mockingly. "Really? How old are you? Seventy-five? No, let me rephrase that because I know seventy-five-year-olds with wilder hair than mine. You're upset because you were turned down for the Sarah Palin gun club."

I glared at her. "You know I'm not politically conservative…"

"Yes, and I am blah, blah, blah," she said teasingly.

As Hasin walked to the hallway he flung open the front door and said, "Girls, girls. While I regret not being able to witness the inevitable brawl which will undoubtedly result in hair-pulling and the ripping of clothes, I must depart." He bowed at the waist and backed out of the door.

Chloe set her cup in the sink and said to me, "See you in an hour?"

"Wait. You were gone for two days," I said.

"Yeah, so?" she said.

"So, I called you twice on Saturday night and texted and you didn't answer or return my calls," I said. "I really want to know how it went."

With a sincere tone in her voice she said, "I'm sorry. I had such an awesome weekend I didn't think to call you. I'll tell you about it at the debriefing this morning. I'm outta here." She turned and headed for the door.

"Wait! I almost forgot," I shouted at her back. "I scheduled three interviews for the accounting position this afternoon."

Chloe spun around with a look of shock on her face. "Already?" she said. "But you can't leave yet. You haven't been here long enough to know the business."

"I'm not leaving yet. Anyway, the person we hire will need to be trained. It'll be good for us to overlap," I said.

"Oh, that reminds me" she said. "Jane called last night and told me a Mr. Klein made an appointment for this morning about something he has in mind for his wife. So I hope it doesn't interfere with your interviews because I need you to be in the meeting with us. He's a friend of Wade's and I guess he was at the engagement party. So, Saturday's project wasn't all bad."

Great. Chloe's first critique of the project that I painstakingly planned was that it wasn't all bad.

Mrs. Franklin 7

He was following her. Mrs. Franklin was sure of it.

When she came out of her front door on this chilly morning she noticed him standing a couple of houses down. He just stood there, motionless, but when he noticed her he turned and started walking toward the subway station in the same direction she walked every day. Even though he was ahead of her she was certain that his being there had something to do with her.

She had never seen him in this neighborhood. He was dressed in a business suit, nothing strange about that. But there was something odd about his face. His expression was too focused, too deliberate.

When she got to the corner her heart began to race. She was standing right beside him. She stared straight ahead and kept pressing the button as if it would change the signal faster. From her peripheral vision she was sure he had glanced her way a couple of times. The light for opposing traffic turned yellow and she stepped off the curb a moment too soon. He made a noise as if to warn her of oncoming traffic but she kept moving. She was ahead of him now.

As she descended the subway stairs she felt safer. The commuters, though strangers, would help a middle-aged woman if he tried to do anything to her. She entered the subway car and made her way to a seat near one of the exits. He entered the same car and although there were blocks of empty seats, he wedged his way between two people, sitting directly across from her.

She hadn't brought her book today, nothing on which to focus her gaze except for her surroundings. She fidgeted with her gloves for a moment then put them in her pocket. She looked to the end of the car where a young couple was staring intently at a cell phone screen. The woman seated next to her was reading a magazine so she looked at the pictures as the woman turned the pages. Then her eyes moved to the advertisements above the windows and the electronic subway route map blinking the next stop.

From the corner of her eye she could see that the man's head was down. She carefully slid her gaze from the advertisements to the window just behind him and over his head. She looked through the glass at the blackness whooshing past them. She slid her focus down the glass and dared to look at his face. She realized that her gaze stayed a moment too long when he suddenly lifted his eyes and stared straight at her. He smiled. She drew in a breath and looked away.

When the doors opened she made a beeline for the exit but he got ahead of her. She was looking at his back as he ascended the stairs. As soon as she was on the street he turned and walked to the right. She exhaled and turned to the left. He was gone. For a moment she felt silly about imagining such a ridiculous story about this man who was probably just an ordinary businessman on his way to work.

She stopped at a newsstand and grabbed a newspaper. As she pulled the money from her wallet she cautiously glanced in all directions. The man was standing on the next corner waiting to cross at the light. How had he gotten in front of her after turning the other way? He must have changed direction when she wasn't looking and passed her when she picked up the paper. He was standing at the corner where she crossed every day.

She looked to the right. She thought she could walk down the street to the other corner and avoid him altogether, but this was her route. No one was going to intimidate her into going another way. She wasn't going to let this man inconvenience her.

She walked slowly toward the corner to allow time for the light to change. When the light changed she watched him cross the street. But instead of turning right toward her office building, he walked straight ahead and disappeared down the side street. When she got to the corner she waited for the light to change. She looked up the street he had just taken. The sidewalk was clear. He must have gone into one of the stores in the first block.

The light changed and she crossed. Her pace slowed. She breathed in the cool morning air. Once in her building her thoughts focused on the stack of papers upstairs on her desk. Then she saw him, with his back to her, waiting for the elevator. She felt her body shake. How could he have entered the building without her noticing? He was standing in front of the elevator that she was going to take. Then a woman in a business suit walked up to him

139

and said something. When he turned his head to speak to the woman she could see it wasn't him.

How silly she was being. Her imagination was making her crazy.

As she entered the elevator she noticed another woman who had been leaning against the lobby wall. As the doors began to close the woman entered and stood beside her. She was sure she had never seen this woman in her building, but there was something familiar about her.

When the elevator stopped at her floor Mrs. Franklin and the woman walked into the hall. She felt relieved when the woman turned and walked in the other direction. On her way to her office she noticed a custodian rolling a cart toward her. She didn't remember seeing custodians in the hallway so early in the morning. His eyes were riveted on her.

She began to shift the glove in her pocket and it fell to the floor. As she bent down to pick it up she glanced down the hall and her heart made a thud in her chest. The woman had changed direction and was walking toward her.

As she reached for the glove she lost her footing and fell to the floor. The custodian stopped beside her and, without saying a word, grabbed her arm and lifted her to a standing position. Mrs. Franklin collected herself as the woman brushed by her, eyes staring straight ahead.

The woman walked directly to the stairway door, opened it and stepped inside. As the door closed she could hear the woman's shoes clank down the metal stairs. She turned. The custodian was gone.

Chapter 32

I plopped down in my chair, the one facing Chloe's desk that sits just a little shorter than her chair. She was standing next to the file cabinet waiting for the water to boil in the tea kettle. She lit a stick of incense, and as the smoke swirled into the room she swished her hands over her head in a circular motion, as if she was washing the smoke into her hair. She pressed her palms together and bowed to the Buddha. She dropped a teabag into a cup, poured the water, turned and in a relaxed airy voice said, "I'll tell you about my weekend since you're so hot to find out about it."

"First I want to hear about Shannon's surprise. How did it go?" I asked.

Chloe sat and held her cup of tea in both hands as she blew the steam away. "Oh, she was surprised. In fact, she was so surprised she didn't realize it was a surprise party even after the people yelled surprise," Chloe said.

"What? How could she not have known?" I asked.

"First you take an insecure bride-to-be who is starving herself to cram into a size eight wedding gown. Then you watch her have a late lunch of three Bloody Mary's and a few pieces of lettuce. That's how," she said.

"She got drunk?" I asked.

"Yeah, she was upset. I guess our redecorated houses caused a stronger reaction than we had anticipated," Chloe said.

"But was it OK? I mean, she got to the party and Wade was OK with it, right?" I asked.

"He was fine. And I spoke with Shannon yesterday when I dropped off her car. Once everything was explained to her, she was fine too. I think in some back-ass-wards way Shannon got a lot out of the day. Her love for Wade was tested. We wanted her to have an interesting experience and we may have accomplished it, but I'm not sure."

"So what was so extreme about our decorating that caused her to get drunk?" I asked.

"She thought the houses he chose were so weird that she felt she didn't know him. She began to doubt him and their relationship," Chloe said.

"But we expected that," I said.

"She thought he was losing interest in her, you know, getting cold feet," Chloe said. "She even demonstrated her interpretation of the cold feet concept by dislodging the dolphin ice thingy."

"I don't get it," I said.

"Never mind. I think the problem was that she knows me. Because she's comfortable with me she felt free to do anything around me. If I had stopped her from drinking I would have been out of character from my usual personality. So I had to go with it. If she had been with someone she didn't know I don't think she would have said or done the same things. She would have been more polite and less apt to express her emotions," she said.

"Yeah, I think you're right."

"And the day was too long. Shannon and I started with a late breakfast, drove over an hour to the real estate office, saw two houses and spent over an hour at the restaurant. If it had been my party at the end of that day I don't know if I would have been up for it either."

"So what's your conclusion?" I asked.

"Let me put it this way. It was generally a success. I got her to the party without her suspecting anything, but she had too many options. Because of our friendship she was too free to make bad choices and I was limited in what I could do."

"I see. There's a dynamic between friends that you don't get with strangers. In the future we'll need to stick to squeezing people we don't know." I considered for a moment about how inappropriate that statement sounded. I continued, "And we'll need to make sure we don't give the person many options. If Mr. Klein shows up for his appointment today his project will be the definitive test."

"We need to do the squeeze in a shorter period of time," she said.

"Point taken," I said.

"So, aren't you going to ask me why I didn't come home until Sunday?" Chloe asked with a cagey look on her face.

"Yeah. What happened?" I asked.

"I met a guy. He's handsome and intelligent and interesting.

142

He invited me to a party so we had time to get to know each other."

"Where did you meet him, at Shannon's party?" I asked.

"No, he's the bartender at the restaurant," she said.

"The restaurant where you took Shannon? The Roadhouse Grill?" I asked.

"Yeah. I met him in the afternoon. After I dropped Shannon off at the party I talked to one of the band members because he was local and I thought he might know if the bartender was a good guy. According to the band member he was, so I went back to the restaurant and he was still there," she said.

"You spent the night with him?" I asked in a disapproving tone.

"Yes, I did, Mother," she said

"A guy you just met?" I said.

"I didn't have to get Shannon's car back until yesterday. One thing led to another and…yeah, we spent the night on his sailboat." She paused for a millisecond and continued, "The harbor was pretty calm but by the end of the night we had that boat rockin'."

"Sailboat…wait…is his name Chris?" I asked.

"Yeah, Chris, the bartender at the restaurant. He lives on his boat. When Shannon and I were at the restaurant he said I looked familiar and I thought he was just flirting. But later that night I found out he met you the day you scouted the restaurant."

"Later that night?" I asked.

"Yeah, after, you know," she said.

Yeah, I knew. They had talked about me after they did it. Lying there sweaty in his bed they had said my name and talked about me with only air between them, if that. I felt my blood steaming, my heart thudding in my chest. Even though I froze my facial muscles I could feel my body shake.

"Hey, what's the matter," she asked.

"I liked him," I shouted, "I gave him my card and he said he would contact me when he came to Manhattan."

"You didn't say a word. Why didn't you tell me?" she asked.

"Would it have made any difference?" I said as I shot to a standing position. "How about Nick Johnson in high school? You didn't care that I liked him. You had to have him so you glommed onto him even though you knew I liked him."

"Wait a minute," she said as she straightened in her chair. "We

143

talked about that situation years ago. You never told me you liked him until after I went out with him."

"Well, how about, uh…Justin Page? He liked me," I shouted as I slapped my chest with my hand. "When he started talking to you, he thought you were me but you didn't correct him. You just let him believe he was talking to me."

She eased back in her chair. "Once he talked to me it was too late. He already liked me," she said in a smug tone.

I fixed my eyes on her and said, "He's the one who gave you the sweater."

"What sweater?"

I felt singed by the hot arrogance in her voice. My blood churned. I said, "The periwinkle sweater. It was my favorite color, not yours. But he didn't remember that I had told him it was my favorite color when he gave you the sweater."

"You remember that?" she asked.

"So do you. You kept the sweater. It's hanging in your closet."

She lowered her head for a moment and said, "You never talked about any guys you liked. You always kept things to yourself. Then when I made my moves you blamed me for stealing your boyfriends." She bent forward and leaned her palms on the desk saying in a slow deliberate tone, "They weren't your boyfriends, except in your imagination."

I spun around. "No they…yeah…but…we're sisters. You should have known. People were always getting us mixed up," I said, remembering she may have been right about the boyfriends.

"Are you crazy? I'm not a mind reader. And why were you snooping in my closet?" she shouted.

"I wasn't snooping. I just happened to see it," I said.

"You just happened to see it all the way in the back corner of my closet?" she asked.

I gasped. "You do remember keeping it. It was important to you. Admit it!" I shouted.

Just then the bell rang at the reception desk. Chloe and I fixed our eyes on each other. She stood up, closed her eyes, took a breath and slowly pressed her hands to her side. She looked toward the reception area, then at me and said, "There's really no need for us to talk about this again. I didn't know you liked Chris because you didn't tell me. And I'm sorry you can't be happy that I found a nice guy. Now, you and I are going to be professional and embrace this next task, right?"

I glared at her. I sat down with my shoulders slumped. Why did she always have to get the best of me? It wasn't enough that she spent the night with the guy I liked. She had to rub it in by chastising me for being unsupportive of her new love interest. I lifted my shoulders and said, "Yes, we're professionals."

She marched to the door, paused as she reached for the knob and continued through the doorway with a fluid motion and a fake smile on her face.

Chapter 33

Mr. Klein entered the office, followed by Chloe. She introduced us and as she took her seat Mr. Klein took the chair next to mine. He looked like he was in his early forties, refined, someone who had a well-paying white-collar job.

Chloe started with, "Mr. Klein, as you know from talking to Wade, our mission is to deliver the person of honor, in this case your wife, to the destination without her suspecting anything. How elaborate you want the ruse depends entirely upon your desires and your budget. What is your vision for this project?"

He hesitated for a moment and said, "My wife's happiness is very important to me. I came up with an idea to surprise her but I have no idea how to do it, and I definitely don't want to be the one to do it. I want it to be a unique experience for her. I need your expertise."

Chloe said, "That's what we're here for. Give us an overview of what you'd like us to do."

"The party will be simple, minimal decorations, champagne, appetizers and a trio playing soft jazz. The majority of my budget will be spent on you getting her there. I know it's short notice but the event will be in two weeks, Friday night, which means that my wife will be taking the subway home from work two hours prior to the party. So your part will have to take place within a two-hour time span. I would like you to include something that has to do with art, like maybe an artist's loft. Oh, and a fire pole."

"Fire pole?" Chloe said. "Well, Mr. Klein this could involve research, more than one staff member and the cost of minimally remodeling a space. The details depend on what you are willing to spend."

"Tell me what it will cost and the funds will be available," he said.

Chloe didn't flinch. I, on the other hand, caught my breath and began mentally calculating what it might cost to rent a space.

As Chloe asked him questions about his wife and her daily

routine I jotted the information on a pad of paper. He handed Chloe a couple of photos of his wife, which she slipped into a folder. The conversation continued for the next half hour. He explained what subway she would be taking and what time she would be at the station. He was confident that her routine would be the same as usual. He filled us in on the reason for the party and gave us some background about her past. When we were finished we stood and shook hands.

Chloe said, "I'll prepare the contract and email it to you. Don't worry about a thing. You'll have the art theme and we'll prove that we are masters of the *art* of surprise. I promise that your wife will come away with an experience that she'll remember fondly for the rest of her life."

Mr. Klien smiled and shook our hands as Chloe gloated with confidence. After he left the office I spoke first. "Masters of the art of surprise? He's only our second project. I don't think we qualify as masters yet."

"Why not? What we do is an art, isn't it? Devising detailed plans and luring people to their destinations? Not everyone could do this work."

"OK, it's an art…but masters? Let's not confuse the finger paintings we did when we were five years old to Michael Angelo's Sistine Chapel. Baby steps, remember? And remember, you're doing this squeeze, right? You know I'm terrified of doing them."

"Yes, I know," she said, rolling her eyes.

"Another thing…you may need to start thinking about a back-up, you know, someone who can take your place if you can't do it. Because, if this whole squeeze concept works, you'll be doing one after another and you'll need someone, like an understudy, to take your place if something comes up unexpectedly that prevents you from doing them."

"Yes, you're right," she said in an apathetic tone.

"I mean it. I can't do them. I won't be your back-up because I'm terrified. Terrified!"

"If you say the word terrified one more time I will terrify you. Yes, I'm doing it. And yes, I'll find a back-up when we get steady business," Chloe said.

"OK," I said taking a breath. I paused for a moment and went on. "It looks like you have to get to the wife before she gets off the subway. But getting her to go with you is the problem since she doesn't know you."

"Yeah, getting Shannon to go with me was easy. This project will be the true test of whether our concept works."

"I'm starting to get an idea. Well, a series of ideas. One small nudge is not going to get this woman to go with you. We don't want to plan anything that involves force so this is going to involve her trusting you. And we must create a situation in which she has no choice."

Chloe said, "But there are so many choices in this city."

"So we'll make sure she believes that going with you is her best choice, one she can't refuse," I said.

"Hmm, that's going to be a challenge," Chloe said. "So give me some specifics."

"I don't have any specifics yet. Just some inklings. I'm going to take a walk. When I get back I may have some specifics for you," I said as I grabbed my wallet and phone and threw on my coat.

I walked to Broadway and turned uptown. The anger I'd felt about Chloe being with Chris was beginning to subside. After all, she was right. She hadn't known I liked him. But I knew I would file away my feelings under unfinished business and pull out that file at a later date.

The crowds were mixed with tourists and residents. I must have looked like a regular New Yorker, tangled in my thoughts. I would occasionally bump into someone passing me and mechanically apologize.

At first the people passing by were specks in a human blur. Then I turned my attention to the individuals, the people who might become clients in the future. How would I get a woman, like the one pushing the baby stroller, to go somewhere with me? And the middle-aged guy in the apron who was hanging a sign on his shoe repair shop window. What might he and I have in common? How could I convince him to leave his business and go with me? How could I stop the man in the black suit from hailing the cab and make him believe that he needed to walk down the street? What could I do on this crowded street that would make someone think they had no choice but to go with me, to change their course and do something else?

I looked toward the sky. The buildings which had pushed down on me just days earlier didn't seem as oppressive. They now seemed like towers of endless possibilities. Life was not just out here on the street but tucked away in the offices and apartments stacked to the sky. The grid of this town was like a giant Boggle game, where you could not only create possibilities horizontally but vertically, and with each vertical addition came a different meaning, a different possibility. Businesses and empty warehouses and apartments and studios, one on top of another, were waiting for me to incorporate them into my puzzle.

Chloe, Aunt Jane and I had discussed extreme projects using airplanes, boats and helicopters. We talked about crashing cars and breaking the law. But we had to start small. The most important component of a successful plan was to develop a logical sequence of events.

I caught the closest subway, the subterranean addition to this multidimensional urban grid. I studied the people in the subway car. I read the signs above the windows. One poster encouraged passengers to report theft. Another encouraged them to be courteous. I noticed the electronic map on the wall with lights blinking the next stop. I recalled Mr. Klein telling us that his wife only went three stops. When the doors opened at the second stop I mentally counted the seconds it took for the doors to open and close. When the doors opened at the third stop I got out.

Instead of taking the subway back to the office I walked, giving myself time to formulate a plan. I had over a mile to walk. I checked my watch. I'd be back at the office in time for the first interview with the potential bookkeeper.

My plan hinged on using an apartment and an office. Chloe's apartment and our office wouldn't do for what I had in mind. If we really wanted this business to work it was time for us to invest some money. I'd call Dad.

Chapter 34

I took out my cell phone and called Dad's office. The call went to voicemail. I hung up and dialed his cell. He picked up on the second ring.

"Hello," a gruff voice said.

"Hi, Dad. Where are you?'

"At home," he said.

"Are you sick?" I asked.

"Yeah. I thought I'd stay home one day to see if I could get rid of this thing. Jennifer's got me taking vitamins and herbs. She's made an umeboshi plum poultice for my neck. I'm drinking tea with lemon and honey. I think it helped because my voice is a little better than last night."

"Maybe I should call another time," I said.

"It's OK. I can talk. What's going on?""Remember when you said you would help us with this business if we needed help?" I asked.

"Yeah, what do you need?" he said.

"Do you know anyone with an empty office we could use for one night? We'd pay rent if the cost fits into our budget."

"I have one in Soho that's vacant," he said.

"How is it configured?" I asked.

"It's located on the third floor of an office building. It's got a small room in the front, like a reception area, and one huge room in the back," he said.

"Does it have an exit to the street, like a stairwell from the large room?" I asked.

"I think there is a stairwell at the back."

"Great. Could we modify the room slightly?" I asked.

"Like how?" he asked.

"We just need a small portion of the room. We have to make the large room look like a hallway with some closed doors and one small office. Do you think we could get someone to build some temporary walls in a few days?" I asked.

"I think it could be done. Do you want me to ask around for carpenters?" he asked.

"Yes, thanks. I hate to ask you for so much so soon, but if this project works we may be able to rent that office. I'll talk to you about it tomorrow. Feel better soon."

"Thanks, sweetie," he said.

I hurried back to the office. When I got there Chloe was on the phone. I scooted past her and pulled a notepad from my desk drawer. She hung up the phone, looked up at me through the doorway and said, "You thought of something already?"

"Yeah," I said as I jotted some notes, "and I called Dad and I think he might be able to help, too."

"Well, I just got two calls from people who want surprise delivery projects," she said.

"How did they hear about us?" I asked.

"One guy is a friend of someone who was at Shannon's party. The other person is someone Jane talked to last week, a chef or something," she said.

I sat down, looked at the clock and said, "I have to make this fast. The first bookkeeper interview is in twenty minutes. I've come up with a plan but it's going to cost some money. I know we have some money from Shannon's assignment but it may cost more than that. You were telling me we would probably need to rent an office we can modify to suit the different projects in the future. Maybe this is the time to get an office."

"Hold on, you've lost me. Slow down and tell me what you're talking about," Chloe said.

"This project involves using an apartment and an office. If you know anyone who has an apartment we can use for a couple of hours let me know. And the office..."

"We could use my apartment and this office?" she said.

"No to both suggestions, not for what I'm planning. I need a loft apartment, maybe one in the village we can modify. And I need an office with a reception area that leads to a hallway with a few doors and an exit in the back," I said.

"Sounds very specific," she said. "How are you going to find it in only a week and a half?"

"I already found the office. I mean I haven't seen it yet but I described what I wanted to Dad and he has something we can use in Soho. But it's got to be modified. That will cost some money."

151

"You did this all on your...," she paused to look at her watch, "hour and a half walk?" she asked.

"Yeah."

"OK, tell me the plan. Then we'll talk about money," Chloe said.

As I explained my plan Chloe's eyes widened. We would use Hasin in the first part. We would need another person in the second part, preferably a man. Chloe said she knew a guy who would be perfect. He had worked for her occasionally. He was a friend of Hasin's and a fellow actor. She would find out if he was available later in the day and introduce him to me.

When I came to the part about using an apartment Chloe remembered that the guy she had in mind lived in a loft apartment in the village. She was sure he would lend his apartment, especially since we were going to pay him a fee for its use in addition to employing him. I explained Dad's part in modifying the office. She asked a few questions, trying to shoot holes in my plan, but for every question she came up with I had the answer.

I assigned myself the task of drawing rough sketches for the office remodel. I assigned Chloe the task of asking her friend for the use of his apartment and of riding the subway each evening to observe Mrs. Klein.

Chloe said, "If I ride the subway with Mrs. Klein, she'll know my face before the project starts."

"This project involves trust. If she sees you every day or every other day she will either consciously or subconsciously know your face as a fellow commuter. I think it will help establish the trust factor."

"OK, that makes sense," Chloe said. "But I can only do it once next week because I already have appointments on the other four evenings."

"Then I'll do it. I mean I won't have to talk to anyone or lie to anyone. I just have to sit there and observe. And we look alike so...Oh," I said, pausing for a moment. "No, that won't work unless one of us changes her hair color so we look alike."

"One of us?" Chloe said. "Why would *one of us* have to change *her* hair? Women dye their hair all the time. I mean, I could have been riding the subway with brunette hair and then the day before project day I dyed it blonde. When I talk to Mrs. Klein she might remember my drab brown hair and complement me on my new vibrant blonde."

"Mm, thanks for your evaluative observance of my hair color and your less than tactful critique, but I guess it makes sense…sort of," I said. "So you and I can keep our current hair colors. But you need to lose the pink streak."

"Why?"

"Because we don't know how conservative this woman is. You know…your ability to relate to her…the trust factor. Having the streak in your hair may make you seem flakier, less business-like than no streak." I said.

"But the business we're talking about in this project is art, right?" she said. "So the woman is probably somewhat liberal."

"Yes, possibly, but next time use one of those clip-in hair extensions. They're easier to remove," I said.

"But those things are cheesy. I need an element of risk," she said.

"Risk?"

"Yeah, once I dye my hair I'm committed, at least until I find enough time to re-dye my hair," she said.

I was about to google the definition of the word committed for her when the buzzer sounded at the reception desk. The applicant was early.

Chapter 35

I flipped through the papers in the file on my desk. One day to go until Mrs. Klein's party. Within eleven days Mrs. Klein had been observed on the subway six times; habits, probabilities and timing all down, ready to go. The apartment was ready. The office was ready. Aunt Jane and one assistant were scheduled for the event. The actors, including Hasin, were scheduled for the squeeze.

I wasn't satisfied with the accounting applicants I had interviewed the week before so I scheduled three more interviews for early that morning. Once those were done I'd be free for the entire day, since I wasn't working the squeeze.

This would be the test for all future projects and I wanted to celebrate our completion of the set up. When I walked into Chloe's office she was on the phone. She quickly ended her call and hung up.

"It's been a long day. Let's go out to dinner," I said.

"I can't. I have a date," she said.

"With whom?" I asked.

"Um, just a guy," she said as she shifted some papers on her desk.

"Why are you acting so weird? Who is it, someone I know?" I asked.

"It's Chris. He's coming into the city tonight and he asked if he could take me out to dinner. That was him on the phone."

Jane came from the backroom with her purse on her shoulder and a blue chiffon apron in her hand. "Good night, girls. I'll see you tomorrow for the Klein thing. Well, at least you, Chloe. Sophie, have a good day off tomorrow."

"I'll be here in the morning to interview some people for the accounting position. I'll see you then," I said.

"Oh, yes," Jane said. "Have some great interviews then."

"Hey, Aunt Jane, are you doing anything tonight?" I asked.

"Yeah, I haven't seen Stan for a few days so he and I are going to his apartment and, well...," she said.

"What, Jane?" Chloe asked.

Jane held up the translucent apron and said as she blushed, "I'm cooking him dinner and I'll be wearing this."

"Nice apron, Aunt Jane," I said. "I don't think I've seen that one before."

"Yeah, it's new," she said hesitantly, "and it's all I'll be wearing."

Chloe burst into laughter.

My mouth flew open and I said, "Aunt Jane, I'm shocked."

"Why, because I'm an old lady who wants to look sexy for her boyfriend?" she said. "When you're my age you'll understand. We don't age, we just advance. Anyway, you girls have fun tonight. I know I will."

As Aunt Jane turned to leave I noticed a thread dangling from the hem of her blouse. I started to say something but let it go. I watched her close the front door behind her and said to Chloe, "Oh, well, I guess I'll just go back to the apartment."

Chloe said, "I think Hasin is having a guy over. Someone new. Or maybe it's a girl. I don't know."

"What am I gonna do?" I said. "I don't want to hang around the apartment with Hasin and his mystery person."

"Why don't you come with us to dinner?" she said.

"Are you kidding? Either way I'm the fifth wheel. No thanks, too awkward," I said. "I think I'll go to an early movie and then back to the apartment. If Hasin wants privacy he'll have to go somewhere else."

"OK, see you later," she said as she focused on her computer screen.

I grabbed my coat and purse and walked to the closest movie theater. The marquees displayed the latest chick flick, a slapstick comedy, a futuristic CG-enhanced thriller, a psychological crime drama and an animated Disney feature. I wanted to choose something light but I knew that the chick flick would remind me that I had no boyfriend except for David, the piece of crap back in Los Angeles. The Disney movie, no matter what the subject, would make me bawl my eyes out but I was alone so who would care that I'd leave the theater with red eyes and mascara running down my cheeks. I chose the Disney one. I needed a good cry.

After the movie, my puffy eyes and I were walking back to the apartment when I heard a familiar laugh. I turned and saw Chloe and Chris looking in a store window up the street. They were playfully talking and laughing. They hadn't seen me yet so I turned the corner and headed for the office since it was only a few blocks away. I would find refuge for the time being and go to the apartment later.

When I got to the office I unlocked the front door and locked it behind me. I left the reception area lights off, flipped on the office lights and headed for the backroom. Once in the backroom I dropped my purse on the table and headed for the drawing table in front of the windows. I flipped on the task light above the drawing table. Its incandescent glow made the room warm and cozy. One of the windows was open so I pulled up a chair and sat, inhaling the brisk night air.

I hadn't been there by myself at night before. The hum of the city was as close to silence as I had found since coming here. This would be my new secret place to escape from Chloe and Hasin and the bustle of the city streets. The hum was jolted by a sound in the direction of the reception area. I tiptoed to the door and listened. A woman's voice said, "Hello - is anyone here?"

I froze.

The same voice said, "We must have left the office lights on when we closed up today."

It was Chloe.

My heart started to race. I sprinted on tiptoes toward the windows, grabbing my purse from the table on my way. I flipped off the task light and scanned the room for a place to hide. I could hear the two of them laughing and their voices murmuring on the other side of the door. I carefully opened the last cupboard. I stepped in and closed the cupboard doors from the inside. I sat on the couch, trying to slow my breathing.

I blinked through the darkness toward the gnarly tree trunk painted on the back wall. I turned my back to the tree, keeping my eyes focused on the cupboard doors, but I kept imagining the gnarled branches grabbing me from behind and sucking me into the elevator. This room was definitely creepier in the dark than in the light of day.

If I had to, I could make my escape through the elevator, but the rumbling of the motor might alert them that I was here. And ending up alone in the alley at this time of night was not my idea of a prudent escape plan. I stayed seated, slowed my breathing and stared at the cupboard doors.

One second later I heard the door to the backroom open. I heard a faint click and a slit of light emanated from around the edges of the cupboard doors. Too late for the elevator escape. I took deep silent breaths. I could only hear parts of their conversation. He would say something and she would laugh. Then silence, followed by a shuffle and some groans and whispers, then another laugh. He muttered something and she said mmm. What had I gotten myself into? I was about to be a voyeur to what might be an extended sexual encounter. I wanted to plug my ears but I had to know if the two lovers were coming my way. If I pushed the button for the elevator, who knows how long it would take for the doors to open? My only choice was to wait it out.

I could hear feet clomping around the room, like one was chasing the other. Then the clomping stopped and she let out an annoying giggle. Then quiet scuffles, some "ums" and "ahhs" and silence again. I heard a crash and Chloe said, "Oh no, this is Jane's stuff. We shouldn't mess this up. I have an idea, a much more comfortable place."

I heard footsteps coming closer. I think my heart stopped when Chloe said, "You've got to see this."

"What?" he asked. Suddenly there was pounding on the cupboard doors. I jumped and put my hand over my mouth to stop a scream.

"What...we're going to do it in the closet?" he asked. "This could be challenging."

"You'll see," she said.

I put my hands over my eyes hoping to make myself invisible.

Just then the cupboard doors flung open and before they noticed me Chloe reached in and turned on the light. All at once I heard her scream and my scream intertwined into a blood curdling sound that bounced off the walls of the tiny room and rattled the elevator doors.

"Sophie, what are you doing in here?" Chloe shouted as she doubled over and grabbed her chest.

"I could ask you the same thing. But from the sounds I've been hearing I think I know."

"Are you spying on us?" she asked.

"I was here first. And anyway, I wouldn't do that. I was just relaxing here for a while. When I heard you come in I thought you would just show him the office and leave. I thought if I kept quiet you'd never know I was here and I'd be able stay and relax awhile longer."

She stiffened and said, "Have you been crying?"

I shrugged and said, "I just came from a Disney movie."

She relaxed and said, "Yeah...I know how that is."

Chris' eyes met mine and I said in a casual tone, "Hey, nice to see you again."

"Same here," he said sheepishly. "I wish it could have been under better circumstances."

I raised my hand and said, "You two go right ahead with what you were doing. Don't let me cramp your style. This couch is a little small, challenging as you said, but somewhat comfortable. So I'll be on my way."

Chloe's eyes followed me as I walked between them and out the closet doors. Without saying a word I left the office. I made a mental note to bring a can of Lysol with me the next time I sat on that couch.

Mrs. Franklin 6

Mrs. Franklin walked to the bedroom, got down on her knees and slid a box from under the bed. She removed the lid and looked at the row of thin boxes inside. Her eyes followed the titles. The oldest title was "Christmas 1988". That was the year Charles bought the video camera. The titles read 1989, 1990 and so on. There were others like "Fourth of July at Nana's", "Todd's Swim Meets" and "Jen's Recitals".

She pulled out "Jen's Recitals" and went back to the living room. She popped the DVD into the player and picked up Nibbles from her seat. She sat in her chair and repositioned him on her lap.

Charles had taped Jen's dance recitals for nine years. Later they had converted the tapes to DVD's. They had only recorded the dances Jen was in, at least three dances per year since she always took ballet, jazz and tap. A couple years she also experimented with hip hop and lyrical.

Mrs. Franklin's face was transfixed on the screen as the dances rolled by one after another. Within a couple of hours she saw her daughter go from the gawky nine-year-old with braces and frizzy hair to the stunning beauty she was today. A tear rolled down her cheek as she heard her husband's voice narrating.

From the time Jen could walk she had wanted to be a dancer. It was a blessing and a curse to Mrs. Franklin that those dance lessons had enabled her daughter to move away and pursue her dance career elsewhere. Now she was happy just to be able to speak to her on the phone.

How long those days had seemed when she was working full time, rushing home to make dinner and driving Jen to dance class in the evenings. And there were Todd's soccer and swim meets on the weekends. Where had she gotten all that energy?

She realized that her foot was tapping to the music. She whooshed Nibbles off her lap and stood up, swaying into the kitchen, her hips moving with the rhythm. Nibbles shook his head as he wondered what to do after his unexpected displacement. She returned to the living room with a cup of hot tea to find Nibbles curled in a tight ball on the chair. She placed the cup on the table and stood beside the chair. She began to move back and forth, tap step, tap step. She lifted her arms into the air, reminded of her own dance classes when she was a teenager.

She was jolted by an abrupt knock at the front door. She paused the DVD and went to the door. She wondered who would be knocking at such a late hour. She turned on the porch light and checked the peephole. Nothing, probably neighborhood kids playing. As she shut off the light she turned away from the door and the knock came again. She jumped. This time it was heavy and loud, like someone pounding with their fist. Her heart thumped in her chest. She slowly moved toward the door, flipped on the light and looked through the peephole again. Nothing.

She heard footsteps like someone running along the walkway toward the house next door. She slowly unlocked the door and opened it a few inches. With her hand on the knob she looked out onto the empty yard. "Travis, is that you?" she said. Then she heard footsteps again, this time loud and heavy, coming from an unknown direction. Her heart raced. She slammed the door and reached for the lock. Her shaking fingers faltered as the footsteps could be heard clomping up the steps. She threw the dead bolt into place and froze. The footsteps stopped. She could not bring herself to look out the peephole again. It must have been Travis, or maybe the kids who lived on the other side. They were always out after dark, playing in the yard.

She glanced at the clock over the fireplace. Eleven-fifteen. The kids were never out this late.

She hadn't realized it was so late. She took a few long breaths, turned off the DVD and made her way toward the bedroom. The phone rang. Who could have been calling at this late hour, hopefully not a problem with Jen or Todd? She picked up the phone and tentatively said, "Hello."

She heard a couple of clicks and a sound like someone breathing.

"Hello. Is someone there?" she said.

Nothing. Then she heard another click.

She hung up. Could it have been a wrong number?

Chapter 36

When I got back to the apartment Hasin was sitting on the couch with his woman friend from the play. I couldn't remember her name. It was something like Marlene or Maurine. No, I remembered reading it in the program because it was so unique. Her name was Morning, short for Morning Song. But that wasn't her whole name. Her whole name was something like Morning Song Butkowski.

To see her first two names in print made them seem delightful, like birds tweeting in the early dawn, but saying them out loud without seeing the letters made them sound like a funeral dirge. Anyway, I remember her saying she was from California. It's a wonder I didn't meet anyone with that name while I lived there, although while I was at UCLA I did meet a guy with the first name of Electron whose father was a scientist. But I don't think he counted as a Californian because he had been born in India.

So much for unusual names. Having a somewhat common name didn't prevent me from experiencing the cruelty of my fellow classmates. Sophie Hopper...Sophie Horney...Soho...So is a Ho...Sophie the sofa...let's hop on the horny sofa.

I said hello to Hasin and Morning Song Butkowski and assured them I would be leaving shortly. They both assured me that she was leaving soon anyway. Chloe would be home soon and I didn't want to deal with her, especially if she brought Chris back with her. I could find a place to stay for the night and then leave the city after the interviews in the morning. My part for Karen Klein's project was finished so I could get another night away before I was due back on Saturday morning for the debriefing.

I couldn't stay in the city where drop-dead gorgeous men with nebulous sexual orientations were spending time with their co-workers, aunts were having sex with their guidos, probably on the kitchen table, and sisters were romping through offices with men I should have been with. Everywhere I turned someone was about to have sex with anyone but me.

I grabbed a tote bag and filled it with enough clothes and toiletries for two nights. I said goodbye to Hasin and Ms. Butkowski and was out the door. Out on the street I realized that without a hotel reservation I would probably pay at least two-hundred dollars for a room. Dad's multi-level four-bedroom apartment could easily accommodate one more person for one night. And he had already offered me a room if I needed it. I called him on the way and expressed my concern that he was not feeling well. He assured me he was feeling better and urged me to come over.

When I got to his apartment he was in his sweats, as usual. He gave me an affectionate tap on the shoulder but would not kiss me hello, which I appreciated. He voiced concern about me needing a place for the night and I explained that with Chloe and Hasin both having dates, I wanted to give them some privacy. He seemed to understand. Jennifer took me to the guest room and I got ready for bed.

In the morning I was at the office just before the first applicant was scheduled to arrive. Chloe wasn't there yet. Long night, I guessed. She would be working into the evening with Mrs. Klein so she deserved to arrive late. As the seconds passed I tried to snuff out the thoughts of Chloe and Chris' naked bodies entwined. I don't know if I was jealous, envious or just pissed off.

The interviews went well. I hired someone on the spot. It probably would have been more appropriate for me to consult Chloe before offering the position, but screw it. I knew more about accounting and business than she did. And she had the ability to adapt to anyone, except me, sometimes.

I left Chloe a note explaining that I had hired someone. If she didn't like it she could fume about it while I was gone, but I suspected she would be fine with my decision. I took a cab to the nearest car rental agency.

In California everyone had a car, even if it was only a college clunker, so renting a car hadn't been an issue until now. I didn't realize until I was standing in the rental office that I had to be at least twenty-five years old to rent a car. Luckily I had turned twenty-five a few months back.

I took off in the general direction of Connecticut. A few years ago Chloe, Aunt Jane, Dad and I had sprinkled Mom's ashes in the Connecticut River. I think we were breaking the law but we didn't care. Who would know? Mom loved the area where we often camped and that's where she wanted to be. I thought going to the place where we had scattered her ashes would make me feel closer to her.

I drove as far as Essex, Connecticut and got a motel room which had minimum bathroom counter space, but I managed to line up my ablutions like sardines crammed in an invisible can, giving each a nudge to make sure all labels were pointing out.

I changed into black slacks and a dressy top and walked to a nearby restaurant to have dinner. It was early, just before the dinner rush, so I ordered a glass of wine and sat at the restaurant bar. I eyed the illuminated bottles on the shelf in front of me. The labels faced the room but all were a little too askew for my taste. I wanted to turn every bottle slightly so all labels pointed exactly at me, but I couldn't get to them without climbing over the bar. I concentrated on willing them to turn, with no results.

After a few minutes an extremely unattractive man sat two seats from me. He was probably ten years older than I and had a pock marked face, a receding hairline and a bulbous nose. I stared straight ahead and kept saying to myself, *Please don't talk to me.* Then he started talking to me. I was polite at first, just saying one-word answers to his questions, but before long he and I were having an interesting conversation. I don't know if it was the alcohol, but he turned out to be a very pleasant, intelligent and slightly attractive man.

He asked me to have dinner with him and I politely declined. I had planned on having dinner there, but after declining his invitation I felt awkward about eating alone at a table where he could see me so I left the restaurant and picked up some fast food and took it back to my room.

I looked at the clock on the night stand. It was only six. Chloe would be in the beginning of the squeeze. I felt anxious and wanted to call her, but I knew an unexpected phone call might botch the whole thing. I could text but what would I say? I hoped if she encountered any problems and needed my help she'd contact me.

So I waited…and waited.

Chapter 37

The tall, dark-haired woman swiped her card in the slot and pushed through the turnstile. As she walked to the platform she slid back her coat sleeve with her gloved hand and glanced at her wrist. She knew the subway would be arriving in three minutes. After checking that the straps of her bag were securely looped over her shoulder, she folded her arms across her chest and took a rigid stance, the same stance she had taken every day for the past week.

She had changed into flats and had dropped her heels into her bag along with her umbrella, a magazine and the Tupperware container left over from lunch. Her bag felt heavy and awkward, but she could withstand the discomfort knowing that in three minutes she would be sitting down for the rest of her journey home.

Her foot tapped out the seconds. She shifted her weight and tapped the other foot as if the rhythmic movement would bring the subway faster. She pinched her eyes closed for a moment and imagined sitting at home in her sweats and socks. She opened her eyes, stretched her facial muscles and let out a yawn. She glanced at her watch again.

Chloe stood about twenty feet away among the people waiting on the platform. Her blue oxford shirt and black pencil skirt could not be seen under her coat. She wore two-inch black pumps and a nondescript watch with a silver band. She held a tote bag securely in her hand. And most importantly she remembered to wear her gloves.

While others were checking their smartphones and reading newspapers, she kept her hands free and her eyes moving, as Sophie instructed. She smiled at a young mother making faces at her baby in a stroller. She turned slightly and caught a couple words spoken by two students talking about some lecture they'd just attended. Her head moved almost imperceptibly to see the tall woman enter the area.

As the woman inched her way to the center of the platform

Chloe raised her eyes to Hasin who was standing near the back wall, wearing his gray suit. He held a briefcase close to his side. He seemed to be staring straight ahead, but as the woman entered his line of sight he momentarily glanced in Chloe's direction, confirming that this was the woman they'd seen in the photos. She was wearing the black coat and gloves Mr. Klein had said she'd be wearing. And the woman, Mrs. Klein, was right on time.

Chloe's most important articles of clothing were her coat and gloves, because they were black, the same color as Mrs. Klein's. During preparations Sophie had insisted that Chloe wear the same color of outer wear as Mrs. Klein, something to do with being able to identify more closely with the mark. This was also a test for Sophie's theory that had to do with peripheral vision, something about blending in with immediate surroundings.

The adrenaline in Chloe's body sprinted like an Olympic athlete from the tips of her toes to the top of her head, but the feeling didn't come from nervousness like she had felt with Shannon's assignment. Standing at the subway platform she felt a power that came with anonymity. Since she hadn't met Mrs. Klein she could become anyone and act any way which would accomplish the objective. Today's assignment would determine if the new business concept was viable.

The outcome of Shannon's assignment had teetered on the edge of failure. In Chloe's mind, if today's events went as intended they would prove that Sophie's planning was successful. If today turned out well, Chloe was certain that Sophie would stay in New York City and continue to be a part of the business.

As the train appeared Hasin and Chloe moved closer to Mrs. Klein. When the train stopped Mrs. Klein made her way toward the doors. The doors slid open and she didn't notice Chloe and Hasin enter behind her. A few seats were still available but the car was filling up fast. Chloe waited for Mrs. Klein to take a seat and managed to get the seat next to her, while Hasin had to stand at a pole in front of them. Chloe glanced at Hasin for a brief moment. A slight smile curled on her lips, confirming that their positions were optimal for Plan A.

Everything had to be accomplished before the third stop.

Mrs. Klein placed her bag on the floor at her feet. She took a magazine from the bag, opened it and attempted to turn the slick pages. Then she closed the magazine and removed her Armani gloves, the ones her husband had given to her for Christmas. She placed the gloves on her lap and returned to reading her magazine. Days of observation predicted that she would remove these important articles of clothing and she would either place them on her lap or drape them over the top of her bag. Now that they were on her lap, Chloe shot Hasin a look.

Step one, complete. Two stops to go.

Chapter 38

Chloe placed her tote bag on her lap with the logo facing out. Hasin looked down at the bag and said, "Excuse me, what is that logo? I've never seen it."

Chloe said, "Oh, this is a business I'm developing, part time right now. I work with artists and curators in preserving, archiving, shipping, that sort of thing."

Mrs. Klein raised her eyes from the magazine and looked in Chloe's direction. She opened her mouth as if to say something and then, recalling that things hadn't worked out for her in the last week, lowered her head and kept reading.

"Do you have a business card?" he asked Chloe.

"Yes, I do," Chloe said. She handed Hasin a card.

Chloe turned to Mrs. Klein and asked, "I don't mean to bother you, but would you like one of my cards?"

Mrs. Klein kept her eyes on her magazine and said, "No, thank you."

Chloe felt her heart start to race. Mrs. Klein hadn't taken the business card.

Step two, not complete. Not complete!

Chloe didn't want to ask again. That would be too pushy. She shot Hasin a glance that said, *Go to Plan B.* Hasin gave an imperceptible nod.

One stop to go.

Chloe looked at the people sitting in the seats across from her. Most of them were focused on their reading material or their phones, but a few stared straight ahead. She glanced up at the poster above the window which read, "Report subway crime to (800) SUBCRIME." The subways had become safer since Mayor Guilani's campaign to clean up the city because subway riders were reporting crimes. She would have to make this next step fast. She hoped their diversion would work and that none of the passengers would notice.

Hasin placed Chloe's business card into his suit pocket. As he brought his hand out of the pocket a couple of small papers had apparently caught on his hand and fell to the floor. As he bent to pick them up the lock on his briefcase sprung open and papers cascaded out, hitting Mrs. Klein's magazine and sending it to the floor. Mrs. Klein let out a sound of annoyance and leaned forward to pick up her magazine. As Hasin stooped down to pick it up, she straightened. He handed her the magazine and Mrs. Klein's eyes locked on his eyes, giving Chloe the opportunity to slide the Armani gloves from her lap and carefully tuck them under her own leg.

Step three, complete.

The subway car began to make its turn to the final stop. Hasin was still stooped over picking up papers while Mrs. Klein assisted. He raised his eyes to her and said, "I'm so sorry. The lock has never given way before." Then he gave her one look that might have been enough to keep her off balance until the third stop. Even a happily married woman was no match for his dreamy look, but Chloe had to be sure that Mrs. Klein would stay distracted until her destination. Chloe glanced at the subway map above the window, blinking the next stop. She threw Hasin a look that said, *This is it*. With the third stop coming around the corner she would have to keep Mrs. Klein focused on anything but the gloves. She turned to Mrs. Klein and said, "Excuse me, I couldn't help noticing your magazine. You and I might be in the same line of work."

Mrs. Klein turned to Chloe with a look of annoyance on her face. Chloe stared into her eyes with warmth intended to draw her into conversation, but maybe Chloe had tried too hard. Mrs. Klein seemed to slow down. She blinked a couple of times in slow motion and opened her mouth to speak but nothing came out. It was as if Chloe's words had injected valium into the woman's veins. Chloe touched Mrs. Klein's arm, which prompted her to speak just as the train rolled to a stop. It was as if she had forgotten that this was her stop. Chloe had to do something to get her off the train. Now.

Hasin said, "This is my stop, sixty-eighth," and hurriedly stepped to the door. Plan B said that he would now get off at Mrs. Klein's stop, but his announcement was unexpected. Subway riders didn't usually announce to the strangers that they are getting off. His words sounded forced. Maybe he had noticed Mrs. Klein's sluggish behavior and was attempting to turn her attention to the exit.

Chloe couldn't let on that she knew this was the woman's stop. Chloe jerked Mrs. Klein's arm and in mid-sentence the woman hurriedly rose and dashed to the door. Once Hasin was out the door he stopped, set his briefcase on the platform and bent down to tie his shoe, causing a commotion with the crowd exiting the train behind him. Chloe leaned back and sighed. Then remembering the plan, she leaped up and stepped toward the door.

Mrs. Klein was now on the platform, her back to the subway car, angling her way around Hasin, when the doors closed behind them and the train's wheels began to roll. Chloe's heart raced. "Turn around, turn around," she whispered to herself as beads of sweat began to form on her forehead. Mrs. Klein was supposed to realize her gloves were gone and turn to see Chloe holding them inside the door. Hasin and Chloe made eye contact. Her look screamed at him to do something. He glanced at Mrs. Klein walking away.

Hasin shouted, "Excuse me, you left your gloves." Three people turned around, including Mrs. Klein. Hasin made eye contact with her and pointed to Chloe who was now hanging onto a pole with one hand and pressing the gloves up against the glass door with the other. Mrs. Klein looked down at her hands and patted her coat pockets. Then with her mouth agape and a look of horror on her face she watched her Armani gloves disappear into the dark tunnel. Chloe forced back a smile as she watched Mrs. Klein disappear. She dropped the gloves in her pocket and felt like twirling around the pole, but as she turned to see a passenger eyeing her she daintily dabbed the sweat from her brow and took her seat.

Step four, complete.

Chloe felt beads of sweat return to her brow when she realized Mrs. Klein hadn't taken her business card. It was up to Hasin now.

Chapter 39

The woman sitting across from Chloe was glaring in her direction. Chloe wasn't sure who she needed to be at that moment, the Good Samaritan who might end up seeming to explain too much, the aloof passenger who finds people's stuff every day, the business woman engrossed in her own matters. She decided to continue the ruse by chatting about how fortunate it was that the owner of the black gloves had seen her holding them because then she would be able to get them back to her. The woman sitting across from her suggested taking the gloves to the lost and found and Chloe added that she didn't trust the lost and found desk to safely keep such expensive items, but that if the woman didn't call she would drop them off later.

Back at the platform Mrs. Klein said to Hasin, "Oh my God, my gloves. My husband will kill me if I don't get them back."

Hasin said, "Well, that woman has them and by the look on her face she wants to get them back to you."

"But how?" she asked. "She and I don't know each other. I mean, I think I may have seen her on the train before but I can't wait. I need to get them back tonight. How will I find her?"

"Didn't she give you her business card?" Hasin asked, knowing that Mrs. Klein had not taken one.

"No, I didn't get her card," she said.

"I have one," he said digging his hand into his pocket. He brought out the card and handed it to her saying, "Here, take it."

"Thank you so much. You're a life saver," she said.

Hasin looked at his watch and said, "Gotta go. Good luck."

Chloe got off at the next stop. Once out on the street her phone rang. She could see it was a text from Hasin with only four words, "Step two finally complete."

She kept the phone in her hand and let out a sigh as it rang again.

"Hello," she said.

"Hello, this is Karen Klein, the woman on the subway who

lost the gloves," the frantic voice said.

"Oh, yes," Chloe said, "I have them. Your gloves dropped to the floor but I didn't notice until the doors closed and the train was moving. Would you like me to mail them to you or maybe…?"

"Oh, no," she said. "Those were a very special gift from my husband. I wear them every day. He would be devastated if he thought I was careless enough to lose them. Can I pick them up tonight?"

"Sure. Let's see. I have to be at Bio-Link on Thompson just south of Houston in about twenty minutes. They called me in to work late so I'll be there most of the evening. You could meet me there," Chloe said.

"I thought you were in the art business," she said.

"It's a sideline but I haven't quite gotten it off the ground yet. Not enough business yet to make a living," Chloe said. "I work part time at Bio-Link. It's at 155 Thompson, Room 405. I'll be there in about twenty minutes. Ask for Chloe."

"OK, I'll be there in twenty minutes," Karen said, "Oh, Chloe…I really appreciate this."

Step five, complete.

Standing in the hallway in front of Room 405 Karen Klein read the letters "Bio-Link" on the plaque next to the frosted glass door. She entered a small lobby where a young woman was seated at a large reception desk. The smell of fresh paint permeated the room. She walked to the desk and said, "My name is Karen Klein. I'm here to see Chloe."

The receptionist picked up the phone, pressed three buttons and said, "Karen Klein is here to see you." The receptionist hung up. She motioned to some lockers against the left wall and said, "You may see her in the back but visitors must first check in their bags over there."

Noticing the perplexed look on Karen's face, she continued, "Don't worry. You just place your bag in one of the lockers, close the door and take the key with you. When you're finished you come back here and use the key to retrieve your bag."

"She can't come out here?" Karen asked.

"Um," the receptionist looked down at the phone and said. "Looks like she's on a call right now. It might be awhile before she can come out. She'd like you to go in. She doesn't mind if you interrupt her."

Karen hesitantly moved to the lockers. She noticed that some of the doors were closed and the keys were missing. Other guests she presumed. She placed her bag in a locker, closed the door, pulled out the key and dropped it in her coat pocket. She turned to see the receptionist motioning toward a door to the right of the reception desk. The receptionist said, "Just go through that door. When you get inside the hallway it will be the first door on your left. Just knock."

As Karen walked past the desk she read the words on the large sign on the wall above the desk: "Bio-Link, Creating Resources for the Future". As she reached for the doorknob she heard a faint buzzing sound. She opened the door and stepped into a hallway. The door closed behind her.

Step six, complete.

Chapter 40

Karen saw closed doors evenly spaced down both sides of the hall. A man and a woman, dressed in white lab coats were standing half way down the hall having a conversation. When they saw Karen they finished their conversation and went through one of the doors. She walked to the first door on the left and knocked.

"Come in," said the voice from inside.

As she opened the door she saw Chloe sitting at a desk talking to someone on the phone. "Gotta go," Chloe said as she hung up. "Oh, hello. Sorry you had to come all the way in here but I didn't want to leave the gloves at the front desk. They're expensive and I wanted to make sure I gave them to you myself. When the receptionist called me, my other line started ringing so I just told her to send you in."

Chloe opened a drawer, took out the gloves and handed them to Karen.

"Thank you. You don't know how much I appreciate this," Karen said as she extended her hand to shake Chloe's.

"Oh, it was no trouble," Chloe said. "If you hadn't called me I would have left the gloves at the lost and found. By the way, how did you get my number?"

"The man in the subway gave me your business card," she said.

"Good. Things worked out relatively well," Chloe said,

They were both smiling when a loud intermittent noise blared outside the door. Banging sounds could be heard in the hallway.

"What's that?" Karen asked.

"Don't be alarmed," Chloe said in a cool manner, "It's a possible bio leak in one of the labs. Hurry, we must evacuate." Chloe leaped up and grabbed her coat from the back of her chair. "Follow me," she said.

In the hallway Karen shouted over the noise, "But my bag." She turned toward the door to the reception area and Chloe grabbed her arm.

"We can't go that way. The door is secured. You can pick it up it later," Chloe said. "Now hurry."

Chloe coolly walked toward the end of the hall where a heavy metal door was marked exit. The same man and woman who had been in the hallway earlier were entering the stairway ahead of them. A man dressed in a business suit walked down the hall and held the spring-loaded door open as they entered the stairwell. As they descended to the street Chloe could see the concerned look on Karen's face.

"Don't worry," Chloe said. "The labs all lock down automatically. Those clanking sounds you heard were the automatic door locks. The technicians who are in the locked labs have sanitizing showers and the haz-mat team will clear them when they get here. We're required to evacuate right away so we won't be infected. Sometimes it's a false alarm but we still have to wait until we're cleared to return."

"Did you say infected?" Karen asked.

"Yes. The bio-engineering projects produce organic matter that can be infectious to people. But since I've been here no one has been infected."

Once out on the sidewalk Chloe said to Karen, "Excuse me a moment."

She walked to the man in the business suit. She glanced at Karen who was looking around as if she was trying to figure out what to do next. Then Chloe said to the man at a volume she knew would not be heard by Karen, "OK, your part is almost finished. After Karen and I leave, you know what to do. Just lock up when you're done. I'll call you tomorrow."

"Will do," he said.

She walked back to Karen and said, "The haz-mat team has been notified and it's on its way. But this may take hours. This happened before and we couldn't go back inside until the next morning. Do you have anywhere you can go?" Chloe asked.

"No, I don't know anyone around here. My money, my credit cards, my metro card and my cell phone are upstairs in my bag. And I live uptown. It's too far to walk," she said.

"Well, my money and cell phone are upstairs too. Can you borrow a cell phone from someone and call somebody?" Chloe asked, knowing that Karen's husband and friends had been instructed not to pick up.

"No, my husband is in a meeting tonight. His phone is probably off anyway. Even if his phone is on he won't answer it until he's out of his meeting." Karen noticed a young man standing near the doorway of a Duane Reade talking on his cell phone. "I'll see if I can borrow that man's phone and call my friend Julie. She doesn't have a car but maybe she can meet us and bring some money for the subway so we can get home."

Chloe glanced at her watch as Karen walked toward the young man. When he finished his call Karen said, "Excuse me, I'm stranded and I wonder if I could use your phone for one minute to call a friend of mine."

He gave her a puzzled look and hesitantly said, "Uh, OK, lady, but make it fast. I can see the bus a few blocks away. Then I gotta go," and handed her the phone. Chloe saw Karen press some numbers and put the phone to her ear. Without saying a word she handed it back to the man.

"She didn't answer," Karen said.

Chloe couldn't let Karen get any other ideas about being rescued. She had to get the two of them moving. "Hey, I know a guy who lives about a half mile from here. I know he's home tonight and he has a car. He'll take us home."

"A half mile. These shoes don't have much support but I guess it's alright," Karen said.

Chloe put her hands into her coat pockets and her eyes widened as she pulled out a wad of bills. She flattened the paper and counted four ones. "Look, I have four bucks. Not enough for two subway tickets but how about getting a cab?" Chloe said.

"Will four dollars get us there?" Karen asked.

Chloe smiled and said, "I don't think so but it's better than walking the whole way. Let's see how far it gets us. If four bucks doesn't take us all the way we'll walk the rest."

"We don't have too many options. It sounds like our best shot," Karen said with a look of wonder on her face.

Chloe stepped to the curb and hailed a cab. They climbed in and Chloe gave the address to the driver. She said, "Here's four bucks. It's all we have. Please take us as far as this will go."

He turned with a look of annoyance on his face and said under his breath, "College students."

Step seven, complete.

Chapter 41

A smile filled Karen's face as she gazed out the window and said, "This is turning out to be an unpredictable day. I'm glad I didn't have plans to be anywhere tonight or I'd be a nervous wreck right now." She turned to Chloe and asked, "How are you doing?"

"I'm good. The bio leak or false alarm, as it probably is, enabled me to get off work early. And if this is anything like the last bio leak, I'll get paid for the entire shift. So I get to go home and watch the TV show I was planning to record."

Karen smiled and said, "I was looking forward to relaxing in my sweats in front of the TV tonight too. But I'm fine with all this. You know, there are no coincidences. The things that happened today were meant to happen. I don't know why they happened but I'm just grateful that you were the one who found my gloves. Most people would have kept them." Karen paused for a moment and continued, "You know, the gloves were expensive but that's not why they're important to me. It's because my husband gave them to me at a time when we were going through a rough stretch, not financially, but emotionally. They mean a lot to me. And right now a four dollar cab ride and these gloves are all I have."

Chloe smiled and looked into Karen's eyes. She noticed a warmth lingering in her eyes she hadn't seen back at the platform where Karen had taken her rigid stance. Chloe was aware that this woman's cold demeanor had come from some recent disappointments. Chloe had to be careful about how she responded. She ventured onto a limb by saying, "You're right. There are no coincidences. You and I were meant to meet today."

Karen went on. "I've never asked a cab driver to take me as far as my money would go," she said with a chuckle. "About ten years ago I couldn't afford cab rides. I had to take subways everywhere, or walk. And even though I can afford cabs now, I still take the subway to work because it stops directly across the street from my apartment and right beside the entrance to my office."

The driver dropped them off near Seventh and Perry. Chloe and Karen started walking west. "It's only a couple of blocks," Chloe said.

Up ahead they could see a van double-parked with its hazard light flashing in front of a brick building. As they approached the van they saw a man coming out of the building with two large flat boxes in his arms. As the man paused to get his footing on the stairs he awkwardly peeked around the boxes at Chloe and said, "Hi, Chloe, what are you doing here?" His casual demeanor was perfect for someone she had only met once that day they finalized the plans Sophie had arranged.

"Hi, Fred. Possible bio leak," she said.

"Again? Didn't you have a bio leak last month?" he asked as he crossed the sidewalk and shoved the boxes into the back of the van. "Isn't it dangerous to be around all those spores and cells and stuff? Next thing you know you'll be growing fingernails out of your ass. You've got to quit that job."

"Yeah, as soon as I win the lottery," Chloe said. "Our purses and cells are inaccessible, possibly till morning. I used the change in my pocket to get here. Is there any way you could take Karen and me home?"

"Well, I've got to get my stuff to the Smith Gallery tonight. If the two of you could help me get the last large piece into the van, I can take you both home," he said as he eyed Karen. Chloe cringed at the thought of him possibly dropping a flirtatiously inappropriate comment.

"By the way, who is this lovely lady with you?" he said as he extended his hand to Karen. His adlibs were alright for the time being.

"I'm Karen," she said, shaking Fred's hand.

As Karen and Chloe ascended the stairs Chloe turned and said, "You've got to see this place." She was recalling the extensive work they had done to get it looking like an artist's studio.

As they entered the apartment Karen drew in a breath. She looked in all directions, taking in every detail. A large blank canvas hung on a brick wall to the right. A tarp covered the hard wood floor below the canvas and buckets of paint were lined up next to containers of brushes and cloths. The opposing wall was painted white with sketches and designs randomly penciled from floor to ceiling, as if someone's raw, midnight sleep-walking dream had spontaneously spewed forth.

A moss green velvet couch faced the tall front windows and a Tiffany lamp dangled over a tree stump end table. Under the loft was a kitchenette next to a wide wooden rack filled with canvases angled one after another. An iron spiral staircase led upstairs to a loft with a bed and a night stand. A mirrored disco ball hung from the ceiling over the bed. The stair rail was decorated with Christmas lights, and a multi-colored kite was pinned across the ceiling, the tip of its tail adorned with a tiny light bulb dangling just above a small, round dining table.

As Karen's eyes scanned the room she thought of the studio she had before she was married. For a moment she missed those days when her life was harder and income was unpredictable. Then she noticed the brass fire pole glistening next to the spiral staircase. Her eyes followed the pole to where it attached to the ceiling. She looked at Fred and then at the pole and asked, "May I?"

Chloe looked at her watch. A few more minutes wouldn't hurt. Chloe shifted her body behind Karen as she gave Fred a nod.

"Sure. Let me show you how to do it," he said as he grabbed the hand rail and ascended to the top of the stairs. "See this dip in the hand rail? It's a gate. I leave this cloth up here so my hands don't stick."

Chloe could tell he had been practicing before they had arrived. "Just swing the gate open," he said, "grab the pole with both hands, step out and wrap your legs around the pole like this." With that he slid to a pile of pillows on the floor at the base of the pole.

As Karen headed for the stairs Fred tossed her the cloth. Her heart was racing. She followed his instructions and as she flew down the pole her voice involuntarily said, "Eeeeeeeee." She landed with a soft thud, sprung to her feet and said, "I've always wanted to do that."

Chloe momentarily forgot herself and said, "Me next." This delay wasn't in the schedule but what the hell. Another minute or two wasn't going to make a difference. As she landed in the pillows she almost forgot she was working. She and Karen looked at each other and laughed.

Fred gave her a look and said, "OK, we've got to get going." Good ad lib, Fred.

They were looking at a flat package about three feet by four feet wrapped in brown paper. The large wooden frame double-wrapped in paper would hopefully pass for a large canvas inside. As long as someone's finger didn't break through the paper in the process of moving the piece, the illusion would work.

"I think two people are enough. If one of you could get that end I'll take this end," he said as he leaned down to grab the package. Chloe trotted to the other end and lifted it.

Karen moved into the hall ahead of them. As Fred started to back out of the door he said, "Good thing you two stopped by. This piece is more awkward to move than I thought. Hey, I was going to wait for Bret to come home to pick up my last piece from another gallery. It's big and heavy so I can't do it by myself, but since I have two strong lovely women with me, is it OK if we pick it up before I take you home?"

"Sure," said Chloe, "it's alright with me. How about you, Karen?"

"Yeah, I'm in no hurry," she said.

Karen walked ahead of them as they maneuvered the piece down the stairs and held the front door open as they angled their way through. While Fred walked backwards down the front steps, Chloe found her body bending forward as she struggled to manage the weight of the piece whose center of gravity was now over her head. Karen, seeing Chloe's struggle, released the door and lunged to steady it. Chloe, startled by the sudden movement, felt her foot slip and the piece began to tilt away from Karen who was reaching to grab it. Fred managed to lift one arm to stop the piece from falling, but not before a dry rapier-like branch of a tall bush stabbed one corner of the paper.

Chloe and Fred flashed horrified looks as the branch sliced completely through the brown paper.

Karen flailed her hands and shouted, "Oh my God, your painting!"

Fred looked at the ground, contemplating what to say. He lifted his eyes and said, "Chloe, hold still. Karen, could you come around to this side and push. We'll slide the piece so that the branch exits exactly the same way it entered. Less tearing that way."

Karen stepped to the other side and as Chloe and Fred steadied the piece she gently pushed. Once the piece was free Fred instructed them to lower it to the ground. He bent over the torn area, making sure Karen could not see that there was nothing under the paper. He smoothed the jagged area with his hand and jumped up.

"Well, as fate would have it, nothing is lost," he said.

"But your painting," Karen said.

Chloe could see him struggling for the right words.

"Well, um," he said hesitantly. "You're not familiar with my work, are you?"

"No," Karen said.

Chloe listened with her mouth agape. She couldn't imagine what Fred was going to come up with.

"Well, many of my canvases are what I would call…distressed. I occasionally cut sections out of them to accentuate, um, devastation for instance. So fortunately the branch stabbed one of the open areas. See, fate is with me."

Chloe's gaze moved to Karen who was squinting at Fred. She lifted her eyebrows and said, "Sounds intriguing. What gallery is showing your work?"

"The Smith Gallery in Chelsea. My show starts tomorrow," he said, looking at Chloe for approval.

"Hmm, I'll have to see it," Karen said.

Chloe shot Fred a glance that said, *Let's get out of here* and he said, "OK, let's go."

When they got to the back of the van Karen pulled on one of the doors to make more room for them to move. Once the package was flat in the van, Fred swung the doors shut and announced, "I'm going to lock up. Take a seat. I'll be back in a minute."

Their eyes followed him taking the stairs two at a time. They turned toward the van and realized that he had literally meant to take a seat - one seat. They stared at each other for a moment. They had two choices: two in the passenger seat or one in the seat and one positioned between the boxes on the floor in the back. Chloe graciously took the floor, Karen took the seat.

Step eight, complete.

Chapter 42

Karen leaned over the seat and said, "I haven't thought about my old loft for years. It was similar to Fred's. I shared it with an annoying roommate but I couldn't afford it myself so I put up with her idiosyncrasies." She paused for a moment. "I always wanted a fire pole but I rented and I couldn't afford to install one. Now my husband and I live in a very nice apartment uptown and I haven't thought about a fire pole in years. Things have gotten easier and...ordinary."

Just then the door opened and Fred slid into the driver's seat, flipped the hazard lights off and started the engine. It rumbled like a diesel truck. As they turned the corner he said, "We'll just pick up my piece at the Consuelo Gallery. Then I'll take you home."

"Consuelo Gallery, the one in Chelsea?" Karen asked.

"Yeah," Fred said. "My piece has been stored there ever since they closed. It's not too far. They're expecting me."

"I know where it is. My husband and I were going to purchase the Consuelo Gallery. He had done all the negotiating. He's good at that. We signed papers and everything. There were a few setbacks along the way but I thought he had straightened everything out and that it was finally ours. Then a few days ago he got the bad news that the deal had fallen through."

"I'm sorry to hear that," Chloe said.

"Yeah, it's in a great location," Fred said. "Ground floor. I think it's in one of the best locations in Chelsea."

Turning to Chloe Karen said, "When you mentioned your service on the subway I thought how coincidental it is that you are going to work with curators and I want to be a curator."

"I'm sure you'll find another gallery," Chloe said. "There are a lot of galleries in this city."

"Well, I'm discouraged right now. It's not that I just wanted a gallery. You see, my father used to own the Consuelo Gallery years ago before he became sick. You're probably too young, but have you ever heard of Andre Duvall?" she said as she looked out the window at the people walking down the street.

Fred interrupted, "That name sounds familiar? Wasn't he a Pulitzer Prize-winning photographer?"

"Yes, he was," Karen said. "Not many people know that."

Chloe gave Fred a sideways glance. How could she have known when she hired him that he would know this obscure tidbit of trivia about their mark?

Karen went on. "When I was a little girl my father displayed his photographs in the Consuelo Gallery. It wasn't until he became sick that he turned to photojournalism. Even though his later photos were about cancer, they were uplifting and inspiring. When I heard that the gallery was for sale I had to have it. I recently found out that my nephew, who became a photographer because of my father, has cancer. His work is surprisingly intelligent and mature for a seventeen-year-old. Just another reason for the gallery...to promote his work."

She turned to Fred and said, "But enough of my sad story. Fred, when I saw that fire pole in your apartment it reminded me that I've always wanted a fire pole. I had forgotten." She paused, then murmured as if talking to herself. "A dream left over from my younger days. For one moment tonight I imagined putting one in the gallery and then I remembered that we didn't get the gallery. I thought we had it. I was sure of it. Then...just like that...it was gone. How did I get so arrogant?"

For the next few blocks the three of them were silent. Chloe could see the city lights illuminating Karen's profile. The woman sitting in the front seat, the woman without her money, her phone, the support of her husband or her dream, was a deflated version of the rigid woman who had stood at the subway platform just hours earlier. Chloe felt an affinity for her that she hadn't felt until now. She could hardly stand the next few awkward minutes in the van. She wanted to relieve this woman's pain, but Chloe reminded herself that she was working. If things continued to go as planned, this woman, whom she might only know for one day, would likely remember her for the rest of her life. Chloe was certain that she would remember Karen for the rest of hers.

The van pulled up to the front of the Consuelo Gallery and Fred threw on the hazards. "We should make this fast or I'll get a ticket," he said as he jumped out. "I'll need both of you for this one. It's heavy and quite large."

Chloe and Karen got out of the van and walked to the front door. Karen noticed that the windows were still covered in paper, just as they had been for the past month. As they entered the front door, music blasted in their faces and a crowd of people yelled, "SURPRISE!"

"What?" Karen gasped. "Wha', what is this?"

Her husband walked toward her with a glass of champagne in each hand. "I'm sorry, darling, I lied to you," he said.

"What do you mean?" she said as tears formed in her eyes.

"We got it," he said.

"We got it?" she said as her body began to tremble. "You mean..."

"Yes," he said. "The Consuelo Gallery is ours."

She threw her arms around him as champagne spilled from the glasses. Her friends crowded around them clapping and asking questions.

"How did you do this? How did you get me here?" she asked her husband as she wiped away the tears. He looked over her shoulder and pointed at Chloe. She turned to Chloe and said, "Chloe, you did all this? I mean, the subway, the lab, and Fred?" Fred smiled and waved from the doorway.

"Yes, here is my real business card." She handed Karen the card imprinted with "PJ Enterprises - When a card or gift just won't do".

Karen read the card and said, "I couldn't have been more surprised. Now I wish you and I could have done business together. You know...the art business. And Fred...I'd love to see what's inside those packages. Maybe I could show some of your work here in my gallery if they fit in with my theme."

"I'm sorry to burst your bubble but those packages are just frames and paper. They'll be dismantled and used for something else. But maybe your kind words will help me with my real business," Chloe said.

"Absolutely," Karen said as she bounced toward Chloe with open arms. Karen grabbed her in a hug that she thought would never end.

After a long minute Chloe pulled back and said, "I have to tell you that it has been a pleasure to meet you. Congratulations on getting the gallery."

"Thank you," Karen said.

"I've got to ask you a favor, Karen," Chloe said.

"Sure," Karen said.

"Don't tell your friends too many details about what happened today. It's better for my business if people don't know too much. You know, for future business. The less people know, the better."

"I get it," Karen said. She gave Chloe a wide smile and turned back to her friends.

Chloe made her way to the back of the room where Jane was pouring champagne. "Hey, how's it going?" Chloe asked as she pointed to a smudge of something on Jane's blouse.

"Great. I see you made it right on time," Jane said as she attempted to brush away the smudge, smearing it even more.

"Yeah, I surprised myself today," Chloe said. "It's a good feeling."

"So, does this mean we're in business? I mean the new business?" Jane asked.

"Yeah, I think so," Chloe said. "I'll see you Monday and we'll debrief. For now, I'm beat."

Chloe turned to see Karen approaching with a gangly teenage boy at her side. "Chloe," she said, "this is my nephew, Jeremy. Jeremy, this is Chloe."

The boy reached out his hand and said, "Nice to meet you."

Chloe reached out and took both his hands in hers. "I hear you're an up and coming photographer."

"Yeah, Aunt Karen is my biggest fan," he said.

"Don't forget to invite me to your opening. I might become your second biggest fan," she said.

He smiled. Chloe felt a lump well up in her throat. As she turned to leave, Karen said, "Oh…what about my bag?"

Chloe turned and faced Karen. She stepped backwards toward the door and said with a smile, "It's already here."

As Chloe turned to leave she could hear Mr. Klein say to his wife, "Tell me about your day. How was it? Were you really surprised?"

Karen laughed. "Yes, I was surprised. Tonight was one of the most unusual evenings I've ever experienced, but I promised Chloe I wouldn't tell too many people about the details. I'll tell you when we get home. By the way, we've got to get a fire pole."

Chloe chuckled as she opened the front door and whispered to herself, "Last step, complete."

Chapter 43

The Essex Motel room was alright although I wasn't used to falling asleep to the sound of crickets. I was accustomed to being lulled to sleep by the traffic noises of the city. One might think I would prefer crickets to traffic noise but there's something to be said for having a routine, especially when it came to falling asleep.

In the morning I picked up breakfast at a fast food place and drove to the river where we had scattered Mom's ashes. I walked to the shore and stared at the slow-moving water. I imagined the ashes floating on top of the water, dancing their way to the sea, playing in the ocean waves, twirling around dolphins until their essence spread to other continents, with light years between them, like stars in the heavens.

Then I thought of the ashes that never made it to the sea, sunk to the bottom of the river, embedded in the slime, sucked up by bottom feeders or digested by thousands of bacteria. My visualization was ruining the moment. I attempted to shut off my brain but all I could see were microorganisms munching mouthfuls of my mother. I had to get that picture out of my head so I imagined the tiny microbes metabolizing these bits of ash into bubbles of gas that burped to the surface and floated up past the stratosphere. My mother was part of the entire earth and outer space. She was part of everything, queen of the ubiquitous 'I am'.

I wanted my mother to say, "I'm proud of you, Sophie, for having the courage to move so far away from everything you knew, for graduating from college, for returning to help your sister." But metabolized ashes don't have voices. I thought I would feel her presence here in the place where we had said our last goodbyes, but I couldn't feel her. I only felt sad that she was gone.

I dropped off the rental car and arrived at the office about eleven a.m. As I crammed my purse into the desk drawer Chloe came out of the backroom followed closely by Jane. Jane's flowered apron, the one with the plastic cherries dangling from the hem, was spattered with what looked like dirt and her bare feet looked like they had just sloshed through mud.

"But…but…," Jane said to Chloe's back.

"Jane, we need to debrief," Chloe said.

"But I'm trying something. I'm almost there. I just need a few minutes…well, ten more minutes," Jane said.

"OK, I'll start with Sophie. You get cleaned up and join us when you can," she said. Then she pointed to the mud-like substance trailing behind Jane on the floor and said, "Please get this stuff off the floor."

Jane lowered her eyes and dropped her shoulders as if Chloe's words had poked a hole in her and drained all the air. Chloe rested her hand on Jane's shoulder and said, "Jane, you are the most imaginative person I know. I don't want to stifle your creativity. Take all the time you need and I'll talk to Sophie. You and I can debrief tomorrow if necessary. We'll get this cleaned up later."

"Thank you, sweetie," Jane said. She smiled and returned to the backroom. Chloe sat in her chair.

"Well, maybe you can live with this stuff on the floor but I can't," I said as I opened the door and headed toward the bathroom. I grabbed a roll of paper towels and returned to the office. I dragged the waste basket to the middle of the room, got down on my hands and knees and began to sop up the guck.

Chloe swiveled in her seat and leaned back. "How was Connecticut?" she asked.

"It was fine," I said using both hands to swipe the towel across ridges of the clay-like substance.

"Fine, huh?" she said. "Fine. So it was fine. And you're fine?"

"Yes, I'm fine," I shouted, scooting my knees down the now cleaner path on the floor.

Chloe let out a breath and rolled her eyes. "So, do you want to hear about last night's outcome?" she asked.

Without looking up I could sense her derogatory eye rolling. I was glad we were not face to face. I wanted to make this short and get back to the apartment where I was hoping to have some time alone. I pressed my eyelids closed and took a breath. "How did it go?" I asked.

I could feel her lean over the desk and focus her eyes on the back of my head. I stopped and looked at her. She took a moment and then said, "It was the most satisfying experience I've ever had out of bed," she said.

"I'm sure that is saying a lot," I said. "I'll have to mention it to Chris."

"Hey, I'm telling you something important here," she said with conviction.

"OK, go ahead," I said with a sigh.

"When I work with someone who is having an event, they're usually tense. They have expectations. They want to impress people. Some agonize over every detail even though I assure them that the event will go well. But there's a difference with working with someone who doesn't know what's happening to them. They have no expectations. I can't begin to explain the rush of being able to manipulate someone for the purpose of bringing them pleasure. You've heard of athletes getting in a zone?"

"Of course I have," I said. Her dramatics were annoying.

"I got into a zone. I felt a connection with Karen. I can't even call her the mark anymore. She was Karen and I was me. Only I was the best me I've ever been. I felt like I was taking part in changing someone's life for the better. I mean, I know it was the Kleins who bought the gallery. And it's Karen who is going to promote her nephew's work. But it felt good to be a part of that."

I wanted to yawn but I decided to save my disrespectful demonstration for another time. "So you think this business is a go?" I said.

"Yes, absolutely. This is what I want to do. And I want you to do it with me," she said.

I looked down and shook my head. "You know when I came here I only planned on staying until this concept got off the ground and you found a person to do the bookkeeping. It looks like both those things have happened. I don't think you need me anymore."

"Of course I need you," she said. "You're the planner, the organizer, the detailed, anal perfectionist."

"Thanks a lot," I said.

"I mean it in a good way," she said. "You're everything I'm not. I wish you could experience being in the zone. I wish you could feel the adrenaline rush that I get from doing this. Accounting and planning is boring. If you could feel the rush you might want to stay."

"Look," I said, "I get it. You're in the zone now so that's taken care of. And you know how to plan all this stuff. Just follow my procedures," I said. "And as for me getting in the zone, I don't think it's going to happen for me. My personality isn't suited for doing the actual squeezes."

"Sure you can do them," she said. "You're fun...when you want to be."

"Another thank you," I said, "but I can't pretend to be someone I'm not. I get too nervous."

"Of course you can. People do it every day. You're polite to strangers when you're in a bad mood. You say you like a friend's haircut when you don't, right? You worked on plays in high school. Just tap into that experience," she said.

"Yeah, I was the stage manager not an actor," I said. "I was terrified of acting. Don't you remember?"

"OK. Well, high school was...a long time ago. You're grown up now. You can change," she said.

"I don't think so. I've got my plane ticket and I'm leaving next Saturday," I said.

"A week...you're leaving in a week?" she said. She paused and took a loud breath. "OK, but you'll still have time to finalize our next project, right? The one with the guy's birthday party next Friday night? It's Hasin, Fred and me doing it."

"Yeah, most everything is in order. A few details need to be worked out next week. I'm going to write every step on one piece of paper and leave it in your box," I said as I pointed to the box on top of the file cabinet.

"OK, I'll see you back at the apartment," she said.

"OK, see you there."

Mrs. Franklin 5

Mrs. Franklin pushed open the glass door of her office building and started toward the subway. Her cell phone rang. She dug it out of her purse and said, "Hello."

"Hi, Mom," said the familiar voice.

"Hi, Todd. How are you doing?" she said, hearing screams in the background.

"Great. Hold on - girls, stop that, I'm on the phone with Grandma," he said. "OK, I'm back. We were wondering if you can come up for Sara's birthday party two weeks from Saturday. If you take the train we'll pay for it."

"Oh, I think so," she said. "She's five, right?"

"Yeah and she loves anything that has to do with Disney princesses. You know, Sleeping Beauty, Cinderella."

"That's funny. I was crazy about them when I was her age too," she said. "Yes, I'd love to come."

"Good," he said. "I'll call you later about the details."

Her attention quickly turned to a young man walking toward her holding a bouquet of helium balloons. He made a point of looking her in the eye as he passed. She turned to watch him walk away and he turned his head back and gave her a wink. She felt a flutter in her chest. She returned her focus to the phone.

"Wait, Todd. Uh, did you, um…never mind."

"What?" he said.

"Never mind. I love you," she said.

"Love you."

She started to put her phone away, then glanced at her watch and touched a speed dial number and waited. "Hello," the voice said.

"Hi, Jen," Mrs. Franklin said.

"Hi, Mom. How are you?" Jen said.

"I'm doing fine. How are you?"

"I'm rehearsing but I'm on a break right now so I have a few minutes," she said.

"I thought rehearsals were over."

"Yeah, for the other show. But I haven't told you. I got a promotion. It's an intermediate position between headliner and chorus," Jen said. "Pretty cool, huh?"

"It's wonderful. I knew you could do it. It was just a matter of time before they realized you were a diamond in the rough. I'm proud of you," Mrs. Franklin said.

"It's so much work. I've been so busy. But when rehearsals are over I'll be on a regular schedule again and things will be back to normal, except I'll be making a lot more money."

"Great. I miss you honey," Mrs. Franklin said.

"I miss you too, Mom. Hey, remember those videos Dad took of my dance recitals?" she asked.

"Yes, I haven't looked at those in years," she said.

"Remember in fifth or sixth grade when I met my friend Grace in dance class?"

"Yes, I think so. How is Grace?"

"She's doing great, married with a two-year-old son. She and I were talking on the phone a few days ago and we had a disagreement about the costumes in the jazz number. Would you look at the DVD and let me know which costume we wore?"

"Which year again?" Mrs. Franklin asked.

"Fifth or sixth grade. I guess you'll have to look at both."

"Sure. I'll get back to you."

"Oh, I gotta go. I love you, Mom," Jen said as she hung up.

"I love you too," Mrs. Franklin said. She let out a sigh and entered the subway car.

She took a seat and clutched her purse on her lap. The sway of the train was soothing and her eyelids began to droop. With a jolt her eyes opened. She said out loud, "Sara's birthday isn't two weeks from Saturday. Isn't Sara's birthday the twentieth?" Or was she thinking of Ashley's birthday. She sometimes got the girls' birthdays mixed up. Wait…she thought, Sara's birthday was the twentieth, two weeks before her own birthday.

Chapter 44

During the week Chloe and I started a new project I spent most of my time planning preliminary steps while still finalizing the current project, the man's birthday party. Even though Chloe was spending more time with Chris, she and I managed to see each other a lot this last week before my move back to L.A. She usually slipped Chris' name into every conversation, which was a bothersome reminder of why I was leaving in the first place.

Friday morning I woke up later than usual. Most mornings I was up by six-thirty because that's when Chloe usually got up, but Chloe was still asleep. During the night my dream had been interrupted by the sound of her doing something in the kitchen. I had heard the tea kettle whistle and then the sound of something like a spoon clinking in a glass. I hadn't heard her come back to bed though.

I awoke later to the sound of the bathroom cabinet slamming and the faucet running. I opened one eye to see the glow of the streetlight and clamped my eye shut, hoping to continue my dream. I assumed she had gotten up to get Midol or something; her cramps had always been worse than mine. When she returned to bed I heard a glass clink onto the nightstand and what I thought was a box of Kleenex thud next to it. I was surprised that I had awoken twice. I must have been as restless as she was. The rest of the night was uninterrupted. I hadn't even heard Hasin return from work.

I felt an urgency to begin my day. On another day I might have relished having the early morning hours to sit with a cup of coffee and curl up on the couch and read, but I felt too restless to wait for Chloe to get up.

With the current project planned and the new one on its way I was counting the hours until my flight on Saturday. The pressure of finishing the last project had weighed on me, but procedures were now in place and the business seemed to be on its way. Chloe was set to lead the client to his surprise and I was sure that she would pull it off flawlessly.

I picked up my clothes and shoes and stepped gingerly into the hall so as not to wake her. On the way to the bathroom I noticed Hasin's door was closed. He *had* come in late.

Today was going to be my day...alone. I was going to spend the day doing what I wanted to do. I showered and did my hair. I decided not to use the blow dryer since I didn't want to spend additional time or cause noise that might wake her. Once she was awake I would have to be polite and possibly wait for her to take a shower and get dressed. Then she'd want to go over details of the evening's events. Or she and I would do something together. Then Chris would come up in the conversation and I'd be siliently infuriated.

My hair was wavier than I liked it but I didn't care. My accidental hairstyle wasn't that bad. It gave me a feeling of freedom I hadn't felt for a while. I dressed in the bathroom and tip-toed to the kitchen in my socks. I looked around. Every pan, every drawer, every utensil looked like a musical instrument waiting to be played in an orchestra of clanks and squeaks and thuds. I decided to leave everything where it was and go.

I laced up my cushioned walking shoes, picked up my purse and coat, stepped into the hallway and closed the door with a faint click. Once I was out in the hallway I imagined Chloe waking to the click and opening the front door to see me walking away. I made my escape to the closest stairwell. I felt a chill tickle me from behind and I shivered as the stairwell door closed behind me. Once in the stairwell I was as good as gone. If she opened the door now she would be looking down an empty hallway.

The temperature outside was brisk. I stopped to put on my coat. Some papers danced around me like a mini tornado. Steam wafted from the vents in the sidewalk across the street. Men's voices shouting orders to each other mingled with the sounds of motors and horns honking and delivery truck doors rolling open and banging shut. The morning sunlight was inching its way down the sides of the buildings like frosting melting down the side of a layer cake.

Over the past few weeks I had become a subway expert, knowing exactly which one to take and how to switch trains. This morning, while waiting for the train I noticed a rat meandering at the base of the tracks; just one rat, by itself, looking relaxed and well-fed. Its color blended with the black grease embedded around the rails. It was the same size as Peachy, the rat I had in elementary school. I silently said to it, "I know you're intelligent because I used to know and love one of your relatives. You've learned how to survive in this place that seems to have no food. I, on the other hand, left my home this morning to find someone who will cook mine for me."

I got off close to midtown and started walking. Some shops weren't open yet so I stopped at a Starbucks and got a cup of coffee and a blueberry muffin. I took a seat by the window to watch the businessmen and women passing by. I removed the book I had found in Chloe's living room from my purse and began to read. Every few pages I would close the book, take a sip and a bite and look across the street at the vendors' carts. New York wasn't so bad.

I finished my coffee and muffin and checked my watch. Some stores would be open. I had spent the past month borrowing Chloe's clothes. I didn't have any extra space in my suitcase for something new but I could mail it back to LA. By the end of the day I would have my hot New York outfit.

I closed the book, put it back in my purse, threw on my coat and started walking. I was glad I had on comfortable shoes. I went into a couple of shops but didn't buy anything, making a mental note of my favorite items so I could come back later and buy them if I didn't find anything better during the day.

I stopped in a bookstore and spent an hour perusing the shelves for interesting novels. I walked through Rockefeller Center and sat watching tourists taking photos of each other. The brisk morning air was slowly replaced by a balmy breeze. I took off my coat and draped it over my arm.

My coffee and muffin were wearing off so I started walking again with lunch in mind. A sandwich or hamburger just wouldn't do on what was probably going to be my last day alone in New York City. Within a few blocks I found an attractive café.

As I walked in the front door I heard the faint tinkle of Greek music. The room had a high ceiling and was dimly lit. The walls were coarse and washed with a golden hue, the tables draped with yellow table cloths, each one with a candle in the middle. The lunch rush was over so most of the tables were vacant.

I stopped at the podium in the foyer and waited only a moment. The hostess picked up a menu and asked, "One for lunch?"

"Yes," I said. I followed her to a table near the front window. The waiter arrived with a pitcher of water in one hand and a white towel in the other. He tilted the pitcher, carefully pouring the ice-cold water into the stemmed glass. He straightened and said, "My name is George. I'll be your server. Would you like anything else to drink?"

"An iced tea, please," I said.

"I'll be back in a moment," he said.

"Thank you."

He didn't let on that he thought someone who eats alone is a freak. He probably hoped that the tip from one person at a four-person table is worth the effort though. That's why I always tip generously when I eat alone. And the other patrons, they didn't give a damn. They were too busy wondering what everyone thought of them.

I always felt awkward at first. Then I'd go into my self-confidence-boosting mode, getting past the awkwardness by telling myself I had a secret. I was special because I was able eat alone. I was special because I was an independent woman. I didn't need to be with someone to enjoy myself. I had been summoned by an entrepreneur to fly across the country and use my talents and intelligence to develop a New York City business. I had just gotten a new business off the ground. If the people in this restaurant knew what I had done they would have been at my table asking for autographs.

So many singular diners bury their heads in reading material to get through the awkwardness of eating alone. Not me. I didn't need to read a book or magazine. I could easily sit up straight and look at others. Of course I always had enough to think about with all the inconsistencies around me, you know, the crooked paintings, the chairs askew at the tables, the napkin precariously perched on the edge of the person's lap across the room.

After eating lunch and convincing myself that I was the guru of surprise party deliverance, I headed toward Saks on Fifth Avenue. I had been to Saks once in LA but the prices had been too high. Today I thought I'd splurge. After all, the superstar of the event-planning world deserved to dress like a celebrity.

I prepped myself before entering the door by smoothing my windblown hair and positioning my dark glasses on my head. I always felt like I looked rich when I used my dark glasses as a sporty tiara. I stood a little taller than usual, lifting my head the way people with money do. I wondered if any of the sales people would notice that my clothes were not of the same caliber as those of Saks. But then I thought, why should I care what the sales people think? They probably can't afford to buy clothes at Saks even with their employee discounts. They should be grateful that I'm buying something from them.

I was attracted to a table of airy sweaters in my favorite colors. I lifted a periwinkle mohair sweater and held it to the light. I had never seen such a beautiful sweater, delicate and feminine. I pressed it against my chest and for a moment and felt like it was already mine, like it had been waiting for me to arrive. I draped it over my arm. I shuffled through some racks of blouses and chose a couple to try on. After adding a pair of jeans to my selections I made my way to the dressing room.

I'm size seven with no protruding bulges and my skin usually has a healthy glow but I swear, fluorescent dressing room lights make me look like my grandmother in her coffin - puffy, plastic and dead. Fortunately, I convinced myself that all four items would look great once I was outside this flash-freeze ice house. But the periwinkle sweater was particularly flattering even under the stadium lights.

As I headed for the check-out counter I lifted the price tag of the sweater and gasped. Maybe I had read it upside down. I stopped and turned the tag over. I held it closer to see if a smudge or an eyelash had clung to the tag, giving the price an extra digit or two. No, the price was printed clearly. I found the tag on the blouse that had fit perfectly around my breasts. I squinted at the numbers. I puckered my lips and blew on the tag. Nothing happened. Then I brushed the tag with my thumb. The numbers stayed intact. I started breathing heavily. I glanced up to see a woman looking at me. A gold nametag was pinned to her blouse. Martha. I forced a smile even though I felt like someone had punched me in the stomach.

I didn't deserve to be in this store. What made me think I could afford any of these clothes? I wasn't the talented, intelligent person who had gotten a business off the ground. I arrived in New York an out-of-work accounting major who had been offered a pity job from her sister. I was an office worker for God's sake and I was about to fly home to a boxy stucco apartment to live with a roommate whom I didn't particularly like. I had no boyfriend and my family consisted of a practically non-existent father, an absentmindedly idiotic aunt and an annoyingly eccentric, judgmental sister.

I plopped the clothes on a table and gently touched the periwinkle sweater, saying under my breath, "I'm sorry I'm not good enough for you." Tears began to well up in my eyes as I headed for the front door. Something started rising in my throat. I feared that whatever it was might escape from my mouth in an unpredictably horrifying way. What started as an urge to throw up unexpectedly turned to an urge to burst into uncontrolled laughter, or maybe tears. I stopped at a counter, taking deep breaths as I pretended to look at some scarves. I kept my eyes down as I fingered the silky material.

A saleswoman appeared on the other side of the counter saying, "May I help you?"

I wanted to scream. Why were salespeople always forcing me to buy something? Couldn't they tell I wasn't supposed to be there? Did they have to rub it in? All I wanted to do was to take a moment and compose myself. But there she was, in my face.

She reached for a scarf and draped it over her hand to accentuate its translucent quality. I looked up and expected to see a perfectly coiffed over made-up slender supermodel, but the only thing I noticed about her was her kind expression. Behind it I saw that she had worked there for many years, maybe commuting every day because she couldn't afford to live in Manhattan.

She raised her children by herself and resented the people who spent as much money on one dress as she spent on a month's rent. She had put up with spoiled rich girls for decades and here I was about to laugh like I didn't have a care in the world. She deserved to be resentful. But the expression on her face was that of compassion. I think she saw me, really saw me. She must have seen me put the clothes back on the table. She knew what I was feeling.

I touched her hand and said, "You've already helped me just by asking, but I'm sorry, I have to go."

She smiled as if to say, "Everything will be alright."

As I walked toward the door I tried to hold in my laughter. The other shoppers didn't care but two salespeople looked concerned. I waved them away as I clutched my mouth but one salesman looked poised, ready to give me the Heimlich maneuver. His serious expression only made my urge stronger.

When I got out onto the sidewalk my laughter exploded and tears rolled down my cheeks. I leaned against the wall and put my palm against my chest to catch my breath. Most of the passers-by didn't acknowledge me. After all, this was New York City. I was safely contained inside my hysteria bubble. One passerby must have thought I was crying because he gave me a concerned look and I managed to choke out, "I'm OK, I'm just laughing."

I wiped the tears away and began to walk down the street. I cleared my throat and held my head up high, but every time I thought of those price tags an uncontrollable wheeze shot out of my lungs and I doubled over in silent laughter.

Something had happened to me in those few minutes. It was as though every bit of tension I'd felt toward Chloe was suddenly gone. The things I'd been telling myself, the reasons I'd fabricated for being alone, for being right, for being whatever stupid way I was being, didn't matter anymore. It was all ridiculous. All of it. The whole world and everything in it was a joke and I had never gotten the punchline before.

My father wasn't non-existent. I was the one who had stayed away from him. He'd been there for me every time I needed him. Aunt Jane wasn't idiotic. Although sometimes a little ditzy, she was also artistic, sweet and caring. She loved me. And Chloe's eccentricity was something for which I had always been envious. Yes, I envied Chloe. My annoyance at her ability to communicate with people and to see the world in a casual way was because I envied her. And as for her judgmental attitude? I had done nothing but judge her ever since I got here.

I often missed my mother but the thought of looking into Aunt Jane's face and Chloe's face and even my father's face reminded me of where my mother really resided, not among the ashes embedded at the bottom of the river, or even among the stars scattered throughout the universe, but deep within all of us.

I had to get back to Chloe. I had to tell her how I felt.

Chapter 45

As I made my way to the subway I called the office. Aunt Jane picked up.

"Hello…I mean, PJ Enterprises," she said. She sounded out of breath.

"Hi, Aunt Jane. Can I talk to Chloe?"

"She's not here," she said. "Wait a minute. I just need to get these…wait…"

I heard a crash followed by a splash. In the background I heard her say, "Oh, shit on a stick."

"Aunt Jane! Aunt Jane!" I shouted. She had dropped the phone.

After a few deafening clanks I could tell she picked up the phone again. "Crap, Sophie," she said. "I'll have to get back to you. Chloe's not here. I think she's still at home. Bye."

I looked at my watch. It was almost two-thirty. Why was she still at home?

I calleded her number but the call went to voicemail. My pace quickened. I started running. Like the scene in "Breakfast at Tiffany's" where Holly Golightly runs in the rain to find the cat, I was on a mission. I felt the cool air pressing against my cheeks. My hair was bouncing around my shoulders. I was smiling so widely I thought my teeth would soon be clogged with bugs. I had to tell Chloe I was wrong. As dramatic as running wildly down the sidewalk was, it wasn't going to get me there fast enough, even in my comfortable shoes. I came to my senses and hailed a cab.

When I got inside the apartment I called Chloe's name but she didn't respond. I looked into her room and saw a Chloe-sized lump under the covers. An arm was dangling over the side of the bed and wads of tissue had been strewn on the floor. A water glass and thermometer were on the nightstand along with a brown plastic prescription bottle. I walked to the bed and heard a soft snoring sound coming from under the covers.

"Chloe," I whispered, then a little louder, "Chloe."

She groaned. I gently lifted the sheet and noticed her hair was glued to her forehead with perspiration.

"Chloe, oh my God, you're sick," I said as I reached for the wastebasket.

She opened one eye and in a scratchy voice said, "Sophie, I'm sick."

"You poor thing," I said. I grabbed a clean tissue from the box and used it to scoop up the crumpled ones from the floor, tossing them into the wastebasket.

"It must be from the stress," she whined. "My immune system was weakened, you know, getting this last project right. Now that it's over I think my body is telling me to stop and rest."

"But it's not over. What about tonight's project? Why didn't your body keep you healthy for tonight?"

She didn't answer.

"Last night you seemed fine," I said. Then I remembered that I had heard her get up twice during the night.

"I didn't want to say anything but I didn't feel so good last night. I thought tea and honey would nip this thing but I guess it didn't," she said as she turned on her back. "Sophie...I need your help."

"Sure, anything," I said.

"Don't be mad at me," she said.

"Of course not, honey," I said as I brushed her hair away from her face.

"You've got to take my place tonight," she said.

"What?" I stepped back, my heart pounding.

"Tonight? I need you to do it."

"Are you kidding?" I shouted.

"Do I look like I'm kidding?" she said as she coughed.

"Come on," I said, "I can't do it. You know I'm terrified of doing them. We had an agreement."

"Yes, I know but..."

"Why didn't you tell me about this earlier?" I asked.

"What time is it? I've been asleep," she said as her voice trailed off.

"It's three o'clock," I said as I looked at my watch. "What would you have done if I hadn't showed up in time?"

"I don't know. I'm sorry," she said as she reached for a tissue. She blew her nose and tossed the tissue into the air. I managed to

199

lift the wastebasket and catch it before it hit the floor.

"Oh...my...God. Is this your twisted way of trying to get me to do this? Pretending that you're sick?"

"I feel like I'm going to die and you're accusing me of lying? Screw you, Sophie," she said with a crackling whine that turned to an almost imperceptible cry, like a kitten trying to eke out its first meow. She arched her body and pressed her hand on her chest. She took a breath and flattened her head against the pillow.

"And what's this, some fake prescription from Dr. Bob?" I said as I picked up the bottle. I read the doctor's name on the bottle out loud. "Doctor Rubinstein? Who's that?"

"Hasin took me to the clinic this morning. I thought the antibiotics the doctor gave me would kick in in time for me to do the thing tonight. But they haven't." She coughed again. Her eyelids began to sag and she started to drift off. With her eyes closed she said, "I can't do it, Sophie. I'm begging you. I know you can do it. You planned the whole thing. You know every step. If you don't do this our business will fail."

"That's why I kept telling you to get a back-up, you know, an understudy," I said. I dropped the wastebasket to the floor and started pacing. I said over and over, "I don't know."

She opened her eyes, reached for my hand and said, "I kept thinking you would be my backup. I kept holding out, hoping you'd stay. And now you're going home and...and..." Her words trailed off to a whisper but I heard her say, "I love you."

She was asleep.

My eyes grew to the size of hubcaps. What was I about to do?

Mrs. Franklin 4

Mrs. Franklin passed by the glass wall of her manager's office on her way to get her second cup of coffee. She noticed a woman seated with her back to the glass facing him. He lifted his eyes as Mrs. Franklin passed, then quickly lowered them and said something to the woman. Mrs. Franklin couldn't hear what they were saying, but she sensed something peculiar in the way he lowered his eyes without acknowledging her. The woman seemed to say something back to him and he lifted his eyes and smiled at Mrs. Franklin in a way that was too deliberate. This wasn't like him. Something was unusual about this woman's presence in the office. He was hiding something.

With cup in hand Mrs. Franklin walked back to her desk trying to think of a reason for interrupting his meeting with this mysterious woman. She panned the desk for anything that justified interrupting him. She decided to pick up a file folder and walk past his office again. It was something she usually did.

As she passed the glass wall the woman was standing. They shook hands and he ushered her toward the door. Mrs. Franklin continued and stopped at the drinking fountain down the hall, leaned over and eyed the doorway as she took a sip. When the door opened she wiped her mouth and began to walk back toward her office. The woman came out and walked in Mrs. Franklin's direction. She was pretty with hair too puffy for her stature, probably a wig. OK, so maybe they used cheesy wigs as disguises. They had to do better than this.

The woman gazed into Mrs. Franklin's eyes. Mrs. Franklin steadied her path and stared back. The woman formed a sincere smile and said, "Hello." As Mrs. Franklin passed her manager's door he called her inside.

"Arlene, the woman you saw me speaking with in my office is Ms. Fletcher, a consultant who will be assisting me with something of a confidential nature. If anyone asks you about her, I'd appreciate it if you would let them know that I can't divulge any information at this time."

"Do I need to be concerned?" she asked, hoping to see a bead of sweat running down his forehead.

"No, not in the least," he said. "As my executive assistant you will have full disclosure when my work with her is complete. But in the mean time I expect you to dissuade others from fabricating rumors. You know what I mean? Ms. Fletcher is a young, attractive woman and my wife, who as you know is often here in the office, should be spared the pain that vicious rumors can cause."

"Yes, sir," she said. Of course he was concerned. For the past eight years rumors hadn't bothered him, but today he was concerned.

He was in on it. She was certain of it.

Chapter 46

Chloe hadn't meant it, the screw you thing. She had never reacted that meanly with me. It was the fever talking, although I probably deserved it after accusing my pitifully sick sister of deliberately deceiving me. My watch read three-ten. I reached down and smoothed Chloe's hair away from her face. She looked like an angel. "I love you too," I said. I knew she couldn't hear me. I don't know why it was always so difficult for me to say those words to her, but saying them today was easier than usual.

I went into the hall and closed the bedroom door behind me. I grabbed my phone and called Aunt Jane. I walked to the living room and began to pace. The phone seemed to ring forever. I whispered, "Pick up, pick up."

She finally picked up and said, "PJ Enterprises."

"Aunt Jane, this is Sophie," I said with urgency in my voice. "You're familiar with tonight's squeeze right, the one with the guy's birthday party?"

"Sort of. All the stuff is here and Hasin and Fred are supposed be here in about half an hour," she said.

"OK, things have changed. Chloe is sick," I said.

"Oh my goodness, she seemed fine yesterday. I hope she's not too bad," Jane said.

"She'll live," I said, "but I have to take her place tonight."

She responded with a series of "Oh's", the first being that of absentminded acknowledgment, the second indicating a slight grasp of the situation, the third announcing the realization that Hell must have indeed frozen over.

"Hasin has the car, right?" I asked.

"Yeah, he's probably picking up Fred right now," she said.

"OK, I gotta go. I'll see you in a while," I said as I hung up.

I dialed Hasin's cell. He must have had his earpiece in because he got it on the first ring. "Hello," he said.

"Hasin, this is Sophie. Where are you?" I asked.

"I'm on my way to Fred's," he said. "How are you?"

"Not so good. Chloe is sick and I'm taking her place tonight."

"Yeah, I took her to the clinic this morning. She thought she'd be better by the time this thing went down tonight. I guess not, huh?" he said.

"Yeah. Um, since you're already on your way to Fred's I'll get a cab and meet you at the office. I'm leaving right now."

"See you there." He hung up.

I dashed for my purse, ran down the stairs and onto the street. I noticed clouds forming overhead. A light mist fell like a veil over my face. It was beginning to drizzle. Just great. I jogged a block to Broadway and hailed a cab. Traffic wasn't too congested and within a few minutes I was at the office. I walked into the backroom to find Aunt Jane with her arms tangled in what looked like fifty feet of cellophane.

"Hey, Sophie, could you grab the scissors over there?" She pointed to the table in the middle of the room. "I need a little help getting this stuff off of me."

Without saying a word I grabbed the scissors. Aunt Jane stood still and extended her arms out to her sides. I started at her shoulder and slipped the blade between the transparent mummy wrap and her arm. Then I started clipping. Aunt Jane said, "Everything's in locker number three, the clothes, shoes, purse, procedure sheet and badge. I think it's all there, but you might need a little more make-up. I have some with me. I can help you with that. And a clip or two for your hair."

"OK. We need to be there just before five, right?" I asked as the last piece of cellophane dropped to the floor. "By the way, what is all this stuff?"

She pointed to the three-foot-high, nondescript cellophane sculpture on the table. "I'm working on the centerpiece for the Weller Shipping anniversary party. It's hard to explain. They want some kind of sculpture made out of shipping supplies so I've been experimenting. I haven't come up with the final design yet."

"OK, good luck with that," I said tentatively as I headed for the locker. I had selected the clothes for this night but I had not tried them on. Fortunately Chloe and I were the same size so I already knew they would fit.

I opened the locker door to find the women's navy blue business suit. I lifted the hanger and turned it to get a look at both sides. We had made a good choice in finding a look that was business-like as well as feminine. I noticed that the neckline would definitely show some cleavage, what little I had and the skirt was short but tasteful.

I placed the hanger over the door and reached for the navy pumps with the four-inch heels and placed them on the floor in front of me. These were going to be a challenge. I bent down, untied my shoelaces and slipped off my shoes. I grabbed the locker door for balance, lifted each foot and removed my socks. I slipped my feet into the pumps. As my body rose off the floor I felt like my head would graze the ceiling. I would need some practice walking in order to make a convincing performance. I took a few steps and realized that the less time I spent in the shoes, the better. I removed them and set them on the floor.

I took the purse from the hook inside the locker and opened it. Inside was some jewelry, a little gaudy for my taste, and the badge. The purse was large enough for anything else I needed to take with me. I would transfer some of my personal items to it.

I picked up the badge and tilted it toward the light. I was staring at what looked like a child's toy. I hoped I wouldn't need to use it but if I did, a quick flash of the plastic trinket would have to suffice. It reminded me of what was going to be the most difficult part of the night. A dash of fear shot through me and I realized that I would need a fresh swipe of deodorant before starting.

Chapter 47

"Come here, sweetie," Jane said as she patted the barstool next to the table. "Let me touch up your make-up. You've got to be alluring tonight, and maybe a little slutty."

"Yeah, don't remind me," I said as I took a seat.

"And that hair...we've got to do something with your hair. But luckily you're a beautiful girl," she said as she removed some items from the make-up kit. She grabbed my head in both hands and angled it toward the light. Then she opened a bottle of foundation and poured a small amount on her finger. As she dabbed my face I began to relax.

"Aunt Jane, how long were you married to Joe?" I asked.

"Twenty-four wonderful years," she said.

"How did you do it? I mean, how did you make it work for twenty-four years? I can't even make a relationship work for a year," I said. "And lately I can't manage as much as a day."

"Well, first of all you don't settle for the first person to come along. You try people out. You take time to get to know them. Sounds like you've been doing that. If they're not right for you, you say 'Next' and try another one. Most importantly - you find someone that you like, who likes you," she said.

"But I want to be in love with someone who is in love with me," I said.

Jane paused and looked into my eyes. "I mean it, Sophie. Sure you can be in love with someone who is in love with you. Everyone wants that. But you need to find someone who likes you, someone who you really like. There's a difference. Find someone you trust and respect. Someone you can laugh with. Someone you can have bad hair days with or be bitchy with on those PMS days." She paused. She put the foundation back into the make-up kit and took out some blush. Then she chuckled. "Someone you can fart in front of or you're going to have stomach aches all your life. Because when the spark fizzles - and it will - what you've got left, if you truly like each other, is an affection that surpasses all of that infatuation crap. And having a man like Joe and now Stan, who will forgive the occasional gastric upheavals, is a blessing."

"Thanks, Aunt Jane," I said. She could see I wasn't convinced. She went on.

"It's funny. People talk about being *in* love like it's a place to be or a strong feeling. And when the feeling is gone it means the love is gone. But love is something else. I think love is what we do. It's when we're so annoyed with the other person we want to scream. Then we remember that love means coming through for them when they are down. Love means being there for them even when they can't be there for us. When we do that we find the love again and again as if anew."

She stopped and tears formed in her eyes. She blinked and smiled at me. "Sophie, I know what I'm about to say might make you feel uncomfortable because I know your relationship with Chloe has been strained in the past few years. But what you're doing tonight is love. You're coming through for Chloe even though you don't want to. I know how scared you are of doing this, but you're doing this because you love her. I know you're annoyed that she hadn't trained a back-up person and she has suddenly been forced to rely on you. But somewhere deep inside her she knows she can count on you because the two of you love each other."

She threw her arms around me in a loving embrace. I hadn't thought of it that way. I had just told Chloe I loved her for the first time in years, but my own words hadn't sunken in until Jane said them. Chloe and I loved each other.

I held her and said, "Thank you, Jane."

This time she knew I meant it. She pulled back and held me at arm's length. "Hey, that's the first time you've ever called me Jane."

"What do you mean? I always call you Jane."

"No, you don't. You always call me Aunt Jane," she said with a tear in her eye. "I like you calling me Jane. It makes me feel like we're friends."

"OK, Jane," I said as I grabbed her again and we rocked back and forth laughing.

We were still hugging when the door opened and Hasin and Fred entered the room.

"Ooh, girl on girl action," Fred said, stopping for a moment, staring in our direction. "Hey, aren't you two related? So this is like incest or something."

"Shut up, Fred," I said as Jane and I released our hold.

"You boys better get dressed. You too, Sophie," Jane said. "It'll be time to leave soon and the three of you need to coordinate before you go."

"Yes, Mother," Fred said as he went to his locker and opened the door.

Jane slid across the room and gave him a little slap on the back, saying, "Hey, watch your mouth. I'm not that old yet. Well, not mentally anyway."

As Fred began to change his clothes Hasin slinked toward me with fingers extended in a ghoulish manner. Taunting me, he said, "Hey, girl. So you're taking Chloe's place tonight. Are you scared?" He stretched out the word scared.

"Fuck you, Hasin," I said with a smile.

"Oooooh, I've never seen you this feisty," he said. He opened his locker with a flourish.

"I'm here to do a job. And I'll do a hell of a job at that," I said with conviction.

"As long as you don't give the mark a job," Fred said as he grabbed a plastic police badge from the locker. "Or I might have to arrest you."

"Fred, you have a one-track mind," I said as I took the suit from the door and picked up the heels. "Now I'm going to change in the bathroom. I hope you two boys can control yourselves while I'm gone. Jane, talk to them. Make sure these two don't forget that they're straight tonight."

"Hey, that's a low blow," Fred said. "Sorry Hasin."

"As long as you don't blow Hasin while I'm gone, Fred," I said as I walked to the bathroom. Even though both of my hands were full of clothes I managed to lift my bird finger at him as I backed in the bathroom and closed the door.

As the door closed I could hear Hasin say, "She's on fire tonight."

The suit fit perfectly. The shoes...well...the shoes were another story. They fit fine but I predicted that if I could get through the evening without screaming in pain or falling on my ass I might accomplish an Oscar-winning performance.

When I finished dressing I stared into the bathroom mirror and a wave of terror swept over me. For a moment I willed my reflection to be Chloe, not me. I opened the bathroom door to find that Hasin and Fred were almost ready. They were wearing white dress shirts with dark suit pants. Hasin was still adjusting his shoulder holster. If things went as planned, the mark wouldn't see it. But just in case things didn't go well the holster and gun would have to be revealed.

We had decided that uniforms would not be appropriate for this project. Badges would be enough to identify our two male characters. We didn't want to attract too much attention, and now that I was looking at these two men in their suits, I agreed that suits had been the better way to go.

Fred looked up and said, "Lookin' good. Not too slutty, not too businesslike."

"Thanks, Fred. Hasin, could you come here for a moment? I need to ask you something," I said, motioning for him to come to the bathroom. He entered and I closed the door. I took a breath and asked, "What do I do? How do I do this? What do I say to the guy?"

"What do you mean?" he asked. "You planned the whole thing. You know exactly what to say."

"Yeah, but I don't know how to talk to guys. I get tongue-tied. I say stupid things. I saw you in that play. You know how to talk to women. You know how to talk to men. Tell me what to do."

He put his hands on my shoulders and said, "OK. First, take a breath. Relax." I closed my eyes, inhaled and let the air out slowly. He continued, "Now look at me." I opened my eyes and looked up to see his face inches from mine.

He said, "Sophie, listen to me. Successful acting is not the same as pretending. When I have a love scene with a woman I can't pretend to be attracted to her or people will see through me. I must truly find something attractive about her. Everyone is attractive in some way. You just have to look for it and see it within them. Tonight, when you see it in him, and you will, you may feel a passion that will carry you through the assignment. If not, then think of something else you're passionate about and let that carry you through."

"But what do I say?" I asked.

"When you see him as an attractive person you'll find the words. Don't be afraid of him. He's just a human being like the rest of us," he said.

"What if he's not attracted to me?" I asked.

Touching my cheek with his palm he said, "Your silky skin, your smile, the warmth in your eyes. You're a beautiful woman with passionate conviction who is feisty and honest. How could he not be attracted to you?"

For a long moment he and I stared into each other's eyes. I broke the silence with, "Thank you."

I felt myself being drawn to him. His face formed a smile mixed with a look of regret, like he was about to say something and changed his mind. He dropped his gaze and said, "OK, let's get going."

When I came out of the bathroom with an armload of clothes Fred gave me an inquisitive look. He would just have to keep imagining what happened in the bathroom because I wasn't saying a word. I put the clothes in the locker and grabbed my purse and the set-up purse. I removed my cell phone from the set-up purse and slipped it in my bra to make sure it wouldn't show. I removed the cell phone and placed it back in the purse. I transferred a few items from my purse to the set-up purse then I picked up the sheet from the locker and said, "OK, we've only got a few minutes. Let's go over the plan. The car has gas, right?

"Right," Hasin said.

"And our cell phones are charged and ready?

"Yes," they said in unison.

"Hasin, you have your phone? I want to make sure you can hear what I'm saying in that apartment. I can't be left in there on my own. I need you guys to be there at the right time."

"Yes, to everything," Hasin said.

"OK, we three drive to the building. Hasin and I get out and Fred pulls into the alley. We go into the building. I take the elevator to the thirteenth floor. Hasin takes the elevator to the basement and meets the building super in his office.

"Wait," Fred said. "What if I can't stay in the alley? I mean, what if a cop comes along and I have to move the car?"

"Then call Hasin and let him know you've moved. If you're forced to move, just drive around the block and come back to the same spot. It's unlikely that someone will force you to move the car a second time," I said. "Next, I walk down the stairwell to twelve and wait. The mark has already been told to stay at his office until five-fifteen. I might be waiting for a few minutes. I'll

210

have my cell ready to speed-dial Hasin. Hasin, once you see my call, wait one minute, sixty seconds, that's all. If things go according to plan this is the last time I'll be able to contact you. The only reason you would get another call from me is if something goes wrong. Then you go to Plan B. It's written on the sheet."

"Got it," Hasin said.

"Hasin, give us five minutes. Once you're done with that you can go to the apartment. It doesn't matter how long it takes for me to get there as long as you're there in time. When you hear me talking on my phone you need to be close by. You know what to do next, right?"

"Right," they both said.

"OK, let's do it," I said. I took a breath. "Wait, I have to pee."

"Didn't you just go?" Jane asked.

"Yeah, but I need to go again. I think it's my nerves. But I'll be fine," I said as I trotted to the bathroom.

When I came out Jane said, "Hey, how about a good luck hug?" She held out her arms and gathered us together. "Break a leg, kids."

"Thanks, Jane," I said with emphasis on the word Jane.

She smiled. I opened the cupboard and the three of us entered the rabbit hole. My heart was racing and my legs were jelly.

Mrs. Franklin 3

Mrs. Franklin exited the subway and began her ascent to the street. Coming down the stairs toward her were unfamiliar faces. How could this be when she had been exiting the same train every morning at the same time? There must have been others who had taken the same transportation every day. Why hadn't she noticed them before? Maybe she had never really looked at the people passing her. Come to think of it she usually wasn't looking at anything. Her thoughts of the workload sitting on her desk formed a haze around her as she walked. What else was there to think about?

But today she was looking at everyone who passed by. As she got to the top of the stairs she smelled the aroma of food cooking at a street vendor's cart. Had this cart been there before? A well-dressed man at the front of the line said to the vendor, "Hey, Charlie, give me the usual." The vendor's cart must have been there all along.

The walk from the subway to her office seemed longer than usual. The buildings were shiny. The motors and honking horns and tapping footsteps created a rhythm around her. She took a breath. The air tasted particularly fresh.

She felt like she was seeing everything for the first time. She took a moment to study her own office building. Had she ever really looked at her building, even that first day she had gone for her interview so many years ago?

Pigeons dotted the windowsills. She silently counted the floors and windows trying to locate her office. Then she realized her office faced the other side of the building. A smile came to her face.

As she entered her building she looked at her reflection in the glass doors. The glass seemed to elongate her form. She looked thinner. Maybe skipping those bowls of ice cream after dinner the past few nights had started to pay off. She lifted her torso as she entered the lobby.

Her body shuttered as a chill crept up her spine. Maybe she wasn't seeing things differently. Maybe today really was different. Maybe the people who passed by her were different. It had been two weeks since she had found out about the impending event. Maybe she was different.

Chapter 48

Hasin, Fred and I entered the elevator that would take us to the hallway to the back dock where the car was parked. Fred pressed the down button. We descended with a jolt and a few clanks. Hasin said, "Wouldn't it be ironic if this elevator stopped between floors and we were detained for a long time?"

Fred and I stared at Hasin who looked like he knew he had just said the wrong thing. I said, "Take it back."

"What?" he asked.

"Undo it. Say something positive," I said.

"OK…um…tonight is going to be a success," he said.

"Good."

I think we all held our breath until the doors opened on the ground floor. As we approached the car I scanned it for signs of vagrants' pee stains. A man was huddled beside the dock in a small tent-like structure and Hasin said, "How's it going, Sam?"

The man lifted his head and said, "Hey, Hasin, can't complain."

The drizzle was stronger now. Traffic would be slow but luckily we had allowed ourselves enough time. By the time we got in the car all three of us had a layer of moisture covering our hair and clothes. Fred took the driver's seat, I took the back seat and Hasin rode shotgun. I opened my purse and pulled out my deodorant.

"I forgot to do this. I think I need it," I said. I held it in front of me and read the label, "Strong enough to handle any problem." Hmm, I thought maybe the truth in advertising bureau, if there was one, should cite this company for making promises they probably can't keep. Or maybe the UN should get a hold of this stuff and eradicate world hunger.

I unbuttoned my suit coat and removed it. Then I reached inside my blouse and swiped some deodorant under each arm. I placed the deodorant back in my purse and checked my cell phone. It was turned on and Fred's and Hasin's speed dial numbers were set. I placed my phone back in my purse and folded my arms on my lap. I think my leg was shaking. Or the car had bad shocks, I couldn't tell which.

As we pulled up to the front of the building Hasin turned around in his seat and said, "This is it, Baby Girl." I just stared at him. I wanted to respond with a clever wisecrack but my mouth was a bag of cotton balls. Hasin and I opened our doors and stepped to the curb. We didn't look at each other. Fred pulled into traffic and drove around the corner. Hasin and I made our way to the front door. He held the door for me and followed me inside.

The lobby was small with two elevators on the left wall. It was just after five o'clock on a Friday and most of the employees were gone. I headed for the second elevator and pushed the up button. Hasin headed for the first elevator and pushed the down button. The elevator cars arrived at the same time. I entered my elevator and pushed the button for the thirteenth floor. As I turned and faced the elevator doors I was staring at a mirrored wall across the lobby. I could see Hasin enter his elevator and press the button. He turned and faced the doors. He was looking straight ahead. As the doors of my elevator closed I saw him draw in a breath and release it. I don't think I was breathing at all.

Chapter 49

The elevator passed the twelfth floor without stopping, as expected. According to the information we received, no one would be going up from twelve at this time of day. The doors opened on thirteen. For a millisecond I thought about the stigma related to the number thirteen and I felt my palms get sweaty. Then I remembered that I had invented a ritual a few years ago to proclaim the number thirteen lucky. I entered the hall and made my way to the stairwell. The sooner I got to twelve the better, as long as I could stay out of sight once I got there.

The four-inch stilettos were beginning to rub the skin off my heels and my toes were crammed at the tips. Is it masochism, vanity or stupidity that inspires women to wear these pillars of pain? These were definitely chosen for effect, not comfort. I had chosen them so that Chloe would look sexy. It would take more than a pair of shoes to accomplish that for me.

I had placed bandaids on my heels but they weren't helping at all. I carefully walked down the stairs. One misstep in these towers of torture would ruin the plan. When I got to the metal door with twelve written on it I carefully opened it and looked down the hallway. It was empty. I marched in the direction of the mark's office, which was up ahead on my right, across from the elevators. Just before getting to his office doors I ducked into an alcove.

I took my place behind the large, plastic, potted plant which our company had placed in the alcove a few days earlier. My fingers tingled with anticipation as I pulled out my cell phone and held it to my ear. With the phone to my ear a passerby might think I was merely trying to have a private conversation.

Where was the man? I checked my watch. OK, it had only been three minutes. But standing for three minutes in those heels must have been as agonizing as having my feet buried in the hot coals of Hell. I was perfectly still and my feet were throbbing like there were tiny motors down there grinding away. I'd take my Nikes over these devil shoes any day.

216

The plan was that the mark would come out of the door on the right and walk across the hall to the elevator. At least that's what his friend had told us. His friend had made sure the mark would be leaving the office after five o'clock. If he decided to take the stairwell, which I was told he never did, I was screwed. I had formulated a flimsy Plan B but I prayed that I wouldn't need it.

I checked my watch again. Five minutes had passed. Where was he? My mouth felt like I had just eaten a dirt burger. I poked around in my purse and was reaching for my mouthwash spray when an office door opened and a man and a woman walked into the hall and stood directly in front of the elevator. The man pressed the button and they waited. Their backs were to me but as the man turned to say something to the woman I could see that his profile was not that of the man I'd seen in the photos. The elevator arrived and they got in.

My tongue was still as dry as a rice cake and just as thick. I was reaching for my lip gloss when the office door opened again and a man walked to the elevator. He pressed the down button and waited with his back to me. I could tell from the back of his head that he was the one. He turned slightly, revealing his profile…mmm…nice, better than the photos. I held my breath. He wasn't supposed to turn all the way around. He probably wondered where the loud rumble was coming from. It was my heart playing *Wipeout* in my chest.

Could a healthy twenty-five-year-old have a heart attack? If so I hoped it would kill me because I wouldn't survive telling Chloe that I had just bungled the assignment. She should have been the one standing there behind the stupid plant, wearing Satan's stilts. But sometimes you do things for family that you wouldn't do for someone else. I made a mental note to remind her of that later.

My finger was poised over the send button. I couldn't move too soon. I couldn't let him see me emerge from behind this ridiculous plant. He had to think I had come from the stairwell so I couldn't make my move until he was in the elevator.

As he stood there looking at the numbers flashing above the doors, I felt something wet under my blouse. I dabbed my armpit with my hand. Perspiration. I hoped it wouldn't drip down my face or show through my blouse. I mean, the whole idea was that this guy was supposed to find me attractive. He wouldn't be attracted to a sweat ball. I began to reach for my antiperspirant even though

217

I was sure I'd already used enough.

Too late. I jumped at the ding of the elevator doors opening. I pressed send on my phone, waited for him to step one foot inside the door and lunged from behind the plant. I turned off the phone, shoved it into my purse and shouted, "Wait, hold the door." I hobbled toward the doors as they slid toward the middle and threw my arm forward to block them from touching. My arm fell short by one inch. Then I saw an arm extend from the inside the elevator and flatten the bumpers on the doors. The doors moved apart. I exhaled and ran inside.

As the doors closed behind me I turned around, faced the doors and stared. We were alone.

Step one, complete. Who knows how many to go?

Chapter 50

I was panting, as femininely as possible of course. He had to think my shortness of breath was caused by running from the stairwell, but it was really because of nervousness which adequately substituted for physical exertion. "Whew, could you press lobby? Oh you already…thanks."

He stood beside me near the button panel and watched the floor numbers change. I stood at the back wall and held my purse at my side. He was wearing a suit and tie, his hair was dark and short. Little waves at the nape of his neck told me that he hadn't had a haircut recently and his face had that unshaven look. I liked that look. He turned his head slightly and I could see he was more attractive than I had expected. The photos hadn't done him justice.

I took a breath. I had to engage him in conversation, accomplishing some kind of connection quickly because Hasin's next move would come soon. Here, in society's cone of silence, what could I say that wouldn't make me sound like a freak? Most strangers who find themselves next to each other in elevators deliberately avoid contact. I could start by talking to myself. That would hopefully open us up to conversation without seeming too obvious. I lifted my purse and started rifling through my things. "Now where is my…" I chuckled. "This purse is like a black hole." I glanced in his direction and smiled. "Things go in but they never…."

The red glow of the floor numbers blinked, 7, 6, 5. With a jolt the elevator stopped, a little sooner than I'd expected. I felt relief that Hasin had gotten my page but I had to act surprised so I said, "Oh my God. Why have we stopped?" I prayed that I hadn't over-acted.

"Happens occasionally," he said. "I think it has to do with the renovation a couple floors down. We should be going soon." His voice was smooth and pleasant.

"I hope so. I've got to get off my feet. These heels are killing me," I said.

"Yeah, I know what you mean," he said.

"You know what I mean? You don't look like the kind of guy who wears heels," I said. I didn't know where that came from but I knew I had to make some kind of connection with this man in the next five minutes. I was pleased to see that my comment got a playful expression from him.

He chuckled. "I mean this suit and tie," he said. "I can't wait to get into something more comfortable."

"Thank God it's Friday, right?" I said. That was a lame comment. I was sure my deodorant wasn't providing the confidence it promised. I think my body was vibrating but I wasn't sure. I had to shake it off, get into the zone, whatever that was.

"I haven't seen you before. Do you work in this building?" he asked.

I was thrilled that he initiated conversation but I couldn't let on. "Sort of," I said. "I'm a consultant for a company on the fortieth floor so I've been here occasionally." *Wait...what floor had I said? Had I blown this already*

"But this building only has twenty floors," he said

I laughed a nervous fake laugh that I hoped would work but not make me seem like an idiot. "What did I say, fortieth? I meant fourteenth."

"So why did you get in on the twelfth floor?" he asked.

What was with the interrogation? At least he was talking to me. Anyway, I already had an answer to his question. "Oh, it's a fitness thing. I take the stairs as often as possible but my feet just couldn't take another step in these shoes, so I got off the stairs and here I am."

He leaned against the wall and looked at me like Daniel Day Lewis looked at Madeline Stowe in that scene in "The Last of the Mohicans", the one where he turns to leave and then turns back and stares at her. She says, "What are you looking at, sir?" and he says, "I'm looking at you, Miss." I couldn't believe any man would be bold enough to say that to a woman, especially in those days. He had looked at her like he was stripping her clothes off. Between sips of wine I had rewound that scene repeatedly. Now I felt like this man in the elevator was stripping me with his eyes. He was peeling my clothes off a layer at a time and dropping them to the floor. This box we shared seemed to get smaller and darker and I wanted to cover myself.

"You seem too young to be a consultant," he said.

I had to go with it. Anything for the cause. "How old do you think I am?" I asked as my eyes met his.

"Maybe a couple years younger than I am," he said.

"Oh… and how old is that?" I asked. I think I bat my eyes.

"Twenty-nine, tomorrow," he said.

"Happy birthday," I said.

"Anyway, what I meant to say was that you seem too *attractive* to be a consultant," he said with a smile. I felt the heat of a blush rise in my face. He wouldn't stop staring at me. Normally I would have thought that a stranger staring at me was creepy. But he was relaxed, natural, not creepy at all.

"And you sir are *too* flirty to be alone with me in an elevator," I said as I winked.

I winked? I winked! I wasn't a winker. Chloe was the winker. Had I picked up a flirtatious tick from her? I snapped myself into reality and checked my watch. I didn't have much time. I had to get out the next bit of information before the elevator started moving. "How long do you think it will take them to get this thing going, because I have an appointment downtown?"

"Soon, I hope. I'm supposed to meet my buddy downtown for a birthday drink."

"Do you have a cell phone I can borrow? I must have left mine in my other purse. I need to call my appointment and tell them I'll be late."

"I don't know if cell phones work in here but wait a minute, I think I have it here," he said as he reached into his suit pocket. "Nope, I forgot. I loaned my coworker my phone this afternoon and he didn't return it."

"Thanks anyway," I said.

"This is taking longer than usual," he said. "I wonder if…oh, here we go. Maybe you'll be on time for your appointment after all."

With a clunk the elevator started moving. I looked at my watch. That had been the longest five minutes of my life. As the doors opened on the lobby he pressed his arm against the bumpers and waited for me to exit, then he and I walked side by side to the front door. He said, "Good luck with your appointment."

"Thanks. Have a wonderful birthday drink."

As we approached the doors I knew I couldn't let him get

away. By now the rain was coming down in torrents. The weather report had said chance of rain, but this was a downpour. Summer was just around the corner. One would think the rain would have subsided by this time of year, or was I thinking of California weather? However, the rain would make the possibility of staying with him easier than I had anticipated. He stopped beside me at the door and we both stared through the glass.

"Oh no, it's pouring," I said. "And I didn't bring my umbrella. My hair will be a frizz mop."

"Yeah, and it'll be hard to get a cab," he said, "but I have to get downtown."

"Hey, we're both going downtown. How about sharing a cab?" I said. I hoped I wasn't being too forward but what the hell. It wasn't me talking. It was Ms. Four-Inch-Heel-Wearing Consultant talking.

"Sure. Good idea," he said. "Wait here." He pushed the door open and walked to the curb while I stayed inside. His bio hadn't revealed that he was such a gentleman. I could see him raise his arm at taxis as one after another passed by. It took a few minutes for a cab to finally stop. He waved for me to come out and opened the back door of the cab. I hobbled as fast as I could and got into the back seat. I slid over and he sat beside me. Step two complete.

Chapter 51

Now that I was in the cab I could relax, at least for the time being.

"Two-fifty-seven East Twenty-Third," he said to the driver.

"Oh my God," I said, "my hair is drenched. And I'm sitting in a puddle." Then I looked at him and laughed. He was soaked. For a moment I forgot I was working. I knew I had to stick to the plan so I said, "I can't go to my appointment like this."

"You do look pathetic. Beautiful but pathetic, Miss..." he said as he moved a wet strand of hair from my face. The touch of his hand felt like electricity pulsing through my body. I wanted to melt. But the plan! I had to stick to the plan!

"Sarah Hannigan," I blurted. Where did that come from? "You look a little soggy yourself, Mr...."

"Reynolds...John Reynolds," he said as he extended his hand to shake mine.

"Well, Mr. Reynolds, it's a pleasure to officially shake the hand of the birthday boy." We held onto each other's hands a little longer than a normal handshake. Then I went on, "Why is this traffic stopped when I'm supposed to be....These city drivers don't know how to drive in the rain. I'm definitely going to miss my appointment."

"Hey, I'm stopping at my apartment to change before meeting my friend. Why don't you come up and use my phone and dry off? I have a blow dryer you can use too."

I was glad he suggested it before I did. I guess my whining had done the trick.

"Your hair is short, I'm surprised you have a blow dryer," I said. Of course I was going to take him up on his offer. I was just making conversation.

"I've never used it," he said. "It's a remnant of a recent break up. This is the first birthday in two years I'm spending with a guy instead of a girlfriend."

I believe he was hinting that he was single. I wanted to wrap my arms around him and say, "It's alright. I'll be your girlfriend," but instead I said, "Well, I'd love to dry off and call my client from your place if it's OK."

The taxi came to a stop and the driver said, "That'll be seven-fifty."

"Here you go," John said. "Keep the change."

John got out and extended his hand to help me. The rain had subsided to a drizzle. We entered the apartment building and took the elevator to the eighth floor. He unlocked his apartment door and we entered. It looked like a bachelor pad. The living room was fairly neat with some mismatched furniture that was clean. A bicycle was propped against the wall next to a small dining table. The kitchen counter was strewn with papers but other than that, the kitchen was surprisingly tidy with just a couple unwashed dishes in the sink. A flat screen television was mounted on the wall above a cabinet in the living room and CD's and DVD's were stacked on a shelf.

"Nice place," I said. "May I use your bathroom?"

"Sure, it's over there. And there's the phone," he said pointing to the end of the kitchen counter. He took a step into the bedroom, removed his jacket and draped it neatly on a chair.

"Thanks," I said as I made my way to the bathroom. I locked the door behind me and pulled the phone from my purse. I flipped the switch on and positioned it in my bra. I checked myself in the mirror to make sure the phone didn't show. By now I couldn't have peed if you paid me so I flushed the toilet, exited the bathroom, walked to the kitchen counter and picked up the phone. I called Hasin and waited. He picked up on the second ring.

"Hi, Sophie," he said.

"Hi, Manny. I guess you've already left," I said.

"So my name's Manny now?" Hasin said. "Blah, blah blah. Did you get any yet?" He was trying to make me laugh. I'd chastise him later.

I went on. "Sorry I missed the meeting. I was stuck in an elevator without a phone and then stuck in traffic. I'll call you to reschedule. Oh, I just want you to know I'm at two fifty-seven East Twenty-Third, Apartment..." I shot an inquisitive look at John. I didn't want to give him the impression that I had memorized his entire address.

"Apartment eight-ten," he said.

"Apartment eight-ten," I repeated. "The guy who lives here is
224

John Reynolds. He was kind enough to let me use his phone. Talk to you tomorrow."

Hasin said, "Talk to you in a few minutes, baby," and hung up.

"What was that about?" John asked.

"Just making sure that if I go missing they'll know where to start looking," I said with a smile.

"You think I lured you up here to do you bodily harm?" he said.

"No...not really," I said as I walked in his direction. "But I think you may have lured me here to do bodily something," I said. My heart began to flutter just saying the words but I think I managed to keep a flirtations expression on my face.

He walked closer to me and said, "So...would that be so bad?"

My mouth dropped. I cleared my throat and said, "No, it might be nice." I couldn't tell where my script left off and my feelings took over. My instinct told me to step away from him but I had to go with it. I had to stick to the plan. "You have beautiful green eyes. I hadn't noticed until now," I said.

I had noticed, damn it.

He said, "And I could swim in your azure blues. Maybe I'll have to miss my appointment too." He gently rested his hand on my waist. His touch was too much. I wanted to melt in his arms but I couldn't give in. I had to turn it around.

"Um, before we go swimming let me ask you this. If I stay here awhile, let's say one hour or so, I may need cab fare to get home. Could you give me cab fare?" I asked. I drew closer to him. Our faces were almost touching. I could feel his sweet breath on my skin. I wanted to kiss him but it wasn't in the plan. Not yet. I had to remind myself that whether I meant what I was saying to him or not, I was working.

"Ah...sure...if you need it, I guess," he said hesitantly. He wrinkled his brow as if he knew something else was coming. So here it came.

"I mean if cab fare was, let's say...two hundred dollars. Would you be willing to give it to me to swim in my azure blue eyes or to have me do bodily something to you?" I was starting to sweat again. This was painfully awkward. Where was my deodorant when I needed it?

"Two hundred dollars for cab fare," he raised his voice and

pulled away. "Where do you live, Connecticut?"

"No, I live here in Manhattan," I said, slowly drawing my palm up his arm.

"Wait a minute, what are you saying?"

"I'm saying I like you a lot." The next words that came from my lips disgusted me. "What would it be worth to you for me to stay awhile?" I said.

"Are you joking?" he asked.

"No, no joke," I said. I hated this. I wanted to shout that I was just kidding, about the money that is. I wanted to scream out for him to just take me. No charge. But I forced a seductive look on my face and hoped he wouldn't throw me out the door.

"Oh, I see," he said, "two hundred dollars? How about three hundred? Oh, what the hell, how about five hundred?" He was agitated now. I began to shake so I pulled away from him. I couldn't tell how long I'd be able to keep him talking. Where were Hasin and Fred? They should have already arrived.

The look on his face was that of disgust. He said in a sarcastic tone, "How about a thousand or maybe two…"

He was interrupted by a knock at the door that made me jump. He rolled his eyes, walked to the door and opened it. Fred and Hasin were standing in the hallway.

Chapter 52

"May I help you?" John asked.

Hasin and Fred flashed their badges. Then Hasin in his best Brooklyn accent said, "Officers Minelli and Mercer, NYPD. May we come in?"

"Sure. What's this about?" he asked.

As they entered the apartment Hasin said, "You are under arrest for soliciting prostitution."

"What?" John blurted.

"We have it on tape, sir," Hasin said.

John turned to me and said, "Are you kidding? I was joking. Who would pay a stranger a thousand dollars to…"

Fred reached out and spun John around. "Hands behind your back. You are under arrest," he said as he pulled John's arms behind him and grabbed a set of hand cuffs from his pocket.

Now John was staring at me. "This is bullshit. And you're a cop too? Miss Sarah Hannigan is a cop?" he said.

I could hardly breathe. I wanted to run to him and tear the cuffs away from his hands and kiss him all over, but instead I pulled myself together and said, "It's Officer Bradley and you are under arrest, Mr. Reynolds." The names just kept coming. Hannigan, Bradley - I don't know where they came from. I suppose I could have used my real name but for some reason I kept changing it, editing the original plan I had so meticulously prepared. Maybe it was because I couldn't bring Sophie Hopper to say the words Sarah Hannigan had said to him. Maybe it was because Sophie Hopper truly liked this man.

"This is entrapment to say the least," John said as he squirmed. "This is crazy. I need to make a phone call."

"You can make a call from the station. For now it would serve you better to cooperate," Fred said sternly.

We silently exited the apartment and got into the elevator. We were lined up along the back wall, four across, Fred, John, Hasin and me. Just as John opened his mouth to say something the elevator stopped and the doors opened. A gray-haired woman hunched over to a height of about four foot ten shuffled into the elevator with the help of a cane. When she saw John she smiled.

In a strong Irish brogue she said, "Hello, John. Lovely night don't you think?"

"Yes, Mrs. McCaffrey," he said as he twisted his body and lifted his hands from behind him. "It's a very lovely night, except for these."

"Oooh...seems you've gotten yourself into a predicament," she said. "Would you like me to give these two gentlemen a whack with my cane so you can give them the slip?"

"Thank you, Mrs. McCaffrey," he said with a chuckle, "but this will all be straightened out in a while and I'll drop by and tell you about it tomorrow."

"Oh good. Tomorrow is good. I've made a new batch of cookies and they should still be fresh tomorrow."

"And how is Patrick? Does he need a walk?" he asked.

"Oh yes, always. But I need a walk myself, so I'll be taking him. You're welcome to join us. Oh, I do need a light bulb in the ceiling changed, if you don't mind," she said.

"Sure, I'll see you tomorrow," he said.

Hasin and Fred looked at each other. I think they felt as guilty as I did about arresting this delightful man. The doors opened to the lobby and Mrs. McCaffrey shuffled out the door. As the three men passed her, John swiveled around and began to walk backwards. "You take care of yourself, Mrs. McCaffrey."

"See you tomorrow John," she said with a bob of her cane.

He had a genuine affinity for this little wisp of a woman. I pictured the two of us at eighty, shuffling down the street holding hands. Sophie Reynolds sounded good. Mr. and Mrs. John Reynolds. What was I thinking?

The car was parked in front of the building. A red blinking light sat on the dash. Hasin and Fred must have placed it there, probably to get a temporary parking spot, probably also a felony. I would have to talk to them about it later. Hasin got in the driver's seat while Fred got in the back seat with John. I took the passenger seat. I removed the light from the dash and turned it off. With the light in hand, I gave Hasin a sideways look. He knew what I meant.

Step three, complete.

We drove in silence for a couple blocks. I wished I could have taken John's face in my hands and kissed away all his doubt. Then he began talking directly to me - to the back of my head, that is.

"You think you got me on soliciting prostitution, Sarah or Bradley or whatever the hell your name is. You could tell I liked you. I wasn't looking for a prostitute and you know it. This is nuts. I haven't done anything." Then he turned to Fred and said, "And you haven't even Mirandized me."

"Being Mirandized the moment you are arrested is what they do on TV because they have to cram every bit of info into a one hour show. We can Mirandize you anytime. But before you're Mirandized you can say anything you want and it can't be used in court. Do you really want the things you're saying right now to be admissible in court?" Fred asked.

"Hell yes," he said. "I don't care what I've said because I'm innocent."

Hasin pulled the car into an alley, turned off the ignition and he and I got out. Fred opened his door and got out. As he stood on the sidewalk with his hand extended he said to John, "Come on, get out."

As John exited the car he said, "Where are we? What is this?"

"An unscheduled stop. The commander is inside," Fred said as he took John's arm.

As we entered the building adjacent to the alley John said, "What is this place? This isn't the..."

Just inside the door a chorus of SURPRISE hit us like a hurricane.

"What?" John said. His puzzled look turned to a smile. Fred removed the handcuffs and John's hands moved freely. The crowd of people started cheering and moving toward John. A young man ran up to him and said, "Hey, bud. Happy birthday."

"Kyle, did you do this?" John asked.

"Yeah, well, the whole office pitched in. Cool, huh?" he said.

"You mean the girl, the cops..." John asked.

"Yeah, did you know? I mean, were you really surprised?" he asked.

"Well, I thought something was weird but...yeah. I thought the next time I'd be talking to you was on the phone asking you to bail me out of jail," he said as his eyes scanned the room. "Hey, you got Ted to come. I talked to him on the phone a couple of days ago. He didn't say a word."

"He wouldn't have missed it. And look over there," Kyle said pointing toward the back of the room. "Almost everyone from the softball team. Wait here. I'll get you a brew."

In a few minutes the people crowded around John disbursed into small groups. I walked up behind him and said, "Mr. Reynolds, I'd like to introduce myself." My heart was pounding.

He turned around. With a disappointed look on his face he said, "Who are you now, Sarah what-ever-your-name-is or Officer whoever?"

"Neither. Here," I said, handing him my business card.

He read it out loud, "Sophie Hopper, PJ Enterprises-When a card or present won't do." He shook his head and smiled, "Yeah, you got me."

This was my one chance to turn things around. I had to make it count. As I felt my eyes moisten I quietly said with a smile, "Since I got you can I keep you?"

He was taken aback. His facial expression softened and he said, "Well...I...don't...know."

"John, this is the most difficult thing I've ever done. I usually plan these things and my sister is the one who does them, but she got sick today and I had to take her place. I was terrified." I took a breath. "But I meant it when I said I liked you. Unfortunately I was in the middle of a work assignment."

He looked down at the card and then at me. "Yeah, I meant what I said to you, too. So why don't you stay for the party?" he said. I could see it in his eyes, that same look he gave me in the elevator.

"I can't. I'm still working," I lied. I wanted to stay. There was nothing to do for the rest of the evening besides talking to Hasin and Fred, debriefing of a sort, but I felt uncomfortable and unprofessional taking him up on his offer.

"Oh, I get it. You're going to lure some other unsuspecting guy tonight?" he said.

"No, just business stuff that has to be taken care of," I said.

"Well, maybe I'll see you around."

"Turn over the card," I said. He flipped the card and looked at the number written on the back. "It's my personal phone number."

I started to turn and then I stopped and turned back to him. "I'm so embarrassed about the things I said to you. You know, the money, pretending to be a…well…um…I'm not really like that. It's not me, I mean I…" I took a deep breath and said, "I hope you call me." I reached my hand out to him. He hesitated and then took my hand. It wasn't exactly a handshake. The feel of his hand in mine brought a smile to my face. He smiled too.

"Happy birthday, John," I said as I turned to leave.

"Thank you, Sophie."

Mrs. Franklin 2

Mrs. Franklin sat in her armchair, her legs resting on the ottoman, a blanket draped over her feet. An assemblage of devices intended to cement her position for an extended period of time sat on the end table within arm's reach: a phone, a remote, her reading glasses, her latest book and a steaming cup of tea.

After kneading Mrs. Franklin's lap Nibbles settled into a tight ball and a faint purr rumbled in his throat. Mrs. Franklin had gotten her relaxation ritual down perfectly, and so had Nibbles. No need to move for at least an hour, allowing Nibbles to be motionless through his twelfth nap of the day.

Had she succumbed to middle age? Or was it middle age that naturally changed her desires? After commuting and a full day of work she deserved to sit and breathe and close her eyes. This was a luxury she had postponed for years. Now that she was no longer doting on a husband, she was the one glued to the chair.

After her son and daughter were grown she and her husband kept working at their full-time jobs, saving for their retirement. But her husband didn't make it to retirement. Now here she was, sitting in her comfortable chair with her cat on her lap and her television tuned to the most tolerable show of the hour. Retirement had become a dream that seemed farther away every day.

She tended to go for the documentary channels like *National Geographic, The History Channel, The Biography Channel*. These programs were stimulating to her. But most of the shows, no matter how interesting or informative, went unwatched as her body surrendered to exhaustion.

Her eyelids sagged and the television voices began to scramble in her dream. She pressed the off button and resumed her nap, trying to pick up the dream where she had left off. Nibbles' purr revved with anticipation. No television meant it might be time for lap movement to launch him to the floor. After a couple minutes the purr subsided. Maybe it's our old age, she thought, that teaches us it's alright to do nothing, like practicing for what's ahead in the afterlife. She had never understood senior citizens who just go, go, go.

It was already ten-thirty and she had to be up at five. She lifted her knees and flung Nibbles to the floor. She picked up the phone and the cup of tea and carried them to the kitchen. She poured the tea in the sink and set the cup on the counter. As she placed the phone on its cradle she noticed the copy of the contract next to the notepad. She picked up the contract and returned to the living room, sat back in her chair and put on her glasses. When she came to the words, "anytime, anywhere, and for an undetermined period of time" her body shuddered. What had she agreed to?

Why had she allowed herself to pick up the contract right before going to bed? Now she would be awake all night thinking about it. She reassured herself that when the time came she would be able to handle it. After all, someone believed she could handle it.

Chapter 53

I was attempting to block out the mindless chatter bouncing across the front seat of the car. Hasin and Fred knew to let me alone for a few minutes. I rolled down the back window, leaned my head against the seat and let the breeze wash over my face. The rain had stopped and the air passing over my skin was cool and clean. I leaned my head on the window frame and closed my eyes. My eyes fluttered as droplets flew from the windshield and landed lightly on my eyelids. I couldn't recall the last time I felt this content. I opened my eyes and saw that the clouds were gone and the sky was blacker than usual. I turned my face toward the heavenly void and thought I saw a star twinkle between two skyscrapers. I sat up straight and rested my forearms on the front seat.

"Is this what being in the zone feels like?" I asked. "Because it feels wonderful."

Hasin turned slightly and said, "No, you're too mellow to be in the zone right now. You were in the zone when you were talking to Mr. Reynolds in his apartment. I could sense it when I was listening in."

Fred interrupted, "Yes, my dear. What you're doing right now is like having a cigarette after sex and basking in the glow."

"Thanks, Fred. I can count on you to put a sexual spin on any subject," I said as I swiped the back of his head with my palm.

"Hey, watch the do," Fred said, "or I may have to take you down to the station for assaulting an officer."

Hasin lifted his hand from the steering wheel making circular motions in the air saying, "Your ability to say the right thing to him came from being in the zone. It was beyond planning, beyond rehearsing. It was as if Sophie was gone and your character took over. I mean, didn't you feel it when you were talking to him?"

I thought for a moment and said, "Yes, I did. It was electrifying." I felt a pang of guilt. I hadn't been acting when I told John I liked him. What I said to him was meaningful to me. Maybe

234

I hadn't been in a zone, maybe the power I felt came from being able to say exactly what I thought. Then again, maybe being able to say exactly what I thought came from being in the zone. I wasn't sure what it was. I was exhausted thinking about it.

"I have to confess something," I said. "I meant it when I told him I liked him. So maybe I wasn't in a zone. I told him how I really felt."

"So you like the man. So what," Hasin said. "Think about everything you said and did up until that point. Could you have said those words to him as Sophie? I don't think so. Because the Sophie I know gets tongue-tied at the thought of flirting."

"You've noticed, huh?" I said.

He went on. "Telling him you liked him was one tiny smidge of the evening. You pulled off everything perfectly. You were so convincing that I would have paid you two hundred dollars, and I prefer men."

Fred added, "Well, I thought you were good but I wouldn't have paid you because I don't need to pay women. Sometimes they want to pay me though."

"Fred, get over yourself," Hasin said. "Sophie, tonight you rocked."

"I did rock, didn't I?"

Chapter 54

The guys dropped me off at the apartment before taking the car back to the office. I hobbled barefoot up the stairs, holding the devil shoes in my hand. I unlocked the apartment door and dropped the shoes and the purse on the floor. I hung my coat on the rack and poked my head around the corner into the bedroom. The bed was unmade and a new pile of tissues was on the floor. Chloe wasn't there.

I walked to the living room and found her sitting on the couch wrapped in a blanket with her legs tucked under her. She was holding a cup in both hands and blowing on what seemed to be hot liquid. The hair on the top of her head looked like a twisted pile of spaghetti and she had no make-up on her face. Her eyes were focused on the television, which was muted.

"How are you feeling?" I asked.

She stared straight ahead. In a gravelly voice she said, "Oh, I'm a little better. How did tonight go?"

I sat in the armchair, propped my feet on the coffee table and crossed my ankles. I thought for a moment about how I wanted to present the night's events to her. There was a distinct possibility that I was about to swallow my pride for the first time in years and tell her she was right.

She stopped blowing into the cup and looked up at me.

"Well," I said, "I may have been wrong about fearing the squeeze. Everything went well tonight, very well. And I've discovered in the process that...I liked it."

Her eyes widened and she set the cup on the coffee table. "Tell me more," she said with a childlike excitement.

I leaned forward and said, "I was really nervous at first but after a while it got easier. As the evening went on I felt like I could manipulate the situation any way I wanted to, maybe too much. I felt a power I had never felt before. And it was fun. In fact it was the most fun I've had in years."

She straightened her back and cleared her throat. In a powerful voice she said, "You did it. You experienced what I've been talking about." Excitement bubbled inside her. She unwrapped the blanket and leaned toward me. "Sophie, you were in the zone."

I felt a smile spread across my face, "I think I was," I said. For a moment we were smiling at each other. Then I had to ruin the moment by saying, "And I met a guy."

"You met a guy?" she said with a puzzled look on her face. "What do you mean you met a guy? How did you have time to meet a guy when you were…wait…who is he?"

"John Reynolds," I said.

By the look on her face I knew I would either have to crawl under the seat cushion or steady myself for a sobering reprimand. The prelude to the dreaded reprimand was her leaping from the couch and pacing across the room. Her strides were long and her arms were flailing over her head.

"The mark? I give you one assignment and you fall in love with the mark. You can't do anything right," she shouted.

"I didn't say I was in love with him. And, wait a minute. You met Chris during Shannon's project."

"That's different. He wasn't the mark," she shouted.

"OK, what about Karen Klein? Look how attached you got to her. Remember, you said something like…um…she wasn't the mark anymore…she was Karen and you were you…ah…the best you you've ever been."

She stomped into the kitchen, opened a cabinet and removed a wine glass. She picked up an opened wine bottle, popped the cork and filled the glass.

"What are you doing?" I asked as I twisted in my chair and watched her take a sip. "Aren't you sick?"

"Oh, who cares?" she said.

"What's with this new energy, the pacing, the flailing?" I said.

She stared at me. I paused and thought for a moment. Then I stood and said, "Were you even sick today? Please tell me you were actually sick and that your hours of convalescence are what cured you."

She took another swig, set the glass on the counter, leaned on both palms and said, "No, I'm not sick."

"What?" I shouted. "You mean you were never sick?"

She began walking, the wine glass in one hand, her free hand waving in the air. "I just thought if I could get you to experience one squeeze you would love it and you would stay here and be a part of this business. But how can you do it when you like every guy who comes along?"

"I don't know. What business is it of yours anyway?" I said. "So, you're not sick?"

She set down the glass and walked to the living room. Her tone softened. "Yes. I'm not sick. I'm sorry I lied to you. I had to do something. I couldn't let you leave without letting you experience this. I had to get you to know how fun it is to do this job and now you know. But you just can't fall for every guy who comes along. You'll get hurt."

Now it was my turn to reprimand her. "First of all, it's none of your business if I get hurt. I'm a grown woman and you're not my mother, or even my big sister for that matter. You lied to me. You knew I was terrified and you pretended to be sick to force me into it? What if I had failed? Were you going to blame me for ruining the business?"

I closed my eyes and gave my head a quick shake. I didn't know if I was trying to shake out my disapproval of her or the reality of what she had just told me.

She rested her hand on my arm and said, "That's how you and I think differently. I knew you could do it all along. I knew you wouldn't fail."

I clenched my jaw, pulled my arm from her grasp and continued to shake my head. "Of course you knew I wouldn't fail because you planned this all along. You allowed me to spend all those hours meticulously designing the project that was intended to squeeze me, no, not squeeze me because that term is too nice, but dupe me and humiliate me. Were you all in on it? Were Hasin's compliments to me even real or were they bullshit like everything else tonight?"

Before she could get out any words I ran to the bedroom, slipped my feet into my flats and headed for the door.

Chloe shouted, "Wait!"

"I have to process this," I shouted as I took my coat from the rack and grabbed my wallet. Without looking back I slammed the door behind me.

Chapter 55

The lights glistened off the sidewalk, still wet after the rain. The neon signs adorning the businesses reflected off the cars like slick cellophane. It was a house of mirrors where every light from every building was multiplied down the street as far as the eye could see.

With my hands securely clenched at the bottom of my pockets, I began walking north. I willed a path to open in front of me as I bulldozed my way up the crowded sidewalk. The couples who passed me had been cooped up in their apartments waiting out the storm. Now they were clinging to each other for warmth and laughing at being able to finally go outside and move their legs. For me this was just another Friday night, alone.

I hadn't thought about David in days. What had happened to us? I wanted to call him and ask him what to do, but I knew that if he bothered to answer his phone he would say just the right words to get through the conversation without conflict. He had a knack for making me feel special even if it was only until I hung up the phone after which I would process his gibberish and realize that it meant nothing. Two months ago I had been content just to hear his voice on the answering machine. Tonight nothing short of him begging me to come back to Los Angeles would satisfy me, an absurdity which I knew would never be uttered from his lips. I was glad I left my phone in the apartment.

I wanted to go back to the party and have John look at me the way he had in the elevator and again when we said our goodbyes. But it had all been a lie. I'd get to the party and probably find him fondling some girl he had plied with alcohol. What made me think such a thing? How could I possibly judge this man I had just met? He had seemed like a gentleman, balking at the idea of spending time with a less than reputable woman. Even when he was ranting at the fake police officers he was articulate, reasonable and confident. He hadn't used profanity. He hadn't gotten violent.

I was a few hours away from flying back to Los Angeles and I

239

couldn't think of a reason to go. I had only a couple of friends there. No boyfriend. No job. All I could think of were the reasons why I shouldn't go. I had to find a reason to stay that had nothing to do with my irritating sister. There had to be something more.

I wanted someone to tell me what to do.

I wanted Mom to tell me what to do.

I stepped to the curb and held out my hand. When a taxi pulled to a stop I opened the back door, climbed in and gave the driver the address. I rode silently with my hands in my pockets. The driver didn't start up a conversation with me. Maybe my rigid body told him I was a New Yorker now. No need to talk up the local restaurants with this hardened individual.

The taxi pulled up to the apartment building. Once outside I noticed the doorman holding a leash and stooping to pet a Chihuahua wearing a diamond encrusted collar over its mohair sweater. A pink bow was taped to its head and its toenails were iridescent pink. I wasn't surprised that a penis could be seen dangling between its legs when its male owner came through the door wearing practically the same outfit. The dog's owner held out his hand as he sashayed to the doorman who let the leash drop effortlessly into the man's palm. "Thank you, Harold. Come, Thor," the man said to the dog as they wiggled their way down the sidewalk.

Harold, who had only met me once, made a beeline for the entrance. He leaped sideways and opened the door for me. He gave me a nod like he recognized me but he didn't use my name. The man at the desk asked me who I wanted to see. "Frank Hopper," I said.

"May I have your name?" the man politely asked.

"Sophie Hopper."

He picked up the phone and dialed a number. He said, "I have a Miss Sophie Hopper here to see you." He hung up the phone and motioned toward the elevator. "Have a nice evening, Miss Hopper."

I couldn't believe Dad was home at this hour on a Friday night.

I stood alone in the elevator imagining John Reynolds next to me. How was it that I managed to be alone on a Friday night in the most populated city in America?

I felt small standing in front of my father's double entry doors.

As I raised my fist to knock, the door opened and I saw my father standing dressed in sweats and a ragged t-shirt, his favorite since I was a child. The shirt had a few more holes than I remembered and I was amazed that it was still intact.

"Hi, honey. Are you OK?" he asked. "Why didn't you call?"

"I left my phone at Chloe's. If you're busy I can come another time," I said.

"Of course I'm not too busy for you. I was just concerned. Come in. Come in," he said.

"Is Jennifer here?" I asked.

"Yeah, she's in the kitchen. Let's go in here," he said as he motioned toward the living room. "We can have some privacy."

"Does she know I'm here?" I asked.

"Of course, she'll be in in a minute. She's in the middle of conjuring up some kind of facial mask thing with eggplant and barley or something," he said as he sunk into the couch and I took the armchair next to him. "So what brings you out on this rainy night at..." he glanced over his shoulder at the clock over the mantle, "Ten forty-five?" He paused and lowered his head as if he were looking over the rims of glasses. Then he very deliberately and slowly said, "Sophie."

"Dad, it's Chloe," I said.

"What happened?"

"Oh, she's just being Chloe and I'm being me, you know, like oil and water. We don't mix."

"Hmm, I think I may have to disagree with you." He paused. "I don't think you two are *that* different."

"Not that different?" I yelled. "She's a nut and I'm...I'm...boring. I'm serious and boring." I pressed my head against the back of the chair and groaned.

"You're not boring, you're just careful. You tend to think a lot about things, maybe over-think things."

"You think?" I said. "Sometimes I think so much I drive myself crazy."

"So tell me what happened," he said.

"I'd been thinking about staying here in New York, you know, being part of the business. Then a few days ago Chloe and I had a falling out over a guy. What's new? Anyway, tonight I had to do the squeeze because Chloe was supposedly sick and..."

Dad interrupted, "The squeeze?"

"Yeah. We didn't like the word prank so that's what we call the part of the project that's designed to actually get the mark to their surprise event."

"OK, go on," he said tentatively.

"Well, I was scared to death but I did it and it went great. In fact it was wonderful, that is until I found out she pretended to be sick. I think the entire project was bogus. She had me go to all the work of planning the project for nothing. How can I ever trust her?"

He thought for a moment and said, "You just said tonight was wonderful, didn't you?"

"Yeah, I thought she was right about the squeezes being fun until I found out I was the one being squeezed," I said. "I hate that word now. It's intended to be cute and nice and now it just reminds me of what a fool I am."

Dad looked at me with love in his eyes. I said softly, "I really liked that guy, the client we were getting to his party. And idiot that I am, I thought he liked me too, until I found out none of it was real. It was the first time in my life I could talk to a man without jabbering like an idiot. I feel humiliated."

Dad noticed tears welling in my eyes. He reached out and patted my hand, calmly saying, "So why don't you talk to her? Let her know what you will and won't do. Let her know what's acceptable to you," he said.

"Oh, so I can invest my money?" I blurt. "I don't know if she even cares if I stay as long as she gets my money. It's the first thing she talked about when I got here. Since then she's backed off, partly because you helped us with the fake office, but now the only reason why she wants me here is so I can hand over my money."

He let out a breath and said, "OK, I guess I have to come clean. You see, honey, Chloe doesn't really need your money."

"She told me she didn't have much of her inheritance left and she knew I had mine and that she needed an investor until the business started making more money."

"Well, that's not entirely true. She's a much better businesswoman than she lets on. And even though she seems hair-brained at times, she tends to recover quickly and move on." He paused. "Please don't tell Chloe I told you this but she came to me about two months ago with her new idea for the business and she wanted you to be a part of it. She'd been trying to think of reasons why a logical person like you would want to pick up everything and relocate three thousand miles away for a job that hadn't been tested yet. At that time I told her I would invest if she needed me to. Then when Shannon quit Chloe had the perfect opportunity to ask you to come here. Once you were here she thought you'd stay if she asked you to invest."

"But that doesn't make any sense," I said.

"Yeah, well, that's Chloe. She thought you'd feel compelled to stay if you thought the business would fail without your money. But she doesn't need your money, she just needs you. She loves you and misses you."

"She told you that?" I asked.

"Yes, she loves you. And she told me that she had no idea how complicated these projects would be until you got here. Your logical thinking and your ability to meticulously plan these scenarios is crucial to the success of the business now. But that's not why she wants you to stay. She wants you to stay because you are her sister and she loves you," he said.

"Really?" I asked, feeling new tears welling in my eyes.

"Yes, and I haven't told you this but I'm proud of you for having the courage to move away and graduate from college. And I'm proud of you for coming back to help your sister. Most of all I missed you and I want you to stay too."

"I missed you too, Dad," I said.

"One more thing," he said. "You said that because she fooled you into doing the…ah…squeeze, you can't trust her."

"Yes," I said.

"Isn't this business all about deceiving people into having unique experiences, about creating ways in which people might look at things differently, about surprising them?"

"I guess so," I said.

"You said you had a wonderful time tonight, right?"

"Yeah, until I found out…"

"She enabled you to do something you never would have done. I'd say your loving sister's squeeze on you was a success. Wouldn't you?"

I saw a tear in his eye and suddenly I couldn't stop my own tears. I jumped off the chair and flung my arms around him. Just then I heard footsteps coming down the hall. Jennifer shouted,

"Did I hear Sophie's voice?"

"Hi, Jennifer. We're in here!" I shouted.

She entered the living room wearing sweats and a t-shirt that rivaled Dad's. She said, "Hey, what's with the cry fest?"

"Dad's just lecturing me on family values," I said with a wink. "I can't believe I winked again. See how she's influenced me."

"Who? Me?" Jennifer asked.

"No…Chloe," I said.

"Is everything OK?" she asked.

I looked at Dad and in unison we declared, "Yes."

"OK. Well, come in the kitchen, young lady. I'm giving you a late night facial.

Chapter 56

By the time Dad dropped me off at Chloe's apartment it was almost one a.m. Chloe was asleep in her bed. I turned on the light and tapped her on the arm. She opened her eyes and said, "Sophie. Where were you?"

"Hi, sorry to wake you," I said.

"Hey, are you OK?" she asked as she sat up.

"Yeah. I just want to say I'm sorry. I was wrong. Your squeeze on me was phenomenal. Hasin and Fred and Jane were great. They didn't let on. And John Reynolds, or whatever his name is, was very convincing."

"What do you mean?" Chloe asked.

"Well, they were all in on it, right?"

She sighed and said, "When I told Hasin that you were leaving New York, he was the one who suggested that I get sick and have you take my place. And Fred knew. But Jane wasn't in on it. You know how she is about keeping secrets. And John Reynolds wasn't in on it. The real squeeze was on him. It's really his birthday."

"So all the planning I did really was for John Reynolds' project?" I asked.

"Yes,"

"And when he flirted with me and when he said he liked me he meant it?" I asked.

"Well, he meant it as much as any man means what he says when he's talking to a woman he's attracted to. I guess that's for you to find out," she said.

"Why didn't you tell me?" I shouted.

"Because you ran out of here so fast I didn't have a chance. I tried calling your cell phone and texting but there was no answer."

"I didn't take it with me. It's still in the setup purse, turned off."

"So what are you going to do?" she asked.

"You mean am I staying in New York City?"

"Yeah, will you stay?" she said, her voice slightly cracking.

245

"Well, I'd like to. But you and I have to get some things worked out, according to Dad. And I agree with him," I said.

"Is that where you were tonight, at Dad's?" she asked.

"Yeah, I think he's very insightful,"

"Me too. I know that you and I will work out everything. We're grown up now. I'm grown up now. So, will you give us a chance? Will you stay?"

For the first time in our relationship I felt that she was on the defensive. She sincerely wanted me to stay, not because of the business but because she loved me. "Yes, I'll stay," I said.

Chloe leaped from the bed and threw her arms around me.

With my arms wrapped around her tightly I said, "But under one condition."

"Anything," she said.

"You have to promise me something."

"Anything, just name it," she shouted.

"You have to promise me that you will never, and I mean never, pull another squeeze on me."

She pulled back. With a mischievous look and a wide grin on her face she said, "You know I can't promise that."

I sighed and said, "I know."

Mrs. Franklin 1

Mrs. Franklin stood against the back wall with her purse clutched at her side. She felt small, sandwiched between businessmen dressed in suits and women in their high heels and big hair. She was like poison oak in a forest of towering pines, the plant you avoid, the one you don't touch.

An attractive woman entered and two men stepped aside to make room for her. Mrs. Franklin noticed one man's eyes follow the curves of the woman's body while the woman's eyes focused intently on the floor numbers blinking above the door. The woman sensed the man's attention but she didn't let on - being ogled by men was an everyday occurrence for her. For Mrs. Franklin it was not even an annual occurrence.

The doors opened and people disbursed. Mrs. Franklin caught a glimpse of her reflection in the metallic elevator wall. She was certain that no one in their right mind would pay any attention to a woman of her age and girth. Since menopause the weight had been more difficult to keep down. When Charles was alive he hadn't minded. He had put on a few pounds himself.

She hoped the elevator wall was warped like a fun house mirror that distorts one's reflection because if this image was a true likeness of her, then she had to face the fact that she had become practically as wide as she was tall. Her gray hair didn't help. She used to dye her hair. But now why bother? She had earned every one of her gray hairs and she was going to wear them defiantly. These men didn't know a good woman when they saw one.

The certificate was wedged between her sweaty palm and her purse straps. She loosened her grip and wiped her hand on her dress. She hoped the appointment would be short since she had to be back from her lunch break in forty-five minutes. A few minutes here or there really didn't matter since she had been on time for years. One long lunch shouldn't make a difference.

This was probably a scam anyway. Some company swindling old women. But when she got the certificate in the mail she had checked the postage. First class, not that presorted standard stuff. That's why she decided to keep the appointment, because whoever sent the card paid for first class postage.

The elevator stopped. She stepped out and as the doors closed behind her she noticed the directory on the hallway wall. The building was well-kept with classic Art Deco embellishments and transoms above every door. Some were ajar and she could hear faint sounds of phones ringing and people talking inside as she passed. She got to room 1212 and double-checked the number on the certificate. PJ Enterprises was printed on the frosted glass door.

She took a breath and entered a small reception room which had one desk in the middle, a couch and an end table next to the entry door, two closed doors on the back wall, one on either side of the desk. The room smelled freshly painted. Original paintings were tastefully hung on the walls.

A young woman was sitting at the desk with a pen in one hand and a phone in the other. She motioned with the pen for Mrs. Franklin to have a seat, mouthing the words, "I'll be right with you." Mrs. Franklin eyed the name plate on the desk: Courtney Deeter.

She took a seat, put on her reading glasses, picked up a magazine and began flipping through the pages.

She overheard the woman say, "We do not offer a group plan at this time but the group concept may be just around the corner. I'll place your name on our list and we'll notify you if we develop a service that suits your needs." She jotted something on a pad of paper and said, "No…thank you. We here at P.J. Enterprises are always open to new ideas. Goodbye."

She hung up and said, "I can help you now."

Mrs. Franklin closed the magazine, slid the glasses to the top of her head and walked to the desk. "Ms. Deeter, I'm here to see about this gift card I received in the mail," she said, holding out the certificate.

"Please have a seat while I get this file," the woman said, motioning to the chair in front of the desk and taking the card from her. "And please call me Courtney." She exited and returned with a manila folder in her hand.

She said, "Mrs. Franklin, this is an anonymous gift, which means I am not allowed to reveal the name of the giver. And with this particular service we require the recipient to come to the office in person to get your permission to perform this service."

Mrs. Franklin let out a long breath and said, "It sounds so mysterious."

"Well, that's sort of the idea. You see, our company started as an event planning business. You know, parties, weddings, receptions, fund raisers. We recently added a service to secretly deliver people to their surprise events.

"But if this is supposed to be a surprise, why would I get this card?" Mrs. Franklin asked. "Now I know that someone is going to surprise me."

"This new service is different than our surprise event service." She removed a sheet from the folder and said, "In a nutshell our contract states that within the next two months your surprise may involve anything, anywhere, for an undetermined period of time. The nature of this gift is only limited by the price the giver paid. Even the person who gave you this gift does not and will not know the means by which we will accomplish the desired outcome."

"But I have a full-time job. How can I be interrupted without notice?" Mrs. Franklin asked, "And if I don't know who gave this to me how do I know it's something I want?"

"We have an extensive screening process. The person who purchased this gift cares about you and is doing it for what they think is your best interest. I assure you, when the time comes you will be available. There is no need to be concerned that this will impact your life negatively."

"I mean, if I knew who gave me this…"

"It could be anyone - a friend, co-workers, your husband," Courtney said.

"I'm a widow," Mrs. Franklin said.

"I'm sorry," Courtney said, shifting in her chair.

"That's alright. It's been awhile. My son lives in Connecticut with his wife and kids. I see them a few times a year, mostly holidays and birthdays." Mrs. Franklin paused and looked into Courtney's eyes for a hint as to whether her son was the culprit. Nothing. Mrs. Franklin went on. "They're so sweet. They're always trying to get me out of my routine. Maybe they bought this for me."

"Sounds like they care about you very much," Courtney said.

"My daughter and I talk on the phone every week, sometimes twice a week, but I haven't seen her in three years and I miss her terribly. She's a dancer at the Paris Hotel in Las Vegas. Her schedule is so full. She's always trying to get me to come visit but I'm afraid to fly and I can't get enough time off work to drive or take a train. And it's expensive, you know, I'm saving for my retirement." Mrs. Franklin slumped as if her own words had just sucked the energy from her body.

"Look, our mission is to surprise people with interesting experiences." Courtney opened a drawer and placed a stack of papers on the desk. "Here are testimonies from recipients who were delighted with their results. Believe me, we wouldn't be in business if we didn't know what we were doing."

Mrs. Franklin glanced at the stack of papers and back at Courtney. "You're not going to tell me who gave this to me, are you?"

"No." A warm smile filled Courtney's face.

"Well, someone believes I am up to this. That's encouraging," said Mrs. Franklin.

"I believe you're up to this and I just met you," said Courtney with a playful expression.

"I don't need to arrange time off from work?" Mrs. Franklin asked.

"You don't need to do anything. In fact we prefer that you do nothing. It's written in the confidentiality agreement you'll sign. And anyway, how could you ask for time off when you don't know exactly when this will happen?" Courtney pulled a business card from a drawer and said, "Here is my card. If you ever have questions or just need to talk, pick up the phone and call me. It doesn't matter what time of day or night. If I can't take the call, leave me a message and I'll return it as soon as possible," she said.

Mrs. Franklin saw the sincerity on Courtney's face. Her eyes moistened. "Maybe I do need to get out of my routine," she said.

"All it takes is your signature," Courtney said as she pushed the contract across the desk.

Mrs. Franklin slipped the glasses from her head to her nose and reached for the pen.

Chapter 57

Courtney Deeter, the recently hired assistant bookkeeper and receptionist adjusted the computer at her new desk in the reception area. For the first time since Jane had opened the business the front desk had a person stationed during regular business hours. The smell of fresh paint wafted through the room. The new couch, end table and lamp were in place. The end table was stacked with tabloids and health magazines chosen by Chloe.

While Courtney was settling into her new surroundings Chloe sat behind her desk and I sat in my chair across from her. We were about to begin the brainstorming session for the newest incarnation of our service.

Chloe had received a request from a woman who lived in Las Vegas. The woman, a dancer at the Paris Hotel, had heard of our service through a friend of hers here in New York City. The request was similar to our previous requests in that it involved us getting someone to go somewhere without them suspecting that a surprise was waiting for them. But this project didn't involve a surprise party and it was not going to take place entirely in New York.

Chloe lifted the file folder from the desk and said, "Here's our first global event client."

"What do you mean global?" I asked.

"I mean we will be taking the person out of the New York area. The request is simple. And I think it's good that we start with something simple. You know, baby steps before we run. All we have to do is fly this woman to Las Vegas."

"And where is this woman starting from?" I asked.

"Here in New York City," she said.

"OK. Sounds simple," I said. "So we arrange for a plane flight and figure out how to get her to the airport? It's doable. And if I may say, boring."

"No, no, no baby sister, we have to get her to Las Vegas…without her knowing it," she said.

251

"Without her knowing it?" I blurted. "You mean she can't know she's flying on a plane?"

"That's right. She's deathly afraid of flying. She won't go if she knows she has to fly. And a long train trip or road trip just won't create the surprise factor our client is looking for," Chloe said.

"And who is our client? The dancer, right?" I asked.

"Yes, the woman's daughter," she said.

"And the daughter thinks this is something her mother wants?" I asked.

"Sure, I screened her. I asked all the questions. And like I said, her mother won't fly but she desperately wants to visit her daughter, and she won't take time off work to drive or take a train because she thinks she can't be away from work that long, and she thinks she can't afford the trip."

"So, do you have any ideas about how we might do this?" I asked.

"Well, I've thought it over and I think it's time we go with Doctor Bob," she said.

"What can Doctor Bob do?" I asked.

She leaned back in her chair and an impish look formed on her face, the look that tells me I'm in for the bomb blast. "Well...uh...like I said, this woman can't know she is being flown to Vegas."

"What? He's going to drug her?" I shouted.

"I talked to him. He has this stuff that's safe, and...well...I think it's time for us to go to Plan Z. There's no other way."

"How on earth do you find professionals who are willing to break the law?" I asked.

"Did I say anything about breaking the law?" She leaned forward and raised her hands like she was directing a plane into a terminal. "Just stay focused. Remember the adrenaline rush you got with our last project? The less you know about my part in this, the better," she said.

"And how are we getting a drugged woman through security at the airport?" I said.

"I know a guy..." she said.

"A guy who's going to single-handedly eliminate airport security?" I said.

"No, a pilot," she said. "Remember James? We talked about

him a few weeks ago."

"That guy you dated a couple years back?" I asked.

"Yeah, he's got a small jet at Teterboro. There's less security there. My idea is that we put her in a wheelchair and roll her to the plane. She'll look like someone's napping grandmother."

"Oh my God. You're serious. We're going to drug a woman, put her on a plane and fly her to another state." I imagined the handcuffs cutting into my wrists, my life of waking up every day in a cubical, peeing in front of strange women.

"I'm working it out in my head," she said. "I think we can do it. But of course I need you for the details."

"What about getting the woman back here?" I asked.

"Her daughter will take care of that," she said.

I leaned back, folded my arms across my chest and said, "What if I say no?"

"I hope you don't, because this project is the beginning of our expanded service."

I stared at her. She continued, "I see it in your eyes. You're as interested as I am. You just need to get over the fear."

"OK...OK," I said as I took a deep breath. "Tricking someone into getting to their surprise party only takes them out of their routine for a few hours. Taking someone to Las Vegas entails more than just a few hours. This will take the person out of their routine for days. Does this woman have a job?"

"Yes, she works full time at a firm in Manhattan," Chloe said.

"How can we kidnap this woman for a vacation in Vegas when she has a job?" I asked. My voice got higher with every word. I continued. "If she doesn't show up for work she'll get fired. Unless..." I paused. Something shifted. A thought plunged into my head.

"Unless what?" Chloe asked.

"We'll have to tell the recipient about the gift ahead of time," I said.

"But if we tell her ahead of time it won't be a surprise," she said.

"We won't tell her that she's being flown to Las Vegas. We'll tell her that an anonymous person has given her a gift which will occur at an undisclosed place and time. Then it will still be a surprise. She'll expect something to happen but she won't know what it will be or where or when it will happen."

"But how will she arrange for time off from work if she doesn't know when it will happen?" Chloe asked.

"Let's see. What if we send her a gift card notifying her that she must come here to our office to find out about the gift? When she meets with us...no...that won't work. She can't meet us. I got it. Now that Courtney is stationed out front she can inform the woman of the gift. Since the woman won't meet us, we can still do her squeeze perfectly, like contacting the employer to arrange her time off. Hopefully her employer is willing to go along with the plan."

"Sounds good. You know how convincing I can be. I'll get her employer to give her time off," Chloe said. "For this squeeze I want my name to be Ms. Fletcher."

An involuntary chuckle popped out of my mouth and I asked, "You mean like Ms. Fletcher in seventh grade?"

"Yeah. Remember when I would purposely call her Miss Fletcher and she would correct me by saying, it's Mzzzzz."

I laughed and said, "Yeah, that was funny. She never let you get away with calling her Miss."

Chloe planted her elbow on the desk and propped her chin on her fist. She stared past me in a contemplative manner and said, "So, we're getting her on and off the plane."

I mirrored her stance and said, "Uh huh."

She snapped out of her trance and said, "OK, that's it. Let's get to work."

"You know, I don't think getting her on and off the plane is enough. It's too ordinary, too boring. Of course she'll have a great time in Vegas once she gets there but she won't even experience anything along the way if she's drugged. Do you have any more info on the woman?"

Chloe straightened and glanced at her notes. "Here's what her daughter said about her. She's worked at the same full-time job in Manhattan for twelve years. She takes the subway to and from Brooklyn every day. She lives alone in a house that she and her deceased husband purchased about thirty years ago. She has no hobbies or outside interests. When she gets home from work she usually relaxes with her cat and falls asleep in front of the television."

"Oh my God," I blurted. "Getting her to Vegas is definitely not enough. We need to shake this woman up. She needs to get a life and we need to give it to her."

"How do we do that?" she asked.

"Give me a copy of your notes. And call her daughter. Get any other info you can on this woman, like if she has ever had any dreams or goals. There must be more to her than what you told me. No one is that dull."

"Good girl, I'm on it," Chloe said.

Just then Jane appeared from the backroom, wearing goggles and a yellow rain coat. She said, "Chloe, can I show Courtney what I'm working on?"

Chloe and I looked at each other and smiled. Chloe said, "Go for it, Jane."

Jane poked her head through the door to the reception area and said, "Hi, Courtney. Come with me. I'm going to give you a tour of the backroom, including the rabbit hole."

"The rabbit hole?" Courtney said with an inquisitive look.

As they moved to the backroom Chloe followed. I grabbed my sweater and my purse and was gone.

Chapter 58

Outside the air was pleasantly crisp. My sweater was enough. As spring teetered precariously on the edge of summer I made my way north.

My phone rang inside my purse. I picked it up and answered, "Hello."

"Hello, Sophie," the velvet voice said. "This is John."

My heart fluttered for a second. "Hi, John. How are you?"

"I'm doing great. It's taken me a few days to get over the party. I wish you had stayed."

"Thanks. Me too," I said.

"I was wondering if you want to have lunch with me today," he said.

"It sounds good but I'm in the middle of something right now. How about dinner?" I suggested with a twinge of embarrassment at my newfound courage.

"Dinner is better," he said. "Should I pick you up or do you want to meet me at the restaurant?"

"I'll meet you," I said.

"OK, I'll find a place. What kind of food do you like?" he asked.

"Anything is fine. Pick something you like," I said.

"OK, I'll call you back."

"OK, bye. Hey, wait," I said before he could hang up. "You are aware that I am not a vice officer, right? I'm a normal, non-prostitute kind of girl. I mean woman. I mean, I don't generally do those things on the first date, paid or not. Although I'm not a prude. I'm a healthy twenty-five year-old with a normal sex drive. When I say normal I mean... That is to say, I do... I mean I won't... I mean, I didn't suggest dinner because..."

"Sophie," he interrupted.

"Yes."

"Everything will be alright. We're just having dinner," he said in a soothing tone.

"Thanks," I said.

We hung up.

As I dropped my phone in my purse I said to myself, "Just having dinner? We'll see."

My feet stepped a little lighter on the pavement. I closed my eyes for a moment and felt the cool air drift over my face. This was my real office, the place where I got all my ideas, outside on the sidewalk where everyone lived. The people passing me were like me. For a short time they escaped from their tiny offices and tiny apartments to be cradled in the arms of the city. Our electricity passed down the conduit of the city sidewalk, our eyes connecting in thought, our bodies brushing by each other, the vibrations of our sounds mingling into the urban song.

Like the stone archways and vaulted ceilings of European cathedrals, the skyscrapers drew my eyes to the heavens and reminded me of the mysteries of the universe. My mother was up there and inside both me and everyone I loved. The metal, brick and glass facades which had pressed down on me like weights just weeks earlier were now monuments to human beings' wondrous accomplishments.

I used to think I needed a protective cloak of solitude wrapped around me. I didn't need anyone, especially family. I thought my solitude gave me peace. But being alone just enabled my mind to chatter nonsense in my ears. I can be alone in a crowd as much as I am alone in the rabbit hole, one of my new special places.

But today, this was my special place, out on the street among the living, where every light, every sound and every face coming toward me gave me a new idea. There were so many projects to plan, puzzles to solve and people to meet. The people walking by me didn't know it yet but they were waiting for me to surprise them.

I felt my hand wrapped around the straps of my purse, recalling that I'd cancelled my plane ticket and received a refund. A few hundred dollars was back in my checking account and my debit card was nestled in my wallet.

I now had a full-time job with the promise of lucrative projects to come. I was on my way to becoming a Master of the Art of Surprise. And the two most surprising things were that I no longer cringed at the thought having my sister back in my life and I actually had a date with a really hot guy.

I turned a corner and headed for Saks where a periwinkle sweater was waiting for me.

The End

www.ingramcontent.com/pod-product-compliance
Lightning Source LLC
Chambersburg PA
CBHW021027130626
46552CB00005B/1721